D0200431

THE
REAL
JUSTINE

THE
REAL
JUSTINE

STEPHEN AMIDON

PEGASUS BOOKS
NEW YORK LONDON

THE REAL JUSTINE

Pegasus Books LLC
80 Broad Street, 5th Floor
New York, NY 10004

Copyright © 2015 by Stephen Amidon

First Pegasus Books cloth edition September 2015

Interior design by Maria Fernandez

All rights reserved. No part of this book may be reproduced in whole or in part
without written permission from the publisher, except by reviewers who may
quote brief excerpts in connection with a review in a newspaper, magazine, or
electronic publication; nor may any part of this book be reproduced, stored in a
retrieval system, or transmitted in any form or by any means electronic, mechanical,
photocopying, recording, or other, without written permission from the publisher.

Library of Congress Cataloging-in-Publication Data is available.

ISBN: 978-1-60598-865-8

10 9 8 7 6 5 4 3 2 1

Printed in the United States of America
Distributed by W. W. Norton & Company

For Caryl, as always.

THE
REAL
JUSTINE

PART ONE

PART ONE

ONE

HE ALMOST MISSED HER. IF HE HAD NOT GLANCED DOWN Water Lane, it would have been just another day in which she was lost to him. Even then, all he saw at first was a woman arguing with a man in a leather jacket. They stood beside a white Mercedes that had been badly parked on the narrow street. The early evening light, already depleted by a thick layer of stationary cloud, barely reached them. City people, Michael thought, as much as he thought anything. Transplanted Brooklynites, or weekenders with a place by the river.

It was only after he had taken a half-dozen steps that something stopped him. A feeling, both powerful and obscure. Will, sluggish from pizza and the day's race, kept going.

"Hold up," Michael said.

His son turned, ready to protest, but Michael was already heading back. Even though the woman was facing away from him, he understood now that it was Justine. The man with her was big, a few inches over six feet, with broad shoulders beneath a fissured leather jacket. His hair spilled from a disintegrating ponytail. A tattoo of what appeared to be a snake covered the right side of his neck. There was an aura of violence about him. He looked capable of doing harm.

Michael started down Water, but before he had taken two steps, Justine slapped the man. It was a hard blow, but he did not flinch. She went to hit him again but he grabbed her wrist, spinning her partially around. She struggled in vain to free her gripped arm. And then she was speaking.

"You're ruining everything!"

Michael started to run. The closer he got, the more ragged the man looked. His long hair was dirty, his face all jagged angles, his eyes sunk deep into his skull.

"Hey!" Michael said.

The man's eyes flexed at the sight of a rapidly approaching stranger. He held up his free hand.

"It's cool," he said, his voice a strangulated growl. "We're cool."

Justine saw him now as well. Her eyes were filled with anger and fear. They were nothing like the eyes he remembered. It took her a moment to recognize him.

"Michael."

That single utterance of his name carried many meanings. Recognition, despair, a warning.

"It's all right," she said. "Just . . ."

"That's right," the man added. "We're good."

Michael looked back at the man.

He said to the man, "You should take your hands off her."

The words had just come. The man had three inches and thirty pounds on Michael, and appeared to know about what happened when men faced off in alleys.

"Okay, you have zero seconds to get the fuck out of my shit."

"I'm not going anywhere until she tells me she's all right."

"Michael, it's fine, just . . . no!"

Her last word was directed at the man, who had released her, but only so he could grab Michael's windbreaker. There was real power in his hands. His face came close. His eyes were disease-yellow. His breath was feverish; he smelled of chemicals and rot.

"Leave now or I will fuck your shit up forever."

There was a frozen moment. And then Michael astonished himself. He threw a left. The part of his brain that launched the punch probably intended a tree-felling roundhouse; in reality, his fist struck the bottom of the man's jaw with roughly the same effect as Justine's slap. A jagged bolt of pain shot through his index finger. The word *mistake* registered in his mind. The man released Michael's jacket with a short, hard shove. He balled his hands. Justine was right there now, grabbing at the man's shoulders, pulling in vain. I am fighting, Michael thought. I have finally found her and I am fighting a stranger on Water Lane and I am about to get my shit fucked up. Forever.

"Stop it!"

They both turned. Michael followed their gaze. Will stood a few feet away. With his tousled hair and baggy sweats, he looked pupal and unformed. His eyes were bright with terror, but there was a determined set to his jaw as he held up his cell phone.

"I'm calling 911."

"No!"

Justine had spoken, her voice charged with panic. She was shaking her head, her eyes wide, pleading.

"Michael, tell him not to."

"We're out," the man said. "Come on."

He took hold of Justine's arm. There was no threat of violence now. It was a gesture of protection. Justine looked over her shoulder as she was led to the passenger seat, shaking her head at Michael, begging him not to follow. The man slammed her car door and hurried to the driver's side. He looked very different now. Fight had switched to flight.

"Wait," Michael said. "Justine . . ."

But they were not waiting. The engine erupted and the car lurched into reverse. Michael leapt aside and looked for his son. Will was already flattened against the brick wall. The car sped by. For an instant, she was close enough to touch, separated only by tempered glass. Her eyes were fixed on the dashboard, as if she was willing herself not to look at him. The car reversed up the street, careening madly, almost striking the wall. The driver barely paused as he joined River Street. He cut the wheel hard to the right, putting the car into the northbound lane. There was a horn, but no impact. And then they were gone. The alley was silent. Diesel fumes filled the air.

"Dad?"

It was only when he once again saw the terror in his son's eyes that Michael understood his own fear. Sweat chilled his skin, adrenaline churned through his stomach and chest. His injured finger had begun to throb so painfully that he wondered if it might be broken.

"What the hell?" Will said. "Who was that guy?"

"Some lunatic."

"But you *hit* him."

His son's voice was an amalgam of blame, alarm, and wonder.

"I just . . ."

Finishing the sentence would have required more air than Michael could currently draw into his lungs. He desperately wanted to see where Justine had gone, to ask her what the hell was going on. But he was having trouble commanding his body. He placed a steadying hand on the brick wall as he thought about the man's enraged yellow eyes, the stink of his hot breath.

"Dad?"

"Just give me a second here."

After spending several seconds holding up the wall, Michael led his son from the alley. Will hesitated as they neared River, worried that the man in the leather jacket had returned. But the Mercedes was long gone, as Michael knew it would be. His own car was parked three blocks away, too far to attempt any sort of chase. Not that he would have done anything with Will in tow. Chase, he thought. Fight. The insane, reckless absurdity of the situation was settling over him now like a serious case of the flu. He should have never challenged the man, especially on a secluded street in the company of his fourteen-year-old son. But it was Justine, suddenly there after nine months of absolute silence; nine months in which he had searched for her occasionally and thought about her constantly. It was Justine, slapping a crazy person a few hundred yards from where he had first met her.

He drove slowly north along River, looking for any sign of her. Will remained silent, shooting his father troubled sidelong glances. The Mercedes was nowhere in sight. It was not on a side street or slotted into a metered space. She was gone. Once again. As Michael drove, he began to clench his hand and wriggle his fingers. If you could move it, it was not broken. This was what they said. About bones, anyway.

He checked driveways and parking lots. He went south on River, wondering if maybe they had doubled back without him noticing and were headed to the city, where she said she lived. He wished he'd had the presence of mind to get the license plate of that Mercedes. But that was absurd. What would he do with license plate? Google it? Have somebody run it for him?

Will asked, "Dad, what are you *doing*?"

"I'm just . . ."

But he had no explanation for his son, at least not one that he wanted to filter back to his ex-wife Kim. The alley fight would be difficult enough to explain. And so he returned home, where Will descended to the rec room, his safe haven, to plant himself in front of the vast plasma screen and become a lone survivor wandering a blasted landscape. Technically, this was not allowed, but Michael let him go. He needed to think. He had to understand what had just happened. He briefly contemplated calling the police, but he had no idea what to say to them. She clearly knew the man. She had made it plain that she did not want anyone called. And the man had not been violent with her. The violence had come from her. And Michael.

7

He checked his finger. There was swelling now, swamping knuckles and smoothing skin. He poured himself a large whiskey, filled a baggie with ice and went into his office, where he collapsed onto the old salvaged sofa. He had handled things wrong. He had acted without thinking. That was obvious. But she had been so desperate, so defeated. When he imagined her, she was gliding through the city, graceful and assured. Not cornered in an alley. Was this the lover she had talked about, the one she could not quit, the one she hated herself for loving? Michael thought about his desperate, filthy appearance. It did not seem possible. But there was that protective hand on her arm as he led her to the car; the intimacy in that rough voice. If he was not her lover, he was something very close.

It had been nine months since she had suddenly disappeared. She had been smiling and stretching in his bed the last time he saw her, gloriously naked and impossibly lovely, assuring him that she would be right there when he returned. He had met her four long days before that, on a Monday night, when he had no expectations of meeting anyone. He had just spent the holidays alone. It was a bad time for Michael, arguably the worst of his life. His visits with his son were becoming increasingly awkward, as Will slipped deeper into the mood-infested backwoods of puberty. Self-employment was turning into a featureless maze from which he could not escape. His perfectly nice girlfriend Penny had recently broken up with him after he declined her invitation to move in with her. He was drinking too much. A solid night's sleep was a distant memory. A long, solitary year loomed.

He'd arrived home from an afternoon at the public library to a frigid, empty house. Although it was just after five, night was already settling in. There had been a half foot of snow the day before, followed by a sudden melt that had covered Annville in gray slush. The temperature had dipped again; everything was just starting to freeze back over. It was as if the town was being wrapped by a layer of cold, clear plastic. More sleet and snow were forecast. A wintry mix.

Dreading a night spent channel flipping and listening to his laboring furnace, he went to the Moon Temple, the town's second most popular Chinese restaurant. In the lobby, he waved away the hostess and headed into the bar through a gilded arch, so cheaply ornate that it could have been a prop in a play for children. This was the only bar in town that Michael could bear. It was nothing like the dives down in Cheapside, populated by babbling dead-enders, or the Annville Tavern, the burnished yuppie watering hole that always looked like they were getting ready to film a beer commercial inside. Here, there were Naugahyde booths and stools and a big, mirrored, brass-railed bar. The "art" on the wall looked like it had been clipped from a Hong Kong advertising circular. Drinkers left you alone unless you approached them.

The only other clients tonight were an elderly couple who sat in tomb-like silence, the ornate drinks between them looking vaguely toxic, and a fat man, probably waiting to catch a train at the nearby station, sipping a pint of draft beer as he hunted-and-pecked on a laptop with thick fingers. Michael chose a stool at the end of the bar. The bartender was a fleshless woman whose primary means of discourse involved raising stenciled eyebrows. He ordered a Jameson from her and started to read the book he had brought, the story of an infamous murder in 1890s San Francisco that Penny had left on his bedside table a few days before she had left him.

He had only read a few paragraphs when he became aware of someone new in the bar, a woman ordering a drink a few stools down from him. A very beautiful woman. She was completely out of place in here, but also completely at ease. Michael pegged her as another passenger for the next city train. She was one of those women you saw in New York, moving too quickly to pin down. She looked to be in her late twenties, with dark brown hair and very pale skin and big eyes the same color as her hair. There was a sharp, armored cast to her demeanor, a layer of emotional Kevlar that warned off all comers.

Once she had her drink—it looked like vodka on ice—she shouldered her large bag and walked toward Michael. He could not help but watch. She was tall but not too tall; thin but not too thin. Although she was dressed simply, a black skirt and a gray turtleneck sweater and leather boots, her clothes suggested money. She met his eye with a quick, neutral glance that sent a jolt through him. He turned back to his book as she slid into a nearby booth, but looked up after a few seconds. She was absorbed in sending a text, her thumbs rapid and precise. A message, no doubt, for the sleek, confident man awaiting her in Manhattan. Telling him that she would be with him soon.

Michael returned to the forgotten crime, but found it impossible to concentrate. Making some sort of contact with this woman had suddenly become crucial. He chanced another look after what seemed like a decent interval. She was staring directly at him with a playful, low-voltage smile. He tried desperately to unpack that smile's meaning. She could have been acknowledging the fact that they had both chosen such an unlikely spot. She could have been inviting him to join him in her Naugahyde enclave. She could have been telling him to fuck off.

"Is it as good as it looks?" she asked, her voice pitched a little lower than he had expected.

"What?"

"Your book. You seem engrossed."

Her voice was charged with an unexpected irony. She was well aware she'd rattled him. Not knowing what else to say, he quoted the jacket copy.

"A true story of love, lust, betrayal, and murder among America's gilded class."

"That's it? No talking cats? No vampires?"

"There might be zombies. I'm only on chapter three."

She smiled at him, putting the conversation on pause, willing to talk but unwilling to do it across twenty feet of all-purpose carpet. The ball was in his court. He gestured to the empty bench across from her, his hand innocuously upturned in a gesture that was almost supplicating. She scrutinized him for a moment. Deciding. And then she gave her head a slight nod.

"I thought I was the only one who knew about his place," he said.

"You are. The other actual bar I found turned out to be not to my liking."

"The Annville Tavern, right?"

"I spent three hours there this afternoon."

"But it's renowned for its ambiance."

"I guess I'm allergic to quaint."

"It's the darts that get me," he said.

"Right? This isn't Glasgow. Play air hockey like normal people."

"I'm Michael, by the way."

Her hand was thin and cool.

"Justine."

"Wait, three hours?" he asked.

She explained that she worked for a New York art dealer; she had come to Annville early that morning on behalf of her boss, who had been summonsed to testify in a lawsuit back in the city. Her mission was to meet with a would-be buyer who lived in one of the big estates on the river north of town. He was a sickly old billionaire who was thinking about adding a piece of sculpture to his gardens. She'd brought an array of photos for him to consider. The idea was that he would choose one and they would haul it up and give him some time to see if it felt right among his topiary shrubs and gazebos and waterfowl. She had expected to be in and out in an afternoon, but he'd postponed their noon appointment and then kept her cooling her heels all day, waiting for him to send his driver. So her boss had booked her into the Sheraton with orders to stay put and await the buyer's call.

"So who is this mystery man? Have I heard of him?"

"Not allowed to say. Sorry."

Michael held up his hands. He did not want to pry.

"So what about you?" she asked. "Waiting for the train, too?"

"I live here, actually."

Her eyes registered something. Surprise. Disappointment, perhaps.

"I used to work for a foundation called Grammaticus," he added, answering the unasked question. "They moved their headquarters here a few years back and so . . ."

"Used to."

"We had a difference of opinion. I'm currently self-employed."

"You like it? Living up here, I mean?"

"Less and less."

"Why's that?"

"The armies of darkness are on the march and we're sorting our recyclables."

She smiled.

Justine said, "Beneath the civilized surface lurks a cynic. Looks like I picked the right bar."

Her phone squirmed on the table. Her smile collapsed when she read the message.

"Wonderful," she muttered.

"Bad news?"

She shook her head. Not denying it, just saying she was not prepared to explain. She snatched up her drink and drained it.

"You want another?" he asked.

"Now why would I want another?"

He ruled her question to be rhetorical and collected her glass. As he watched the vodka flow he imagined what her mouth would taste like the instant after she drank it. Heat beneath the acid cold. When he returned, he asked her about her work. The alternative was speaking about the weather, or politics, or himself, or some other subject that was beyond his control. She was reluctant to answer at first, but his gentle persistence and the second vodka eventually won her over. She started with her current job. She'd fallen into the business by chance after she'd arrived in New York when she was eighteen, fleeing unspecified misery. That was eight years ago. She had gravitated toward the art scene, primarily because there was not much in the way of admission standards, you could act up at parties, and nobody got up very early for work. There was a man who took her under his wing soon after she'd splashed down; older, wiser, all of that. She called him The Poet in a way that suggested there had not been many actual poems produced. He got old, both chronologically and metaphorically. After that, she'd supported herself with a series of jobs, assisting increasingly successful gallery owners. She mentioned an apartment but did not say what borough it was in, or if she shared it with a lover, a husband, a talking cat. Her boss, who she simply called Rasputin, was tempestuous, brilliant, paranoid, secretive, so cutting edge that he sometimes ventured into illegality.

"You can't blame him for being cagey," she said. "He trades in a product that is one percent genius and ninety-nine percent bullshit."

She told him about other bosses, about artists she had known, self-styled geniuses and spectacular flameouts. The bar emptied completely and Michael suggested they return to his place. She accepted. Outside, the freeze had taken hold; his tires crackled over the glistening pavement as he drove through town. He briefly wondered what she would make of his big, bland suburban house, but she offered no opinion. He sat her on the living room sofa and offered her vodka, but she said she was fine, she'd had just enough. He sat beside her, thinking, *This is happening*. He had never wanted anyone so much. She turned to him and jutted her chin forward, her eyes twinkling with sweet insolence. When they kissed, she was neither eager nor nervous. Her stillness was primed. He put his hand on the back of her neck. Her spine felt brittle. She gently grasped his shoulders; he reached beneath her sweater. The skin was warm and soft and twenty-six years old. Sweet Mother of God, he thought. She flinched slightly as he ran his palm over her breast, but then moved closer to him. He pulled at her sweater, but she gripped his wrists.

"Not in this awful room."

In the bedroom, she raised her arms above her head like a surrendering combatant. The sweater vanished. She removed her thin bra in that articulated, backward motion that had always struck him with wonder. He lowered her onto the bed. Clothes came off. He slid his hand between her legs, crossing faint stubble. She was very wet. It was as if his finger was drawn into her. She gasped and writhed. There were condoms in the bedside table but she grabbed his wrist as he reached for them.

"Don't worry about all that. Just fuck me."

His sense of caution was offline, evidently, because he did as commanded. When he entered her, she lashed her head to the side so violently that it felt as if she was trying to escape from him. But her hands gripped his back and flattened him against her. She was not going anywhere.

She spoke his name, she sighed and moaned, she talked a little filth. He finished too quickly and she did not seem to mind and when he put his mouth between her legs, she acted as if it was something new and wonderful. After a timeless interval her breathing stopped and then every muscle in her body shuddered. They kissed for a long time after that, saying nothing, and then he was ready again. Her head wrenched to the side as before, her eyes shut so tightly that it looked like she'd just been struck. She held tight; it was as if their contact, his cock inside her, was the only thing that kept her from falling into an abyss. After she came he looked down at her. Her eyes were closed, her head still averted.

"Justine?"

She did not answer. He rolled gently off her and stroked her hair until she finally looked at him. It was impossible to say what was in her eyes. It looked very much like nothing at all.

"I thought I'd lost you there," he said.

"That's the point, silly."

She put her fingers on his lips to stop him from offering further insights.

"Just hold me."

She stayed. They made love again, less urgently this time. After, she grew drowsy and sweetly affectionate, idly touching him, responding lazily to his caresses. The Sheraton was forgotten. Outside, sleet gave way to snow, the splintering patter on his roof becoming a thick muffled silence. A guy could get used to this, he remembered thinking just before he fell asleep.

When he woke it was the middle of the morning. She was not in bed. So that was that, he thought. The collector's driver had collected her. But then he saw her scattered clothes, and there was the smell of coffee. She was in the room he called his office, perched efficiently on the sofa, her legs drawn up beneath her. She had wrapped herself in a blanket and her hair was wild over it.

"You're sorta hot when you sleep, Michael Coolidge."

"No word from your guy?" he asked.

"I'm in a holding pattern."

She patted the sofa.

"So it looks like we have some time to kill."

He peeled back the blanket very gently. They kissed and caressed and maneuvered; he wound up on his back and she lowered herself slowly onto him, one hand on the sofa, the other on his shoulder. They moved like this for a long time, longer than he had thought possible. She leaned forward until her hair brushed his face, she reared back and the skin on her abdomen stretched as tight as a snapped sheet. Her eyes were open now, locked on his, pulsing occasionally to register the pleasure she was feeling. But there was something else being communicated. Something very different from pleasure, something he did not understand. Desperation, yearning, defiance—if there was a word for it, he did not know what it could be.

They were together for the rest of the week. The collector remained elusive, her boss told her to stay put. He only left the house for food and drink; she did not leave it at all. Heavy snow continued through Tuesday night, followed by a cold snap. They spent hours in bed or curled together on the sofa. They took baths beneath a skylight he had always thought to be tacky, though now, covered by a layer of ice, it emitted a refracted light that made her wet skin seem polished. She cooked for him, sending him out into the cold with detailed shopping lists for the ingredients to make pasta puttanesca, Dover sole with saffron rice, a veal dish that was her own creation. She'd dated a man who owned restaurants, she explained, and the only things she had taken away from the relationship was an ability to cook and a resolve never to eat bad food again.

Almost unbelievably, there were few awkward moments between them, few of the yawning silences that usually followed the first heated rush. She would disappear into his office occasionally to text someone he assumed to be her boss, but mostly she was happy to be with Michael. They talked for hours at a time. He wanted to know everything about her. She told him about her childhood in an impoverished rural precinct of Indiana, abandoned by an outlaw father, who had betrayed her in some deep, unspecified way, leaving her to be raised by a crazy damaged mother who held regular, occasionally querulous conversations with Jesus. There was a sainted older brother who had been killed in the war; a wild younger sister who had run away at fourteen. There were bad boys and badder men; there were street drugs and car crashes and a brutal runaway week in St. Louis when she was seventeen that let her know the big world could be a whole lot worse than the shabby little one she hated.

Michael was entranced. The divide between the hardscrabble past she described and the cool sophistication currently inhabiting his house suggested that this was a woman of even greater depth and will than he'd suspected. And there was something else that captivated him. A sense of actual mystery; a suspicion that for every detail being offered, two more were being withheld. Her conversation teemed with hints, allusions, dead ends, teases. She never told him the name of her hometown, or if her brother had died in Afghanistan or Iraq, or why her sister bolted. Almost everything was nicknamed. In addition to Rasputin and the Poet, her mother was the Madwoman in the Basement, her father simply The Bastard. Unnamed lovers were described only by graphic particulars—a forked tongue, a cavernous age difference, an acquittal on manslaughter charges.

At the time, the imprecision did not bother him. He just wanted to keep her close. He did not want to do anything that would make her bolt. Later, during the nine long months of missing her, the days of looking for her and nights dreaming about her, he would come to understand the true reason for her evasions: she was cultivating a thicket of brilliant foliage into which the real Justine could vanish.

Although she programmed his number into her phone, the number she entered into his device, he later discovered, was one digit short. She kept her big black bag zipped tight and stowed neatly in a corner of his room, clearly off limits. She wouldn't tell him her last name, claiming she hated it. When he pressed, she came as close as she ever did to losing her temper. He let it go. She'd tell him when she was ready.

Although he knew it did not compare to her life, he told her about Kim and Will and his normal Long Island childhood. They were in the big tub that had not been used since his wife had left him when he ran through his particulars, that strange light falling over them.

"Can I ask you a question, Michael?" she asked, her cheek on his chest.

"I think that's permissible, given the circumstances."

"What happened to you at Grammaticus?"

"Just corporate bullshit." He laughed grimly. "I got caught in the crossfire of the culture wars."

"I think it was more than that," she said after a moment. "You seem, I don't know. Damaged, in some way. Living all alone. No visible girlfriend. Stuck in Nowheresville, spinning your wheels."

And so he gave her an abridged version of his departure from Grammaticus, leaving out the part about his transgression, his *firing offense*. Instead, he said he'd resigned as a matter of principle after they betrayed his most beloved client, showing themselves to be spineless functionaries, capable only of applying Band-Aids to an arterial spurt. He told her about the giddy elation of those early days of freedom, followed by the malaise Justine had so accurately diagnosed.

Michael said, "And now here I am."

She raised herself so she could look into his eyes. There was something serious there, something searching and deep. She put her head back on his chest.

"I just realized why I like you so much."

"Why's that?"

"Because you're just like me. They broke you too."

"Justine, you're the least broken person I've ever met."

17

"Listen to you. Keep that up and I'm going to fall for you."

"And what would be wrong with that?"

"Uh oh. I think we're coming to the part where we talk about if there's another man."

"The question had begun to cross my mind."

"The simple answer is no," she said after a while.

"What's the not-simple answer?"

"Yes."

He waited for her to explain.

"I fell for somebody when I was young. He was older. He was very powerful. The most powerful man in town. It was a big secret—he had everyone fooled. My family, everyone. He was genius at keeping them so close that they could not even see."

She was lost in thought. Michael knew better than to ask any of the questions crowding into his mind.

"And I can't seem to shake free of him. He's still there. Fucking up the program."

"Do you want to shake free of him?"

"More than anything."

"So who is this guy?"

She did not answer.

"Okay," he said. "I give up. No more questions."

"That's probably wise."

"But here's what I'm thinking," he said. "This buyer is going to call soon or your boss is going to give up. Either way, you're going to have to go back to the city."

"And?"

"I don't necessarily want to stop seeing you after that happens."

"That would be nice," she said quietly.

That was where they left it. No actual commitment, but the distinct possibility of a second act. Michael worried that proposing a future for them would overwhelm her, but this seemed unfounded, at least for the next several hours. She became, if anything, even more affectionate. It was not until later that night that there was the first sign that all was not well. He woke to find his bed was empty. He sat up and listened—he could hear the distant murmur of her voice. He went in search of her. Light leaked from behind his office door. She was on the phone. It was impossible to know for certain, her voice was muffled, but she sounded upset. She might have even been crying. He moved closer to listen, but could distinguish nothing. And so he went back to bed and waited. It took her almost a half hour to return. She moved quietly, taking care not to wake him. He kept quiet, even though he desperately wanted to ask what was wrong.

Things appeared to return to normal the next morning. They were making love before either was fully awake. It was late, mid-morning. His cell phone rang just as he got the coffee going. It was Kim. He let it go to voice mail, but then a text appeared, telling him to call her right away. Will was in the vice principal's office. They were talking about a suspension.

He left her in bed, naked and smiling sleepily. He told her not to move and she agreed. There was nothing ominous in her goodbye, no hint of the previous night's sadness. At school, he discovered that his son had broken a piece of lab equipment during chemistry class. There had been shattered glass, the possibility of injury. It might have been exuberance, it might have been malice. It certainly was not the first time he'd acted out since his parents had split up. The school wound up giving him a week's detention with an under-standing that further misbehavior would be dealt with far more strenuously.

Michael was home by noon. He called out her name as he stepped through the door and was greeted by an echoing silence. She was not in the kitchen or the bedroom. He checked the office. She was not there either. But there was a note, written in a loose, elegant hand he recognized from her shopping lists.

Dear Michael—
I'm really, really sorry. It's better if we just leave it at what's hap-pened. Things are just so wrong with me right now. I don't think

you'd like me very much if you knew the truth about me and the world I live in. I really am sorry. You are amazing.

J.

He jumped in the car and raced over to the station. A train had left a half hour earlier. He checked the Moon Temple, but there was no one at all in the bar. It was only when he got back home that he noticed how thoroughly she had cleaned up after herself. The wine glasses, the bed, the bath. Unless he had seen her with his own eyes, if he had not touched her, he would never have known she had been here at all.

TWO

AFTER SEEING HOW THOROUGHLY SHE HAD CLEARED out, he returned to the station, thinking that she might have gone to meet her rich collector. If so, there was a chance he could intercept her as she headed back to the city. He'd offer to help her with whatever she had been dealing with during that late night call. He'd offer her a ride, a sympathetic ear—whatever she needed. He'd tell her that he did not want her to go.

It was then that he discovered that the number she had given him was meaningless. At first, he put it down to a simple error on her part, though it did not take him long to realize her mistake was intentional. He waited through the remainder of the day, occupying a stool at the Moon Temple between departures, haunting the platform as trains approached. She was nowhere to be found. He returned to the station occasionally over the weekend; he looked for traces of her online. Understanding now how vague her descriptions of her life had been. There were no plausible hits when he twinned "Justine" with "art dealer" or "gallery," though he did come up with a handful of gallery owners with Russian-sounding names. Detailed searches produced nothing about her. He tried to find art collectors in the Annville area, looking in vain for a reclusive, aging billionaire surrounded by Henry Moores. The woman simply did not exist.

When he was not searching for her, he sat in his darkened office, sipping whiskey, his thoughts caroming off one another. He would rage at her for her heartlessness; seconds later, he would lacerate himself for scaring her away with his talk about joining her in New York. Deep down, he understood the folly of trying to find her. Hooded gunmen had not bundled her into the back of an unmarked van. She had not suffered amnesia after a blow to the head. It was just a four-night stand. She knew where to find him. She didn't even have to knock—he'd showed her where he kept his spare key, hidden under the Buddha-like stone frog Kim had bought at a tag sale. His number was in her phone. She just was not calling it.

Despite this understanding, he went to the city on the Monday after she left, kidding himself that it was more out of a desire to get out of the house than in expectation of finding her. He wandered Soho and Tribeca and the East Village, he visited the three galleries with Russian-sounding names. There was no Justine working at any of them. He tried other galleries, without success. He had dinner at a bistro on Spring Street and then continued to walk at night, pausing to look into restaurants and still-open shops. It was almost midnight by the time he retrieved his car from the garage.

He knew this was madness, but he needed to find her. He wanted to once again be in that strange glow from the snow-covered skylight as they lay together in slowly cooling water, her cheek on his chest, her legs wrapped around him. He wanted to have her body moving above him on the office sofa, her eyes wide with pleasure. He wanted to once again be in the bar at the Moon Temple at the exact moment he knew that she was coming home with him. Longing coursed through his veins. He was not accustomed to this sort of emotional intensity. He had never been an impetuous person. The only other time he'd behaved this impulsively was with Piney Hills, three years before he met Justine. And that had ended in catastrophe. It should have been a lesson to him. But here he was, walking the city streets like a lost soul.

He'd been at Grammaticus for two decades before he was terminated. They'd hired him right out of Amherst. He could not believe his luck, landing a job at one of the nation's largest, most admired charities. It had been endowed in 1949 by the 91-year-old timber baron Karl Gustav Grammaticus, who, after a lifetime spent deforesting significant sections of his native Pennsylvania, had decided to give something back to the planet. Michael worked in the Social Justice division, where he had recently been promoted from senior program officer to vice president. He was odds-on favorite to become the department's director after his boss, Jaryd Carmichael, took over as the foundation's chief executive.

Grammaticus was not only one of the nation's largest charities; it was also one of its most progressive. Although Karl Gustav had been too busy chopping and clearing for politics—the foundation's charter spoke vaguely of "meeting human needs" and "bettering the planet"—his two sons had been determinedly liberal in their outlook. After their father finally gave up the ghost at the age of 102, they steered the foundation into the activist heart of the 1960s and 1970s, bankrolling antiwar puppet theaters, Native American museums, and alternative pre-schools. The next generation of Grammaticus family trustees might not have shared this commitment—they were too busy wrecking Maseratis and dying of heroin overdoses—but their indifference allowed the foundation's progressive pedigree to remain unchallenged. This had been Michael's time, during which he'd doled out tens of millions of dollars to hundreds of worthy causes. They were heady days. People in slums and on reservations rolled out their tattered red carpets for him. Tattooed men clutching sobriety medallions called him brother; unflappable nuns in armored nylons hung on his every word. He was spending someone else's money to make the world a better place. He was cleaning up messes without getting his hands dirty.

Things began to change once Karl Gustav's grandchildren finally finished self-destructing. The family's fortunes fell under the control of his great-grandnephew, Bertram L. Kiner, whose dazzling pedigree included stints at Wharton Business School and Lehman Brothers. He was also a proud father of five and an active elder in his Baptist church, having forsaken the family's long association with Episcopalianism. Bertram's mother had drowned after stumbling drunkenly from her yacht while it was anchored off Mykonos, leaving her twelve-year-old son with a dim view of his family's free-wheeling ethos. Once in charge, he stacked the foundation's board with market-worshipping cronies and started talking about "fostering efficiency" and "rewarding initiative." Veteran management was eased out. Longtime grantees were cut loose. Applications that would have been a lock ten years earlier were turned down without elaboration. Family values and entrepreneurship became all the rage. Faith-based charities moved to the front of the line. A think tank was in the works.

Michael's Social Justice division was particularly hard hit. Although Jaryd was retained, he began to sing from the new hymnal. His relationship with Michael had once been frictionless; now, his terse memos did not invite response. Michael began to dread going to work. Kim sympathized, but urged him to hold on until he'd lined up a position elsewhere. It was not a good time to do anything rash. The job market was tight. They'd just moved to Annville, site of the costly new Grammaticus campus. Beneath her eminently practical advice was the unspoken message that perhaps it was time for Michael, so long insulated in his cocoon of beneficence, to wake up and smell the coffee.

He tried. He truly did. He dutifully oversaw the quiet dismantling of the infrastructure he'd spent two decades assembling. There would be no more largesse for the guerilla filmmaking collectives, the reproductive health and literacy projects, the halfway houses and the needle exchanges. As for the basket weavers and the career transition center for dancers—they simply had no chance. Many of these groups had been projects Michael had brought into the fold. He fought hard to save some of them, writing long defenses and making impassioned pitches, but there was nothing to be done. The best of his program officers quit. The rest toed the line.

The end came when he was told he was going to have to cut loose the Piney Hills Hunger Project, a food bank serving a desolate rural section of northwestern Louisiana. They were his favorite clients, and not just because they were the first grantee he had ever managed. Although a casual observer might view them as poster children for well-meaning futility, they were in fact an extraordinarily effective outfit that delivered food to an invisible population of migrant workers, elderly shut-ins, and the intractably poor. They were run by Zara Carter-Dokes, a large woman of indeterminate ancestry who loved Michael dearly, and not just because he cut her hefty checks. Michael's biannual visits to their headquarters, a former Woolworths in a decrepit parish seat, were the highlights of his work year. He'd ride along with Zara in her Econoline as she handed out daily bread to people who lived in poverty so deep that it never ceased to astonish him. Zara and her long-time assistants seemed to know the name and life history of every one of the hundreds of people they served. Michael would sometimes pitch in, toting stacked Styrofoam meals through rutted clay yards, ladling oatmeal to shy children, smiling to octogenarians trapped in sweltering rooms whose curtains did not appear to have been drawn in decades.

He had begun to hope that Piney Hills had escaped the axe when the two-line memo from Jaryd arrived. Their application for renewal, pro forma in the past, had been rejected. Michael knew an appeal would be futile. He put off making the call for several days, and when he finally did reach Zara, she announced that she was about to have surgery to repair two failing heart valves. She would be out of action for six months. Her crew could keep things going—just—but there was no way they could find new funding. By the time she got back on her feet the organization would be dead. They needed a year's stay of execution. Zara's message was clear. She expected him to get her the money. Michael said he'd do what he could, a statement that was met with absolute silence.

He asked for a meeting with Jaryd, who listened dead-eyed to his plea, then dismissed it out of hand. If they made an exception in this case, they would have to do so in dozens of others. Michael made some calls to colleagues in other foundations, but it was the same story with all of them. It would take months for an application to go through, even if there had been anyone to write it. And if this was truly an emergency, why wasn't Grammaticus paying?

Michael could not bring himself to call Zara with the bad news. It was not just that his bosses were being bastards. He had become used to that. This was different. This felt like a betrayal of something more than just Zara and the people she served. For the first time in his career, he was being asked to put something of his own on the line. Although he had doled out millions in his time, he had never once risked a thing. His office was climate-controlled, his chair ergonomic; he flew business class and there was always a car waiting. Even the money he controlled was secure, the bottomless fortune left by Karl Gustav Grammaticus was dispersed in amounts a fraction below its rate of growth.

There was something else as well, the suspicion that he had spent the best years of his life trying to make the world just and safe, when it would never be either of those things. The powerful were amassing more power, crowds were crushing anyone who stumbled, noise was drowning out the defeated, ignorance could now move at the speed of light. One need only look at Bertram and his band of true believers to see this was true. And so he decided to continue funding the group. It was a crazy, futile gesture, but the alternative was saying no, and that was suddenly impossible.

It took them three months to catch him. He was surprised when it happened. He truly believed he'd done enough to mask his deception.

26

He'd cancelled their grant, then funneled the money through a Foundation Administered Project that had been left untouched by the new regime. It was only $205,000, a tiny fraction of the great Grammaticus bounty. Considerably less than had been spent on the "strategic summit" Bertram had recently run on Kiawah Island. In the old days, there was every chance he would have got away with it. But these were not the old days. Bertram's accountants were on the loose, scouring the organization for anything brittle that could be hacked away.

Michael knew he'd been busted the moment Jaryd summoned him to his office. His boss took his apostasy, correctly, as a personal affront. Michael had an hour to clear out his office. There was no question of severance or a recommendation. His transgression would make it very difficult to find work at any other charitable fund.

Kim was furious, and it did not look like it was a squall that was going to pass. Real damage had been done to their marriage. He should have told her what he was doing, of course, but he knew what her response would have been. Sympathy, followed by a very reasonable reminder of his obligations and limitations. But he had already decided that this was something he was going to do.

Despite his wife's anger, Michael felt an unexpected elation in the first weeks after he was fired. He told himself he was a martyr; told himself that he was glad to be free. He could write the historical novel he'd been kicking around, the one set during the Whiskey Rebellion. And there was the independent documentary producer he'd funded who was looking for a writer for a film that he was pitching about Bobby Kennedy's final year. There were plenty of things a man of his age and intelligence could do.

Nothing came of his plans. The sense of elation faded, replaced by a dull gray gloom. He'd power out of bed at dawn and brew coffee and sit at his desk and the fog would settle. At night, he'd sip Jameson and watch programs about the Tet offensive or Russia's toughest prisons. He spent a lot of time wondering if he could have done something differently, hidden the funding better or found an alternate source of income. Anything.

And then he heard that Zara had died of complications following her surgery. The news gutted him. Although it was not entirely rational, he could not help but think that cutting the funding to Piney Hills had contributed to her death. The one time in his life he had been asked to risk something, he had come up short.

After that, he stopped acting as if he were undergoing some sort of renaissance. The passage of time did nothing to lessen the blow. In fact, it had grown progressively worse, like a crack in a tempered windshield whose inexorable growth might be too slow to see, but was unstoppable nevertheless. Kim told him he was depressed; she urged him to get help. He made a few appointments, though he wound up breaking them at the last minute. He could not bear the thought of sitting in some comfortable office, staring at Georgia O'Keefe prints and pursuing strategies of health and happiness. He knew what ailed him. He'd failed at doing the one thing he was supposed to do. Help people who actually needed it.

Kim asked him to move out five months after he was fired. She told him he needed to get himself together. He was suffocating her with his gloom. Forty approached, and she did not want to enter middle age with a man who was losing his ability to enjoy their life together. He took a room just off River and set about not getting himself together. Three months later she filed for divorce. He agreed to her absurdly generous terms. Six months after that she was with Douglas and he was back in the house on Locust, keeping an eye on things until the market rebounded. He supported himself by working as a freelance grant writer. There was plenty of work. He knew the lingo. He did not bother looking for anything more permanent. Even if he found someone willing to overlook his transgression, he no longer had the heart for it.

He tried to stay connected to his son, but Will had suffered badly from his father's downfall. His parents' divorce transformed a bright, happy, talkative boy into a glum loner who was badly wounded by every perceived slight, every ill familial wind. Michael attempted to compensate; he tried to give meaningful structure to their weekends and evenings together. But the trips to the cinema and the ball park and the Adirondacks invariably faltered. Michael was not doing the one thing he needed to do. Be the man he was.

Will began to act up. A resinous pipe had been found in his room; scruffy new friends appeared. He cut classes and failed tests. There was a three-day suspension after he talked back to a teacher. Michael understood that this new slacker persona was some kind of funhouse parody of his father's indolence. There just was not a damned thing he could do about it. Kim suggested they get the boy help, but Michael adamantly opposed her. He did not want Will to join the great, shuffling parade of the medicated young. His problems were not chemical. His father had got fired and then his parents split up. No amount of reuptake inhibitors could change those cold, hard facts.

Kim began to find reasons for abbreviating Michael's scheduled visits with their son. She stopped discussing how she was handling the situation. Whatever was going on, Will's attitude had improved recently. He had joined the cross-country team, despite possessing no obvious skill at distance running. Michael had begun to wonder if his son might be getting some outside help after all—his speech was sprinkled with vaguely therapeutic vocabulary. Kim denied it, explaining that he was just getting on with his life.

Left alone, Michael started to date, thinking that might help him back to the land of the living. Finding lovers was not difficult. He was forty-two. He had all his hair and he knew how to listen and his waist was only an inch bigger than it had been when he was at Amherst. He quickly learned the signals and the rituals. The lingering gaze, the quick laugh, the thing with the hair. He'd meet women in the express line at the supermarket, at school functions. His first lover had been Lauren, who'd sold him his Sonata after he downsized from the Audi he'd driven while at Grammaticus. There was April, a dance instructor with a lean body and unmanageable curly hair whose husband was serving fifty months in a minimum security prison for embezzlement. There was a waitress whose name he could not remember, though he would never forget the pierced nipples that he could not stop touching as they lay in bed. With some of his lovers he felt young and adventurous; with others he found himself holding onto the panting miserable body of a stranger, counting the seconds until escape was possible. With none of them, however, did he feel like he was finding his way out of the abyss.

Penny had been his only actual relationship. They'd been lovers for half a year, breaking up a month before he met Justine. Penny was an English teacher at Annville High who wrote quiet, melancholy short stories she'd had no luck publishing. She was Michael's age; she shared his sense of humor and his partiality for morning sex. It had been nice with Penny. But then came the invitation to move in with her and her sheepdog and her pine-scented tidiness and her Victorian novels and her warm, nurturing self. He hesitated and she noted the hesitation and that was that.

And then Justine had come and gone, and everything had changed. Dating became an impossibility. He found himself incapable of even the most basic carnal transaction. So he stopped trying. He knew this was getting ridiculous. Justine was gone. Waiting for her to return was folly. He resolved to give himself until Labor Day and then start over. He'd put his resume out there and hope for the best; he'd start to make a better effort with Will. He'd stop drinking so much and sleeping so late. He'd join a gym and keep an appointment with a counselor to talk about depression, or whatever it was that afflicted him. He'd call Penny.

Nothing came of his planned resurrection. Labor Day had passed, autumn had begun. And now he'd seen her on Water Lane and he was back in his office—who was he kidding, it was a bedroom with a big desk where the bed should be—sipping Jameson, besieged by the same agonizing confusion he had experienced on the day she had left him nine months ago. After settling Will in the rec room, he spent the rest of the night pondering her return. The swelling in his finger had finally gone down, but the pain lingered. No matter how he looked at it, he could not make sense of her presence in Annville. She'd said she was a stranger here and he'd believed her. As for the man with the big filthy hands and the cracked leather jacket, Michael could not even begin to imagine what she was doing with him.

Just after midnight, he went downstairs to fetch his son, and was astonished to find that he had not been playing video games at all, but rather reading a history textbook. Michael was tempted to remark on this, but he knew there was a good chance that anything he said might be construed as a criticism. Once his son was in bed, he retreated to his own room. Falling asleep was not hard—he'd had three large whiskeys. He was well into deep dreamlessness when the tri-tone on his phone sounded. It took a few seconds for the sound to reach the conscious precincts of his brain. It took him several more seconds to grasp the phone and understand what he was reading on its screen.

This is J. You up? I might be needing your help.

J. Justine. Asking for his help. He wrote back immediately, though with the alcohol and the shock and the lingering pain in his finger, it took him several attempts to get the letters right.

Yes. I am here.

He waited, his mouth dry, his heart thudding. He checked the time. 2:17. Come on, he thought. Answer. Say something. But the phone remained quiet.

He typed again.

Justine?

He pressed send. Still, nothing. He carried his phone to the kitchen, where he chased two Motrin with several glasses of water. After another endless interval, he dialed the number on the screen. A generic voice invited him to leave his name and number. As he spoke, his own voice sounded like a man at the bottom of a well.

He paced the kitchen. He made coffee, he had a piece of toast, he washed his face in cold water. *I might be needing your help.* At least he knew what to expect if he came face-to-face with that yellow-eyed man again. There would be no lashing out, no fourteen-year-old boy in tow. Just Michael. Calm, mature, intractable.

She did not text. She did not phone. He once again contemplated calling the police, but he had no idea what he would say to them.

He did not know her full name, he did not know the man's name, he did not know where she lived or her current location. She could have texted from Annville or Manhattan or just after her plane touched down in Los Angeles. And *I might be needing your help* was hardly a harrowing plea for rescue. Just before three-thirty he sent one more text—*I'm here if you need me*—then went to his room. He lay flat on his back, the phone perched on his solar plexus like a defibrillator. He entered a kind of fugue state, his thoughts drifting without progression or consequence. When the sun had finally risen, he fetched the *Sunday Times* from the front porch, but was unable to focus on anything beyond photographs and headlines. Mid-morning, he called her again, and was once again sent immediately to voice mail.

Will emerged from his room just before ten, the teenaged equivalent of the crack of dawn, to go for a run. After his return, they decided on lunch at the Tastee Diner, to be followed by a movie. At the restaurant, Michael insisted on a booth by a window overlooking River Street, even though it meant a five-minute wait, much to Will's muttering displeasure. He spent the meal picking at a tuna salad sandwich and staring into the faces of passersby, ready to spring to his feet, even if it meant chasing a white Mercedes through the heavy Sunday traffic. After leaving the diner, he led his increasingly exasperated son on an unnecessary walk the length of the town's main street to the old restored cinema, secretly hoping to catch sight of her on the way. The film was about street racing. It was noisy and violent and unabashedly stupid, high-definition gibberish happening in front of his eyes as he waited for the phone he gripped to vibrate.

After the credits rolled, he took Will back to Kim's place. His son's new home was a four-bedroom, five-bath, three-car colonial surrounded by two acres of bluegrass that was perpetually cut into a uniform height and perfectly geometric pattern. It was always disorienting to see Kim in this happily suburban setting. There had been an ample portion of irony in their move to Annville five years earlier, a sense that it was provisional, bracketed by their status as exiled urbanites. They had hated leaving their large Back Bay apartment; their city life.

But Bertram wanted to rusticate the company, and Michael had still considered himself a lifer. So they relocated to Annville, rationalizing all the way along the Mass Pike. Will would benefit from the fresh air. Their real estate dollar would stretch much further. There would be no traffic. Crime was virtually nonexistent.

Since their split, Michael's vaguely ironic stance had turned into out-and-out contempt for the suburban inanity all around him. Kim, on the other hand, had flourished. She came into her own in the town of 32,000, with its enviable median household income, its town-wide goal of a ten percent reduction in energy use by the end of the decade, its sturdy floodwall and its sewer grates warning people that noxious effluent would wind up in the bellies and gills of innocent riverine critters. She'd landed a job teaching second grade at a picturesque elementary school named for a minor abolitionist. She'd joined an all-women crew and spent several mornings a week rowing a scull up and down the river with her seven new sisters. She listened to Spanish language tapes in her car so she could be more effective on the Saturday mornings she worked at the food bank in Cheapside.

Kim's new husband, Douglas, was the sort of rival a jilted man was supposed to like, but Michael could not quite bring himself to do that. He was a partner at McNeil Whitty Munro, the law firm that handled much of the town's legal action. His first wife had died eight years earlier from uterine cancer. He had a son in dental school and a daughter who was currently living in Madrid, trying to market sports drinks to a bemused Spanish public. He was even-tempered, courtly, apparently incapable of pettiness. He served on the town's zoning board. He drove a Lexus. He loved Kim dearly.

The happy couple was in the front yard when Michael pulled up, loading raked leaves into recyclable bags. As always, he was struck by how good Kim looked. It was as if she had undergone a reverse-aging process since the divorce. She'd lost the twenty pounds she'd accrued during the last days of their marriage. She and Douglas were *active*. Hiking and tennis, holidays that included parasailing and ziplines. And then there was the sex, never described but occasionally insinuated. The real calorie burner.

Michael wanted to drop his son and go, but the happy couple's presence a few feet from the driveway made escape impossible. He turned off the engine and opened his door, hoping to make this as brief as possible.

"You guys have fun?" Kim asked as they emerged from the car.

"Dad got into a fight last night," Will proclaimed immediately.

Kim's smile collapsed. Michael cursed himself for not instructing his son to keep quiet.

"What's this?"

"Dad saw this dude arguing this hot chick. You should have seen this guy. He was like some crazy man. And Dad smacked him."

The bravado in his son's voice was wafer-thin; yesterday's shock and terror were clearly detectable. Kim's gaze traveled to Michael. Douglas was watching him now as well, his chin perched sagely on his rake handle.

"You got into a fight?" she asked.

"Nobody got into a fight," Michael answered. "A couple was having an argument that was getting out of hand. I just went over to let them know that people were watching."

"But you *hit* him?"

"There were a few shoves. It was nothing."

"Shoves," Will said with an incredulous guffaw.

"Where was this?"

"Water Lane."

"Where's that?"

"It's the alley off River, right next to the CVS," offered Douglas, the zoner.

"Did you know them?"

"No."

"Yes, you did," Will said. "The woman said your name and you said hers."

Michael was not aware Will had heard that much. But only because he had not asked. Kim was staring at him more closely now.

"She was someone I worked with for a while," he said.

"Who?"

"No, I mean a grantee."

"But if you knew who she was why would you just . . ."

Kim stopped herself from asking him the same question he was asking himself. *Why would you just lie?*

"It really wasn't anything."

Kim was still staring at him, making it clear that the source of her concern was not whether Michael had got his licks in, or if he had some hot chick on the side. He had put their son in harm's way.

"It really was not that big a deal."

"I almost called the cops!" Will said, getting angry now that his account was being downplayed. "I had my finger over the last one!"

"Will," Kim said. "Count."

An awkward silence descended as Will went through some silent anger-management procedure.

"Well, it's amazing what people get up to in public these days," Douglas said.

His bromide had the effect of a nerve gas canister rolled into a bingo hall. In the absolute silence that followed, Kim continued to watch Michael, communicating her confusion and unhappiness with that special telepathy of the once-married.

"Okay," Douglas said, sensing a parental tête-à-tête was about to take place. "We got leaves to rake, young man."

Will shrugged his assent and set off after his new guardian, who would never leave him at the mall, or fight with anyone in an alley.

"He's just being dramatic," Michael said once they were out of earshot.

"Seriously, Michael? A fight? In front of your son?"

"Look, I'm really sorry. It just spiraled out of control. I know I didn't handle it right. I was just worried for this woman."

Kim watched him for a moment. Accepting his apology, but also sensing a deeper cause for alarm.

"Are you sure you're okay? You look—I'm sorry, but you look terrible, Michael."

He was tempted to tell her everything. That he had fallen desperately in love with a woman whose entire name he did not know. That he had just seen her again for the first time in nine months, brawling publicly with a man who was some sort of addict or psychotic. It took Michael a very thin fraction of a second to understand just what a bad idea such a confession would be.

"I've just been having trouble sleeping."

"I thought you were going to talk to somebody about that."

"I will."

She searched his face, ready to offer more advice, more support. And then he saw it. The switch. The ex-wife stutter. Spousal concern giving way to the realization that his life was only her business on every other weekend and some Wednesday evenings. Her son was home safely. Michael was no longer her problem.

"You want to stay for dinner?" Kim asked. "I'm not sure what we're having . . ."

Michael knew that she did not want to feed him. She was simply finding the politest way possible to tell him to get off of her lawn.

"No," he lied. "I'm good."

He drove straight to the station, even though an increasingly loud voice inside him was starting to suggest that his behavior was changing from reasonable concern into something a little less noble. Justine had said she might be needing his help. Which meant that she might not. With every hour that passed, the latter option seemed increasingly likely.

And yet he still went to the station. There was no white Mercedes in the parking lot. The next train was due in fifteen minutes. He scanned the scattered faces in the waiting room and on the platform. They were mostly weekenders returning to New York from their river homes or their luxurious mountain redoubts. He checked the bar at the Moon Temple. She was not there—of course she was not there. He returned to the station as last-minute passengers arrived. The train came and went, its cadenced rumble splitting the quiet night.

Michael walked up and down River for the next hour. The sky was clear; there was a gentle breeze that carried the first sting of autumn. He wound up back at the station twenty minutes before the last train was due to leave. In the hall, a half-dozen people waited, all strangers. Self-consciousness drove him back to the Sonata in the nearly empty parking lot. A van arrived a few minutes later. Four young men piled out, all wearing black suits, all with blond crew cuts. They carried large nylon bags. For some reason, Michael thought they were missionaries.

And that was it. When it was time he went to the platform. The train arrived with its usual prehistoric screech. People got on, people got off. She was nowhere in sight. Okay, he told himself. That's that. Game over. And yet he could not dismiss the thought that she was close; that something beyond a simple change of heart had kept her from sending a follow-up text. It was the same thought that had haunted him in the weeks following her first disappearance. Irrational, baseless, yet undeniable. She needed him in some way. Her departure was not entirely voluntary. His time with her was not finished. He remembered what her farewell letter had said. *I don't think you'd like me very much if you knew the truth about me and the world I live in.*

He waited for a few minutes after the train was gone, in case she came late. Finally, the woman in the ticket office came out and told him he should leave. There would be no more trains that night.

THREE

ON MONDAY, HE WOKE AT EIGHT, WHICH WAS EARLY FOR him these days. Sleeping late was a habit he'd fallen into after it had become clear that dawn would bring no bursts of creativity or life-changing epiphanies. It had been a quiet night. There had been no wake-up texts, no urgent calls, no soft but persistent knocks on the door. The sense of emergency was fading.

He made coffee, checked his email, looked online for news of global catastrophe. Next, he went to fetch the *Annville Call* from the front porch. His elderly neighbor, Mrs. Donald, waved at him from her living room's picture window across the street. He gave her a terse nod in return. The housecoat-wearing busybody had been all chatty smiles and baked goods after they moved in, though once

Kim decamped, her demeanor had become distinctly disapproving. Now, her constant requests that Michael help her with household chores or pick up something at "the market" had a punitive tone, as if she saw herself obligated to inject a dose of domestic obligation into his life.

He ducked back inside before she could beckon for him to come have a look at her leaky faucet. He took the paper to the kitchen to read. Although he had never considered the town his home, he had developed an affection for its local paper. Despite running less than thirty pages, it could sometimes feel as rich as a book, with its police log cataloging folly and bad luck, the letters to the editor that were usually pitched somewhere between the idiosyncratic and the insane.

He rolled off the rubber band. The lead article described the growing fear on the part of the town's authorities that the coming weeks would bring damaging floods in the northern part of the county. Rain had been heavier than usual over the summer, and more was on the way. The good news was that Annville's main streets and business parks and most densely populated neighborhoods would almost certainly remain untouched, as they were protected by the sturdy twenty-foot floodwall that had been built a hundred years earlier, after a series of particularly bad floods.

Michael flipped the paper over and the world stopped turning. He was looking at a familiar face. The accompanying article was titled NOTED PHOTOGRAPHER FOUND DEAD IN ANNVILLE MOTEL. Michael read the words, but it still took him several long seconds to understand that this was the man who had been with Justine on Water Lane. And he was dead. The stylish black-and-white portrait captured him in a much better state from the crazed and ruined creature Michael had confronted two days earlier. He looked smart and strong; aloof and invincible. The sculpted sideburns, the hard mouth and deepset eyes—everything about him suggested confidence and command. The tattoo snaking around his neck looked radiant, just-inked. Cigarette smoke leaked from his nostrils like the exhaust from a vehicle that had just won a high-speed race. He was different, but it was him. And he was dead.

Michael started to read.

Desmond Tracey, the celebrated photographer whose work provoked controversy in the United States and abroad, was found dead Sunday morning at the Valencia Motel in Annville. He was 42. Police are treating the cause of death as an accidental drug overdose. Foul play is not suspected.

"Narcotics and drug paraphernalia were found at the scene," Detective Andrew Maas of the Annville Police Department said when reached for a comment. "The death was unattended. We are operating under the assumption this was an overdose."

Tracey, once a well-known figure on the New York art scene, had faded from public view in recent years. The last showing of his work was in 2005 in Portland, Maine. He was unmarried and is not survived by any children.

Police refused to speculate on what Tracey was doing in the area. This brings to six the number of deaths by suspected narcotics over-dose in Annville this year, a marked increase from previous years.

"It's obviously becoming a problem," Maas claimed. "Drugs are flooding the entire river valley region. Out-of-towners are coming in to take advantage of the fact that we just don't have the manpower to deal with this escalation."

There was nothing about a woman who had summoned the police or been spotted leaving the scene; nothing about her corpse having been found beside the dead man, or pulled from the nearby river. Michael looked back at the photo of Desmond Tracey. He remembered the strength in his hands, the yellowy desperation in his eyes, the acid stink of his breath. Drugs. Of course. Which made sense of the loca-tion as well. Michael knew the Valencia. It was at the northern edge of town, a scattering of huts that backed onto a small swift tributary to the river. It was isolated and shabby. Rooms were always available.

Michael was struck by a sudden surge of nausea. Sweat—it was actually cold—drenched his skin. This man had killed her. He had taken her up to this desolate spot and he killed her and then he killed himself. She'd tried to text for help, but Desmond Tracey had stopped her before she could tell Michael what was happening. Those powerful hands on her pale throat. Desmond Tracey had killed her and thrown her in the river. Or dumped her in the woods. The newspaper said nothing about her because the police did not know she had been with him. Or they knew and were not yet ready to speak publicly about it.

The *Call* always arrived before dawn, which meant that the article would have been written several hours ago, perhaps even the previous night. He needed to see something more recent. He rushed to his computer and searched Tracey's name. The latest article had been published within the hour on a site called the *Gotham Rag*. Its opening paragraphs repeated the information in the *Call*, including the detective's quote. Michael skimmed through the rest of it. There was nothing about a woman, dead or alive. Just a detailed biography of the deceased. He checked several other articles, including a brief mention on the website of a television news channel out of Albany. Still, there was nothing about a woman. Everyone claimed that Tracey had died alone. Unattended.

Michael went back to read the section of the *Gotham Rag* article he had only scanned.

Tracey gained national notoriety in 1996 when In Extremis, *an exhibition of his work at the Albright-Knox Art Gallery in Buffalo, drew both critical praise and strong protests. The photographs focused exclusively on female subjects, many of them dwelling in the margins of society. The show provoked outrage from feminists and religious conservatives alike, driving them into an unholy alliance that accused the reclusive artist of exploiting vulnerable women. Undaunted, Tracey moved the show to the previously third-tier Andrei Klimov Gallery in New York City, where it had a triumphant run. The book based upon it was one of the best-selling art volumes of the year.*

His next exhibit, Varsa, *also sparked controversy when it debuted in 2002. Funded by grants from the Guggenheim Foundation and the National Endowment for the Arts, it included portraits of patients at women's hospitals for the criminally insane in Romania, Haiti, and Guatemala. The exhibit drew furious protests from the Romanian government, which unsuccessfully sought Tracey's extradition to face charges of bribery, larceny, and criminal trespass.*

Although Varsa *confirmed the artist as both a critics' darling and commercial player, Tracey faded from public view in the years that followed. Friends spoke of a steep, drug-fueled decline. There were rumors of madness and homelessness. The last showing of his work was in 2005 at a small gallery in Portland, Maine. Andrei Klimov, whose soon-to-be-defunct Bowery gallery repped Tracey's work for the entirety of his meteoric run, said that the artist recently seemed to be losing his long struggle with the needle.*

"Trace could be a pretty self-destructive guy," Klimov claimed after being reached late Sunday. "People loved him for his edginess, but it could drive you crazy too. He burned a lot of bridges."

The elusive Tracey, who rarely spoke with the press or appeared at public gatherings, was born in Midlothian, Texas, in 1970. His mother, Andrea Atherton Tracey, was raped and murdered when Tracey was eight years old by two men who would later be executed for the crime. Tracey, who was rumored to have witnessed his mother's death, was subsequently raised in a series of foster homes and state institutions, where he claimed in a 2003 interview (with ArtForum Magazine*) he was regularly abused. He briefly attended Texas State University before moving to New York City.*

Funeral arrangements have not been announced.

There was a portal to Tracey's work at the bottom of the piece. Michael clicked on it and was confronted after a fraction of a second by a crowded array of photographs, too small to view in detail. He clicked one randomly. It pictured a very young woman, perhaps a teenager, in a tattered hospital gown. Her exposed skin was filthy, her ankle was chained to an iron bed. Michael could see immediately that this was not some edgy fashion shoot, not some artistic provocation. It was very real, taken in one of those hospitals for the criminally insane in Romania. He clicked another. In this one, a naked woman lay stretched on a gleaming silver gurney. She was young, not yet in her thirties. There was something voluptuous about her posture. Her eyes were pointed directly at the camera, but there was nothing in them, no recognition or light. She was dead. Not posed; not play-acting. But actually, irrevocably dead.

He had to call the police. They needed to know that Justine had been with Desmond Tracey. This man who took photographs of dead and damaged women. They needed to know this was happening. In his panic, he almost dialed 911, but Will had done this out of mischievous curiosity last year, when he was at his worst, bringing two squad cars and a fire engine to Locust Street. The nonemergency number was answered by a curt male voice.

"I'd like to speak to someone about Desmond Tracey," Michael said. "The man who died at the Valencia Motel?"

"Your name?"

"Michael Coolidge."

"What can I do for you, sir?"

"I saw a woman with him on Saturday evening."

"With Desmond Tracey."

"Yes."

"You were with him?"

"No. I just saw them briefly."

"But you knew him."

"No. I knew the woman."

"And her name?"

"Justine. I'm not sure of her last name."

There was a pause.

"What is your relationship with her?"

The male operator said, "She's a friend."

"Where was this, that you saw them?"

"On Water Lane, just off River. This was around five in the evening. They were standing by a white Mercedes and then they got into it and left. I just now read that he had died and I wanted to see if she was all right."

"Do you have reason to think she is not?"

"I don't know. They were arguing."

"What about?"

"I'm not sure."

More silence.

"Is there anything else?"

"She texted me later that night and asked me for help."

"What kind of help?"

"She didn't specify."

"What were her words exactly?"

"I might be needing your help."

There was another pause. Michael could hear clicking. This was all being written down.

"And have you been in contact with her since?"

"No. That's what's so worrying. She won't answer my calls."

"Okay, I'll pass this along to the detective in charge and he'll be in touch. Is this a good number?"

Michael gave him his cell number.

"So should I be worried about her?" he asked before the man could go.

"The detective will call."

Michael hung up. The house phone rang immediately. He snatched it up, expecting it to be the detective, calling with illumination. But it was just a robotic voice asking if he wanted help with his debts. He slept his computer and got his car keys.

He took River Road north. A few hundred yards after the town's center, it became Route 44. Michael had driven this route a thousand times, but it felt completely different now. A place of danger, saturated with her presence. He tried not to think about her in the passenger seat of that big car. He tried to not to think of the look on her face as it raced past him. He tried not to think of her dead, Desmond Tracey's lens pointed down at her.

Homes and businesses lined 44 for the first mile. Down by the river there were the former mills and factories that now housed law firms and software developers and doctors' offices, all of them protected by the floodwall. Grammaticus was there, spread over ten landscaped acres. Development eventually gave way to countryside. It was still Annville—the town was something of a geographical oddity, its limits stretching for almost ten miles from top to bottom. Up here, there were horse farms, antique shops, stretches of dark woods. On the river, big estates, protected by floodwalls or situated on bluffs. It was in one of these he'd always presumed Justine's reclusive buyer to live.

The Valencia was seven miles from Water Lane. The paint on its large sign had been chipped and faded by the elements. Directly across the road was Rustic Arts, a massive barn surrounded by a formation of chainsaw sculptures. The only vehicle in the hotel's graveled lot was a radiant black Escalade. There was no sign of the white Mercedes; there were no squad cars or step vans operated by men in protective gear; no line of people beating the surrounding underbrush. Just him and the Escalade.

The hotel's main office was a small hut adjacent to the parking lot. A dozen cabins of identical design were lined up diagonally behind it, following the tributary as it ran down to the river. A chainsaw began to whine across 44 as Michael emerged from his car. There was a sign slotted behind the front door's cloudy glass. CLOSED FOR SEASON. Beyond that, a small reception area with a counter, chairs, a table strewn with leaflets. It was empty.

He followed the trammeled dirt path that led to the cabins. They were almost ludicrously small, hardly larger than a tool shed. A motorized cart was parked by the last of them. Two people stood beside it, a tall, broad-shouldered man in a dark suit and a short woman with bloated legs. As Michael headed toward them, he caught glimpses of the stream behind the huts, swift and shallow, sparkling in the late morning sun. To his right, a muddy field that held a playground, a picnic area and a scattering of chainsaw sculptures. Beyond that, trees. Wilderness. A place for shallow graves.

The woman spotted Michael first. Her expression was both wary and overwhelmed. She was in her sixties, he guessed, her ankles so swollen that her flesh-colored support hose looked to be on the point of bursting. She wore bright pink rubber gloves and a sun-bleached Yankees cap. The tall man noted the shift in her attention and turned. He looked to be in his fifties, with a strong jaw and short red hair that was beginning to turn gray. He made no effort to hide his displeasure at being interrupted. After a few parting words to the woman, he walked back toward the parking lot. He held Michael's gaze as they passed. There was a cold scrutiny in his pale blue eyes, as if he was trying to place Michael, or figure out what to do about him. Michael nodded a greeting, but the man simply looked away.

"It's getting like Grand Central around here," the woman said as he drew near.

"I'm sorry to bother you," Michael answered. "Are you the manager?"

"Among other things," she said, displaying her rubber gloves.

"Is this the room where Desmond Tracey was staying?"

"And you are?"

"He was a friend."

She squinted suspiciously, thinking about the sort of people who had drug addicts for friends.

"I've been trying to help him with his problems, but we'd lost touch," Michael said. "And now this."

His melancholy *this* worked. The woman shook her head in sour commiseration.

"Yeah, he was here. They took him and his possessions away yesterday. And his narcotics, which were plentiful, evidently. They left his garbage behind, however."

"That must have been terrible. Finding him."

"The husband had the honor. And yes, I believe terrible was the word he used. Among others of a more colorful nature."

"So what happened?"

"Who are you again?"

"My name is Michael Coolidge."

She watched him, wanting more. It occurred to Michael that he should have prepared a story to make himself plausible.

"Do you know who claimed the body?" he asked.

She still looked skeptical.

"I'm just wondering if I would need to take care of that. His remains."

"Oh. Well, the police carted him off yesterday, so you should talk to them. They were poking around here all day."

"Was he police?" Michael asked, gesturing over his shoulder.

"Him? No. I'm not sure what he was. Other than intimidating."

"I'm just having trouble making sense of it all," Michael said.

The very real hopelessness in his voice struck a chord. Something softened in the woman's expression, perhaps at the thought of a friend trying to make sense of it all. She shrugged and looked back through the open door.

"Well, I don't know how much sense you're going to find, because what happened is that your friend overdosed on drugs."

"Was he staying here alone?"

"I never saw no one else. Best I could tell, he came and went at all hours in that big car of his."

"The white Mercedes."

"That's it."

"I didn't see it when I came in."

"They towed it about an hour ago, at my insistence. I didn't want it getting stole and then somebody blaming me for it. You'll have to discuss the car with the police."

"How long was he here? I've been looking for him everywhere."

"Three weeks. We were going to boot him out yesterday because we're closing, which is why the husband came down here in the first place. Normally, we let people be. We're a stop for bikers and those folks are in a permanent state of DO NOT DISTURB, I have learned."

"Did he say why he was here?"

"He told the husband that he was a photographer, so we figured he just wanted to take pictures of the leaves. We get those types, too. Leaf peepers."

"Were you around Saturday night? I mean, when it happened?"

"We live down the road about a hundred yards. So the answer to your question is yes and no. The husband sleeps on a cot in the office in the busy season, but on Saturday there was only your friend here, so we stayed home."

Michael could not think of any further questions.

"Well, I just wanted to see where it happened."

"They're saying he was famous once?" she asked, chatting now.

"Pretty famous. In his own world."

"Well, hell, we're all that!" she said with a laugh.

"No, I mean, the art world."

"The husband intimated as much this morning. Though he didn't go into specifics. He said that the man's artistic taste would not have been my cup of tea. But I guess people like all sorts of things these days."

"He'd fallen on hard times."

"So it would appear."

Something occurred to Michael.

"Was there a camera? Among his effects, I mean."

"Didn't leave much of anything except garbage."

"No photographs? Negatives?"

"Not that I saw. Police may have took it, though to be honest I don't remember seeing anything like that when we were waiting for them to first respond."

"Strange, though. A photographer without a camera."

"Not as strange as putting a needle in your arm for fun. Well, I better get back to make lunch for His Highness. Sorry about your friend. I imagine he had his qualities. Most people do."

She lowered herself clumsily into the cart and sped off. She'd left the front door open to air the place out. Michael waited until she was out of sight, then stepped inside. The room was so small that it was hard to imagine Desmond Tracey in here alone, much less with Justine. There was a stripped bed made of stained wood, a narrow dresser with a mirror. The odor of pine disinfectant was almost overwhelming. There were two doors at the back. The first was for a bathroom that was barely big enough to stand in, the second opened onto a small swept area with a rusted barbecue grill and a blistered picnic table. There were flagstone steps down to a rocky beach that stretched twenty yards to the water's edge. In the stream, he could see boulders shimmering beneath the surface, all the way to the far side. It was too shallow to hide much of anything. Unless the current had taken her downhill to the river.

After one last look at the cabin, he walked back to the parking lot. His phone rang just as he reached his car.

"Mr. Coolidge? This is Detective Andrew Maas of the Annville Police. I understand you have information about Desmond Tracey?"

He listened without comment as Michael recounted the story he'd told earlier.

"And when did you get the text from her?" he asked him.

"2:17 on Sunday morning."

"And what did that say?"

"I might be needing your help."

"And that was all?"

"Yes. I haven't heard anything since."

"Can I have that number?"

Michael told him.

"And you know this woman how?"

"We spent time together earlier this year."

"But you don't know her last name?"

"That's right."

There was a brief pause.

"Is she local?"

"She said she was from New York."

"And you don't have any specific reason to believe Desmond Tracey intended her harm. Threats or anything like that."

"No. Not specifically."

"And would you say that she got into the car of her own accord?"

"Yes. I mean, she was upset, but it wasn't like he dragged her."

It occurred to Michael that he should tell him about her slap, about his own brief struggle with Tracey. And yet he could not bring himself to tell the police that Justine had struck a man who would wind up dead a few hours later. In fact, he was beginning to wonder if making this call had been a good idea, if he might somehow be creating trouble for Justine instead of helping her.

"Is there anything else you'd like to add?" the detective was asking.

"No."

"Okay, I think we have what we need here."

"I'm sorry this is all so vague, but I'm just worried that something happened to her. I mean, should I be?"

"Worried? Well, you never know when drugs are involved, but at this point we don't see any cause for alarm."

"But what about her text?"

"I gotta tell you, *I might be needing your help* can mean a lot of things. It could mean she had a flat tire or wanted twenty bucks or a shoulder to cry on. It's not exactly an SOS."

"And you're not looking for her or anything."

There was a pause.

"No, Mr. Coolidge," the detective said, the timbre of his voice changing a little, growing slower, more wary. "We aren't looking for her."

"Okay, well, sorry to trouble you."

"It's no trouble at all. We always like to hear from the public."

As Michael drove back to Annville, the acid sting of panic that had flooded his nervous system at the sight of that photo in the *Call* settled into a steady buzz of low-level dread. The police were not concerned about her well-being. There had been no sign of violence at the hotel.

His initial fears—that she was in that shallow tributary or the thick woods or the trunk of the Mercedes—were growing less likely. He knew he should take reassurance from this, but he could not shake his conviction that something terrible had happened to her. There was a lot of emptiness up here. There were security gates, private drives. He was beginning to understand that it did not matter what the police said or what was reported in the press. The conclusions arrived at by his rational mind would be ultimately meaningless until he was able to lay eyes on her.

At his house, he checked for new developments. There were a dozen more articles on the death of Desmond Tracey, but there was still nothing about her. The tenor of them all was the same. A narrative was building. A once-celebrated artist had become enmeshed in drugs and died in solitary squalor. Michael searched for news of "Justine Annville," just in case she was mentioned independently of Tracey. There was nothing. Just as there always had been.

He started to look at Desmond Tracey's hectic past for some hint of her, some residue that would suggest who she was to him or where she might now be. According to the interview Tracey had given to *ArtNews* around the time of his second show—the only real interview Michael could find—he came to New York City in 1991, when he was nineteen. He worked as an orderly at prisons and mental institutions, a bouncer at strips clubs, a gypsy cab driver. Anything that allowed him to tap the vein of his obsession. He started calling himself Trace. Some of the photographs chosen for his first exhibition, *In Extremis*, were reproduced online. Now, looking at his work with something like a level head, Michael was able to make a simple determination about the desperate man in the alley, the ignominiously dead junkie in the miniscule hut. Desmond Tracey was good. Very, very good. Brilliant, brave, utterly honest. His most widely reproduced photo, titled *Felonee, Queens, 1995*, was taken in a decrepit strip club. It was a frontal portrait of a dancer standing with her back to a mirrored wall, looking wobbly on stiletto heels. An unhooked, sequined bra top dangled from her throat, exposing veined and swollen breasts that looked as hard as marble. She wore no bottom; there were striations of fat. Her right hand clutched a plastic bottle of Diet Pepsi, her left hand was in the process of tucking a curl of frosted hair behind her ear. In the mirror behind her, there was a nova, the flashing camera. Behind that, a shadowy figure of a man. Trace. Felonee smiled shyly, girlishly, both pleased and embarrassed at having her photo taken. Her expression suggested a drum majorette or a twelve-year-old at her christening, not a fading stripper dwelling in the shabbier precincts of the sex trade.

Women in jail, women in hospital beds, women sitting against rubbled walls. A woman staring serenely at the camera from the back of a squad car just after being arrested for drowning her two children in a bathtub. The virtuosity of the photographs made Michael feel a little squalid. Trace's ability to find beauty in terrible situations was like a kind of thievery. And he was not alone in his unease. Nobody seemed very happy about their reactions to the photos. Critics praised them grudgingly. Many of those who accused Trace of exploitation did so with reluctance as well, almost as if the artist did not know he was guilty of the offense. A piece in the *Nation*, titled THE INTERSEC-TION OF BEAUTY AND PAIN, wondered how "Trace could be so brilliant at his craft without providing any of the usual consolations or transcendence found in art. It makes you suspect honesty is not all it is cracked up to be."

He got in trouble. There were arrests, fights, accusations that he failed to secure necessary permission. There were a lawsuit filed by the parents of a seventeen-year-old anorexic who he had photographed naked on the toilet at her Bergen County home. There were awards and grants, but he never became a fixture on the art scene. He did no group shows, he did not appear in documentaries, there were no photos of him at openings. His second show, *Varsa*, took its name from the Romanian word for "weeds," the nickname given to patients in the country's psychiatric hospitals, administered by the Bureau for the Resocialization of the Mentally Ill. Somehow, Trace had gained access to a number of these institutions. He'd performed similar incursions in Guatemala and Haiti. What was remarkable about these photographs was how subtle they could be. There was no hair pulling or screeching. Madness was evident in a slight skew of the eyes, a twist of the mouth. The most famous was the first picture Michael had glimpsed in his panic and confusion that morning, the young woman chained to the hospital bed. It was titled "Madalina, Cluj, 2001". The sheets bunched around her were streaked with blood, or shit, or both. The flesh beneath the handcuffs binding her ankle to the iron bedframe was swollen and scabbed. Her soiled gown had risen up to her hips, exposing emaciated legs. The scratch marks on her forearms looked self-inflicted. But her face, framed in matted black hair that somehow fell elegantly on the thin pillowless mattress, was beautiful. She wore lipstick; her eyebrows curved gracefully, taut and elegant, like birds riding a thermal. Her wide dark eyes were serene. She was not appealing for help; not begging to be liberated. It was the face of a woman who had already escaped.

After *Varsa*, nothing. Months passed, seasons passed, years, without so much as a single photograph, much less a show. The exhibition in Maine was an attempt at career resuscitation that wound up being little more than a flattened palm pumping a moribund chest. By the end of the decade, mentions had thinned down to occasional diarists wondering whatever happened to the photographer who called himself Trace. The only name that appeared to be currently associated with him was the gallery owner quoted the *Gotham Rag*, Andrei Klimov.

Who was Rasputin. Michael had sensed as much when he first saw the name this morning, but he had been too worried to think it through. He had gone to the Klimov Gallery during his impromptu March walkabout but had not spoken to the dealer himself. Instead, he had been dismissed by a surly young woman who had never heard of a Justine. That was what she'd claimed, anyhow. He remembered the place as being threadbare. But Klimov was Rasputin. Her boss, whatever that might mean. He was the connection. He would know who she was to the photographer. Lover, dealer, subject, fellow artist. Victim.

It was almost five, too late to go to the city now. Besides, he wanted to check the evening trains, in case she had stayed in town to deal with the aftermath of Trace's death. Before leaving the house, Michael brought up the photograph of the woman in the Romanian asylum. Madalina. The one who escaped without moving an inch. He stared into her eerily serene eyes until they almost came alive. Eyes that were animated by a hidden power, a knowledge that made them beautiful amidst all the pain and ugliness. Eyes that held him even more strongly than the iron hands of the man who had captured them on film. What have you seen, Michael wondered, that makes it impossible for me to turn away? Where do you go when you escape?

FOUR

HE FOUND A WINDOW SEAT, EVEN THOUGH THE TRAIN was nearly full when he boarded. His reflection in the scored glass suggested he was just another yawning citizen headed to the city. Copies of the *Times* and the *Call* covered his lap; his bag was on the rack above him. In his jacket pocket, he carried an envelope containing the thousand dollars in cash he had always kept in his desk at home for emergencies. He also had a small stack of business cards identifying him as a vice president at the Grammaticus Fund.

There had been no sign of her at the station last night, no sign of her anywhere in town. While sitting in his car between trains, Michael called Annville's three funeral parlors to see if any of them had Desmond Tracey's body, thinking she might be with him. Nobody had the man. They all suggested he check with the county morgue, but the woman who answered the phone was only authorized to give out information to immediate family. The morgue was located in the basement of the town's hospital. He drove there during the next gap between trains. There were only strangers in the waiting area and the cafeteria. He also checked the Moon Temple again, the lobby of the Sheraton, and even did a quick survey of the Annville Tavern. Nothing. He returned to his house just before midnight.

The next logical step was to speak with Klimov. If you could call anything he was doing now logical. Once again, he was struck by the notion that it was time for him to stop looking for her. He had done everything required of him. He had offered her his help; he had notified the competent authorities that she might be in danger. And yet even as he deployed these very reasonable arguments, he knew that he would not be stopping. He needed to look into her eyes and see that Saturday's fear was gone. He needed to hear from her that she was all right. And there was the fact—perhaps greater than his alarm or concern—that he simply needed to see her again. Until that happened, nothing would feel right. So he would call the gallery first thing in the morning. He slept dreamlessly for a while after that, but woke up just after four, his heart racing, his mind troubled by the certainty that he had left some crucial thing undone.

He searched again for news of her online. There was nothing he had not already seen. Police were not appealing for information about a woman who had been seen with Desmond Tracey hours before his death. A body was not awaiting identification after being found by hikers or fished from the river. As for Trace himself, fond remembrances and attempts to assess his work were notably absent from the blogs. The stark fact of his demise, ignominious and vaguely cautionary, was all he had left to contribute to the great digital conversation, and even that stream was rapidly drying up. A man—almost famous once, nearly forgotten now—had died, consumed by his own private demons. The world spun on.

The sun rose and Michael understood that calling Klimov would be a waste of time. The man would tell him nothing over the phone. He needed to see him, face-to-face, if he had any chance of learning something. And so he joined the commuters who endured 103 minutes on a crowded train in each direction to take advantage of Annville's affordable real estate, its farmers' markets and hiking trails, its schools without metal detectors. He did not open the newspapers on the journey down. Instead, he watched the river until he started to drift into sleep. But then a terrible image entered his mind. Her body, beneath the muddy irregular surface, as beautifully dead as the women Trace had photographed. The thought snapped him so violently awake that he drew several sharp glances from the commuters around him.

Easy, he told himself. Just keep looking. One step at a time.

Penn Station; the subway downtown; a short walk along the Bowery to the Andrei Klimov Gallery. It was a quarter to ten when Michael arrived. The moment he saw the place he feared the article in the *Gotham Rag* was already outdated; that, like its star artist, the gallery had passed beyond the soon-to-be-defunct. The windows were obscured by large sheets of butcher paper that had not been there during Michael's previous (computer) visit. A darkness emanated from around their edges. He tried the door. It was locked. There was no sign explaining what was happening. Last night, he'd read that Klimov's last show had closed in March; no new ones were scheduled. Michael called the number he'd written down and was sent to a voice mail that did not promise a return call. He left no message. He would not know where to start.

He found a window stool in a café across the street and ordered a cup of coffee as he summoned a photo of Klimov to his computer screen. Taken at an opening three years earlier, it showed a blond, sharp-faced man who wore a pinstriped suit. More Polanski than Rasputin. Which was not exactly a consoling thought.

The morning passed. Michael ordered two more cups of coffee, and then a sandwich. All the while watching the gallery. Finally, just before one, Klimov appeared, strolling without urgency. He wore a well-cut tan suit with broad lapels and flared trousers, the sort of thing that had been popular in the 1970s. Michael hustled out of the café and crossed the street. He did not want Klimov to close the door before he arrived—there was no guarantee he would open it for Michael, or anyone else. He was still in the middle of the street when the dealer got his key in the lock.

"Mr. Klimov?"

Michael had spoken too loudly, too sharply, but Klimov turned to him without surprise, a man accustomed to being called out. He held the inserted key in place. Up close, his eyes were more gray than blue, his lips so small they were almost nonexistent.

"Could I have a word with you?"

"I am no longer in the genius business. Sorry."

There was an accent, not too thick. Russia, or one of its satellites.

"I'm not an artist."

The dealer shrugged.

"You don't look it. But these days, you never know."

Klimov waited, his hand still on the untwisted key. They would be conducting their business in the street for the time being.

"It's about Desmond Tracey," Michael said.

Klimov's expression took on an even more defensive cast.

"If he is owing you money, I cannot help."

"He doesn't owe me money."

"Are you a journalist? Because you guys really should make appointments."

"No, I . . . I saw him. Just before he died."

Klimov's eyes narrowed; his head cocked slightly.

"What do you mean, you saw him? What are you?"

"My name is Michael Coolidge."

"When was this, Michael Coolidge, that you saw him?"

"On Saturday. In Annville."

"All right. You saw him. The guy got around. This we know. Why are you telling me this?"

"He was with a woman I know. I'm worried about her."

"You are worried."

"They were arguing when I saw them. It looked very serious. And then a few hours later he's dead and she's nowhere to be found."

"You are speaking with the police?"

"They weren't all that concerned about her."

"Isn't this telling you something?"

"I'd just like to make sure she's all right. That's all I'm after."

Klimov stared at him.

"Can we talk inside?" Michael asked.

The dealer shrugged and opened the door. He hit a switch as he stepped into his gallery. Fluorescent lights flickered on. He left the door open behind him as he started to move through the empty space.

"Close the door behind you," he said without turning around.

Michael did as instructed. There was a stepladder, there were wires, there were ghostly rectangles on white walls. At the back of the gallery, Klimov disappeared into a short corridor. Michael followed him. There were five closed doors here. Klimov opened the last of these, at the end of the hall. It was his office, filled with boxes, its shelves emptied. He sat behind a desk and started his computer. Unbidden, Michael occupied one of the two chairs opposite him.

"Back in the days," Klimov said, his eyes on his screen, "men are always coming for Trace. Angry men. Sad men. Desperate men. Fathers, husbands. Cops. Lawyers. Trace has a way of getting under the skin with that fucking Polaroid. Had. There are even diplomats. Literally. Romanian diplomats, in a state of dungeon. Everyone should see this once. It is like Dracula on meth."

He shot Michael a quick glance.

"And then there are the others. Men who are doing things to the girls that maybe they are not wanting anybody to know. The ones eager to stay in the shadows."

There was a meaningful silence.

"You are not a shadow man, are you, Michael Coolidge? This woman you are concerned about—she is not somebody who is getting away from you?"

"No."

"You have something perhaps for me that says you are who you are?"

Michael handed him a Grammaticus card. Klimov raised his eyebrows in brief recognition. He flicked at the edge of the card with a long nail.

"So what are we discussing here?"

"I'm trying to find a woman I saw with your artist on Saturday. Her name is Justine. I think she might have worked for you?"

Klimov made a fluttering gesture with those tapered fingers, like he was trying to shake off a cobweb.

"No. Sorry. I know no Justine. Why do you think she worked for me?"

"She indicated her boss was a Russian art dealer and so when I saw that you represented Tracey . . ."

"And what makes you think I'm Russian? Joke. But seriously, I don't know any Justines. Well, Justine Schweppers, in Berlin. Was this woman about eighty? German? Used a cane with a minotaur on the handle?"

Michael did not feel that a response was required.

"This cane—she claims that Picasso made it for her. Please, pick a better lie, lady."

"Maybe she used a different name when she was here."

"Describe."

"Mid-twenties. Dark hair, brown eyes. Very pale. Thin. Beautiful."

"Now you are making me wish she is working here. But, alas."

"Well, maybe she had some other relationship with Trace."

"Excuse me, but before we go further, what might have been *your* relationship to her?"

"We were lovers," Michael said, sensing that any other answer would have conveyed the same information. "She left me in January and the other day she turns up with Desmond Tracey."

"She is a junkie?"

"No. I'm starting to think she may have been Tracey's girlfriend."

"You will have to pardon me if I am laughing here." He was not laughing. "Girlfriend."

"Was he gay?"

"Listen to this guy. Gay. I am literally dying here with laughter."
His face was still stony. "Trace was not exactly for the romance. You
have seen his work, right?"

"Some of it."

"He loved women with his camera."

"I'm not sure what that means."

"The guy was not a sexual man, Mr. Coolidge. His dick did not
work. And I am not talking out of the school here. It was not exactly
a secret to those who knew him."

He noted Michael's astonished expression.

"Right? It is a pisser. Literally."

Klimov tossed Michael's card down on his desk, giving it a little
spin, like he was folding a losing hand.

"Look, Trace is dead. I know this is coming, but still, it is a big
shock. Trace and I have a long history but the last few years—not
happy." He shrugged. "The guy was a junkie. End of story. He'd
OD'd before, you know."

"When?

"Last year. He was dead but they brought him back in the ambulance. To life, I mean. He had to find his own way home."

He shrugged.

"You are concerned for your lover. I see this. But Trace is not a
violent guy with the women. The idea of him doing harm to a person
of the female persuasion—no. With men, this is another story. I've
seen him fuck some men up pretty good. But the chance he is hurting
your girl—no."

"But why was he upstate?"

"People are not shooting up where you live, Mr. Coolidge? They
do not die?" He shrugged. "Maybe he was somebody's guest. Trace
had a way of getting rich people to put him up."

"But he died in a motel."

"Tennessee Williams? Sid Vicious? John Belushi? Jimi Hendrix?
Stop me anytime."

Michael sat in frustrated silence.

"Trace often lived homeless, even when there was lots of money coming in. Although back then they are calling it nomadic. Okay, he owns the place down in Chinatown, but he would sometimes take extending holidays. For a while this really works for him. But then he loses Chinatown and the invitations stop. God knows where he lived this past year. Not the Hamptons, I guarantee this. The mind literally boggles."

Klimov leaned forward and brought his small hands down on his desk. Wrapping things up.

"So, I better get to work," he said.

Michael could not leave it at this. There had to be something more.

He said, "I read that he had taken hundreds of photos that he never used in his shows."

Klimov gave him a guarded nod.

"Do you know where those are?"

"Why are you asking me this?"

"If she's in one of them . . ."

"You think she might be one of his subjects?" He winced. "These are not the sort of girls you want to bring home to Mother."

"Honestly? I don't know what to think. I just have to find her."

"I am sorry. It is not right. Having someone look through his work."

"I'd buy it," Michael said. "If I found a photo of her, I'd buy it."

Klimov leaned back in his chair. No longer quite so intent on wrapping things up.

"You are being serious."

"Yes."

"Just her. I am still waiting for the market to speak. Dead people have a way of staging comebacks"

"Just her."

"Subject to negotiation."

"I'll take a Xerox, Mr. Klimov. I really just want to find her and see if she's all right."

"Perhaps we should establish some sort of a floor. A thousand dollars?"

"I can give you five hundred in cash."

"I said floor, not the basement."

"Seven hundred."

Their eyes held. Klimov shrugged.

"What the hell. The guy is not selling anything in years."

It turned out that Trace's work was stored just a few feet away, behind one of the doors in the corridor. Cash in hand, Klimov became more effusive.

"I took possession of his *oeuvre* right after *In Extremis* opened and he is getting big," he explained as they reached the right door. "He was staying with some lunatics in New Jersey and most of his prints are in a big suitcase."

Klimov wielded the keys but was not yet using them.

"Trace, I mean, he does not care about these things. You know, I am not really sure he was even an artist. And I mean this as a compliment."

He was becoming lost in his memories now.

"If the art world did not exist—and believe me, this is a thought I am consoling myself with sometimes—then Trace still would be getting his hands on a camera. No Guggenheim? Nobody buying him sushi? He robs a liquor store. People use this word obsessive and it is usually bullshit. But with Trace, it is true. Was."

Michael said, "I saw this one photo he did online. 'Madalina?'"

"This is up in Rochester. At the Eastman."

"I can't really stop thinking about it."

"You won't, Michael Coolidge. Not soon."

Klimov finally opened the door. He hit a switch; a track of fluorescent bulbs flared to reveal six filing cabinets arranged against two walls in an otherwise bare room.

"And so here we are," he said. "The Desmond Tracey Museum. Though maybe we should be calling it mausoleum. I swear to God, last time I saw him, it is not clear if he even remembers this stuff was here. Or that he had taken it in the first place."

The room smelled of metal and shadow and dust. Its stillness was absolute.

"Okay, take as long as you need. I'll be in my office."

He pointed to Michael's bag.

"And please do not rip me off, Grammaticus."

"I'm only looking for this one thing."

Klimov scrutinized him for a moment.

"You almost never hear me say this, but I believe you."

And then he was gone, leaving Michael to look for Justine amid the life's work of a brilliant, nomadic, drug-addicted photographer. He did a quick preliminary survey of the six cabinets. Each had three drawers; the top drawer of each had a label. They looked to be in chronological order. The first was "Midlothian/Texas State."

The two after that were both labeled "inextremis"; the next two were called "Varsa." The label on the final cabinet read "Misc." Michael performed a rapid calculation. If Justine's story was to be believed, she had arrived in New York sometime in 2004, when she was eighteen. Which was after *Varsa*. He opened the top drawer of "Misc." and was confronted by the stale morning breath of a long-dormant creature eager to tell what it had been dreaming. The photos were in vertical files. Some rested alone, others were gathered in small clusters. Some were covered by protective paper, others had been slotted into stiff cardboard envelopes. For all his apparent cynicism, the man in the next room was still vigilantly curating Desmond Tracey's legacy.

Michael took a deep breath and started, eager to find her, but also terrified that he would. Trace's obsessions, glimpsed yesterday, were on full display here. The women had fair skin and dark skin; they had black hair and blonde hair and fake hair and no hair at all. They were young and not so young. They sat on unmade beds, in the sprung passenger seats of rotten cars, on the stoops of dilapidated buildings. They curled on hospital gurneys or sat in blinding sunlight filtered through barred windows. What they all had in common was the splintered desolation in their eyes. Their gazes focused inward or locked on invisible vanishing points; some seemed to track nearby hands about to lash out at them. A few seemed defiant, a few were dreamily sweet, but mostly they were just beaten. As Michael pressed on, it became clear that this was the time when Trace was losing his touch. Although there were flashes of the old genius, for the most part the photos here lacked the startling luminosity of those published online; the stripper Felonee, or the dead woman on the gurney, or the unforgettable Madalina.

And then Justine appeared. Just like that, near the front of the second drawer. It was not a Polaroid, but an 8x10, printed in black and white. Her presence in the shot was clearly incidental. The photo had not even been taken by Trace: he was in it, standing in some kind of basement assembly room, surrounded by a small crowd that looked to be about as far from the art world A list as you could be and not find yourself at a church picnic in Nebraska. Two people flanked him. To his right was a tall man with a tweed jacket and a grandiose beard, smiling at the camera as if he had just won the lottery. To Trace's left: a short, disheveled woman in drab baggy clothes. Justine stood behind them, her back pressed against the wall, almost in the shadows, but still clearly recognizable. She looked barely out of her teens, if she was out of them at all. She held a paper cup delicately, as if it were fluted crystal. Her eyes were locked on Trace. Michael flipped the photo. "S. Wessels show." There was no date. He put it on top of the filing cabinet and continued his search.

The second image of her appeared amid the hard-core junkies and the wholly dispossessed in the bottom drawer. There were eight photos, all of them taken at the same time. A nearly identical series. To anyone else, the subject would have simply been an anonymous woman, stretched naked on a rustled bed. Her posture suggested that she was asleep. She faced the camera, her torso completely exposed but her pelvis twisted downward. Inadvertently demure. Her face was hidden by her dark hair and a flared section of blanket and an arm stretched above her head. Although this could never be entered as evidence in a court of law, it was her. Michael was certain of it. He saw it in the color of her dark hair and pale skin, in the shape of her breasts and the curve of her hip. She was completely different from Trace's other women. In this vast catalog of pain, she appeared to be utterly at peace; strong and untroubled. If there was something wrong with her, it was hidden from the camera's eye. Michael removed the first of the photos and placed it with the photo from the opening.

He searched the remainder of the bottom drawer with renewed focus, looking not only for her, but for more evidence of this florid man, this S. Wessels. But that one photo was all he could find. Which was a relief, since the remaining work depicted junkies, pure and simple. The drugs were taking over, infecting Trace's vision with their warped needs. The work had become haphazard, distracted, senselessly ugly. And there were now shots of Trace himself. Hazy self-portraits in mirrors, photographs of him sprawled in lobotomized repose, so poorly composed that he had probably handed his camera to the nearest person and commanded him to shoot. There was a close-up of a needle puncturing leathery skin. Trace's, presumably. Another, taken in a mirror, showed him with jaundiced eyes; lips cracked and crusted. Well on the way now to becoming the man on Water Street.

Michael collected both photos and went to find Klimov. Something stopped him when he opened the door. Voices. He peeked around the corner. Klimov was with two guests, big men in blocky suits, oversized for their chairs. They spoke in low tones; Klimov's haughty ironic smile had vanished. His eyes flickered nervously between the men, his tongue moved across his thin lips. Michael could see that it would be best not to interrupt.

He went back into the archive and started to look at the earlier work, just in case there might be another picture of her, or something that would tell him about S. Wessels. He opened the first cabinet, "Midlothian/Texas State." The yellowed Polaroids—some faded into near-invisibility, others perfectly preserved—all featured the same woman. Andrea Atherton Tracey, according to the careful block letters crammed in their margins. His murdered mother. She was gawkily pretty and impossibly young, her eyes frozen in a permanent state of embryonic panic. Tanned men with ropey muscles often stood nearby in varying postures of control. It was unclear if a young Tracey had taken these photos—he was only eight when she died—but the Polaroids in the lower drawers were undoubtedly his work, produced when he was in his teens. These featured gaptoothed, clearskinned girls, radiant with the Texan sun. He'd coaxed a few down to their bras, but no further. Finally, at Texas State, came the nudes, beautiful shy girls who seemed astonished to find themselves offering their naked flesh to the boy with the Polaroid.

And then New York. The work that was to become *In Extremis*. In the decade before the internet saturated the world with flesh, it would have felt as if something was being risked here. Although there was plenty of nudity and sex, it was a long way from pornography. Trace found beauty everywhere, in the webbing of semen stretched between open lips, the billow of cheap fabric as it fell to the floor, the twinkling vacancy in the eyes of a stripper as she blew a fat client. The intersection of beauty and pain.

And then he turned his attention to his true subjects, the women he found when he somehow gained access to prisons, psychiatric institutions, rehab facilities, even shelters for battered women. Port-au-Prince, Guadalajara, Romania. *Varsa*. His beloved weeds. The risks this big, undeniably American man would have taken to infiltrate these institutions were staggering. In the *ArtNews* interview, there had been hints of bribery, beatings, dramatic escapes from the authorities as he broke and entered a world of leather restraints and iron bars; hells-on-earth where dozens of women were crammed into cells built for two. There was a long sequence detailing the birth of a child, a boy, dead and blue, his mother handcuffed to her bed. And yet all of it possessed one thing that had been lost by the time Trace took the photos in the final drawer. Beauty.

There was motion in the hallway. Michael waited until Klimov was back in his office before he left the archive. The dealer sat staring at his desk, looking dejected.

"You ever do business with Moldovans?" he asked.

"Not that I know of."

"Don't."

Michael showed him the first photo, the nude.

"This is the one you are wanting?" Klimov asked.

"That's her."

"How do you know? Is there an extinguishing characteristic I am missing?"

"It's her."

Klimov sniffed.

"This is not his best work. You know this, right? It reeks of sentimentality."

"It's the one I want."

"All yours. What else you got there? This is a one-picture deal, Grammaticus."

Michael showed him the second photo.

Klimov said, "Seriously?"

"Do you know what it is?"

"Sure. I spent about five minutes there."

"This is Justine."

Klimov looked where Michael was pointing.

"No, I do not know her." He touched the first photo with the edge of the second. "So you think this is the same girl?"

"Yes."

Klimov shrugged. It was impossible to tell if he was impressed or dubious.

"How about this Wessels guy?" Michael asked, pointing at the man with the beard.

"I have no idea who this idiot is. *This*, however," Klimov said, pointing to the frumpy, nondescript woman to Trace's left, "is Susan Wessels."

"Who is she?"

"A photographer. A bad photographer. Trace got me to put her on the books. I have no idea what he saw in her. She had no talent. Zip. Nada. You put her in front of the Chrysler building in an ice storm as a movie star is jumping to her death, she is taking pictures of the pigeons on the sidewalk."

"Do you know where she is now?"

"I might have a number."

Klimov placed the photos on the desk and began to search through a fat Rolodex.

"Do you know who is taking care of him now?" Michael asked. "The funeral and stuff like that?"

"There is maybe an uncle back in Texas." He shrugged. "I have asked them to send me any photographs. I am not expecting much."

He found what he was looking for.

"You are not supposed to call her Susan," he said as he handed the card over.

"What does she like to be called?"

"Our relationship never got that far."

"Can I take both of these?" Michael said, gesturing to the photos.

"Why not. Two for one. Everything must go. I'll walk you out."

At the front door, he extended a small, cool hand.

"Good luck finding your girl," he said. "Just . . ."

"What?"

"You seem like a decent guy, Michael Coolidge." He sighed. "Trace, he was a great artist. But beyond the work, it is not so great. Not these last years. If this girl really was in his life, then maybe you should just head back upstate with your photos and your memories."

"I have to make sure she's safe."

"In Trace's world, that might be too much to be asking for, you know?"

FIVE

HE CALLED THE NUMBER KLIMOV HAD GIVEN HIM THE
moment he left the gallery. A woman's dour recorded voice directed
him to leave a message. Michael explained that he was a friend of
Trace's and urgently needed to talk. He did not say more. He could
hear his exhaustion and uncertainty. It was not necessarily the voice
of a man who a stranger would want to call back.

If Klimov was to be believed, then Justine and Trace had not
been lovers, at least not in any way Michael understood. Trace was
impotent. He did not have lovers. He loved women with his camera.
Michael could certainly feel the intimacy and the adoration in the
photographs he had taken of Justine. Of all those shattered women.
So, he thought. There you have it. They were lovers. Except they

weren't. Good work. You've figured everything out except the part that explains who she is, what she was doing with Trace, and where she is now. Seventy-two hours had passed since he had seen them together on Water Lane. With the train and a hotel and his unexpected entry into the world of art collecting, he had spent over a thousand dollars and every waking second looking for her. And yet her connection to Trace was still an utter mystery.

Once he was in his room, he searched online for anything he could find about S. Wessels, who did not like to be called Susan. There were no photos of her; the only example of her work was a photograph on a moribund blog. It depicted a car burning on a barren stretch of highway as four dejected cheerleaders looked on. It was a clever shot, but nothing special. She had taught photography at a night school in Brooklyn five years ago. She had taken part in a group show in Weehawken, another in Brooklyn. And that was it.

Michael lay down in the stiff bed and examined the photos he had found at the gallery. He started with the S. Wessels show. He was certain that it was taken soon after her arrival from her small Indiana town. Perhaps Justine was already entangled with the older man she had called The Poet. She looked both diffident and bold, her eyes locked on Desmond Tracey, like he was the only other person on the planet. But why? Was it just some sort of crush? He was already into his decline. Not yet the ruined man Michael saw three days ago, but also a long way from the powerful presence in the black-and-white portrait that had been so widely reproduced after his death. What did the girl lurking by the back wall see in him? If she was ambitious, if she wanted to make the scene, what was she doing in a shabby basement instead of some high-end gallery, where the drinks really would have come in fluted glasses instead of paper cups? Why would she choose Trace and not someone triumphant, or at least whose fortunes were rising? And why would she stay with him as the fires of his self-immolation consumed him? He wondered if it was a case of unrequited love. Was his impotence the great hurt that had been inflicted on her? Desmond Tracey could not give her what she needed and yet she could not quit him. He did not see it. The damage she spoke of seemed more acute than simple denial.

He looked at the second photo, the nude, but placed it face-down on the bed after just a few seconds. Nothing good would come from staring at that for very long. He knew that he should probably get some sleep, but he was far too keyed up. After a short scalding shower, he headed out, walking the city until dark, trying to form an image of her life there, though all he could come up with were fragments that he could not even begin to fit together. He had dinner at an Indian place on Lexington, aromatic food and a large Kingfisher. He bought a pint of whiskey and two bottles of water on the way back to the hotel. After checking online for new developments, he propped himself up in the uncomfortable bed and started to flip through the channels as he sipped the liquor from a small, permanently clouded glass. He turned off the television after a few minutes and picked up the nude, his free hand moving down his body. It was a conclusion to the day that was both shameful and logical. After all, what the hell else was he going to look at? What else was he going to do?

His phone rang just after midnight. He was in the semi-conscious stupor that now seemed to be passing for sleep.

"You called me earlier," a suspicious voice said without introduction. "I don't know you, right?"

"No. I'm . . ."

"How did you even get my number?"

"From Andrei Klimov."

"And why do you want to talk about Trace?"

"I saw him on Saturday. Right before he died."

There was a long pause.

"You saw him? Where was this?"

"In Annville. He was with a woman I knew. Justine."

There was another long silence.

"He was with Justine?" she asked, her voice very quiet now. "Seriously?"

Michael's heart was hammering against his ribs.

"You know her?" he asked. "You know Justine?"

"Inasmuch as anyone does, sure."

"Do you know where she is?"

"Who are you, exactly?"

"I'm her friend. She texted me for help late Saturday but I didn't hear anything after that."

"She texted you for help."

"At two in the morning. And then she disappeared."

"All of this on the night he died."

"Yes."

"Why? What sort of help did she want?"

"That's what I'm trying to figure out."

"And nobody else has heard from her? The cops, nobody?"

"Not that I'm aware of."

There was a long pause. Come on, Michael thought. Come on.

"Okay," S. Wessels said. "I can meet you tomorrow. I'll text you after they tell me where I'm supposed to be."

A slamming dumpster woke him at dawn. He felt woolly and confused. Hungover, yes, though there was more to it than that. His exhaustion had somehow grown more acute as he slept. His dreams had been populated not by Justine, but by the other women he had seen in Trace's archive. They were both desperate and alluring; they seemed to dwell in a state that was both dead and alive. Reaching for him from their cots, speaking to him in a language he could not understand.

He checked for news about Trace, but all that had been added since he last looked were a scattering of comments on various blogs. These ranged from the elegiac to the venomous. One person said that he was a conniving junkie who had stolen $300 from him. A woman who had Madalina as her avatar claimed he had been killed by the Romanian secret police. There was a thread on the *Gotham Rag* debating whether he was a genius or a misogynistic fraud. Someone called him a low-rent Helmut Newton without a darkroom. There was more, but it was all static and marginalia. Nobody knew anything. The echoes would end soon. To the great world, Desmond Tracey truly was becoming a forgotten man.

Just after nine, S. Wessels texted him an address in Alphabet City, instructing him to meet her there at 11:30. There was no explanation of what sort of place it was, or what she would be doing. He left the hotel and went for a late breakfast to kill time, which seemed to be moving very slowly now that he was on the verge of meeting someone who knew Justine. When he finally arrived at the location, he found the street barricaded to traffic, although nobody stopped Michael from navigating around the sawhorses. He passed buildings whose walls were covered by graffiti and cartoonish pictures commemorating neighborhood saints.

The number she had given him turned out to be a badly damaged four-story building. Its facade had collapsed, exposing several rooms in its upper two floors; bedrooms and kitchens, their furniture and wall hangings there for the world to see. Michael had seen headlines about this while searching the news. There had been injuries, a few of them severe. The damaged building stood alone, flanked on either side by communal gardens. Sturdier barricades protected it, these clearly intended to be impassable. Pedestrians were being shunted to the far side of the street, where cops and Dayglo-vested officials mixed with civilians.

Michael approached the barricade. Two men in hardhats stood inside, gazing up at the damaged facade. There was a third person, a tiny woman dressed in black cargo pants and a hooded sweater. Her yellow hardhat looked like it was about to engulf her face. She frowned at the screen of a digital camera. Michael recognized her from the exhibition photo.

"Ms. Wessels?"

She squinted up at him with her small, closely spaced eyes. Her frown remained intact.

"I'm Michael Coolidge."

"You look exactly like you sound on the phone," she said. "Do you know how rare that is?"

Michael had nothing to say to this.

"Give me a couple minutes to wrap this up."

He walked across the street to watch as she took photos of the wreckage. She moved nimbly over the rubble, as if it was her natural terrain. It was almost a half-hour before she finally ducked gracefully under the barrier to join him. She gestured to the hardhatted men with her pointy chin.

"I wish these guys weren't here. I have this fuzzy old teddy bear I could put right . . . there."

She pointed the camera at a small tumuli of plaster and brick. There was a thundering noise at the end of the street. A great shuddering crane had appeared, its downshifted motor revving as workmen moved the barricade aside.

"Come on," she said. "I got everything I need."

They walked in silence to a café one block to the west. It was a spacious overly lit room centered around a long table where old men in berets played board games in silence. S. Wessels chose a table beneath framed photographs of people who must have been famous in another culture. Men with austere moustaches, women who looked like they sang songs about betrayal and the sea. They ordered coffee. Speaking in a dry affectless monotone, Wessels explained that this was her day job. Law firms paid her to document accident scenes for lawsuits. Car crashes, fires, workplace havoc. The idea was to catch the pathos in the wreckage. The waste and the needlessness of it all.

"You remember that party boat that sank in the East River last New Year's?"

"Vaguely."

"That was me. You want my advice? If you get a chance to die in a tux, take it. It looks as good as you'd think."

"Does your teddy get a lot of use?"

"Listen to you," she said. "Let me tell you something. You know where I was before coming here? The hospital. Falling masonry and six-year-old faces do not play well together. I bet the fuckers who owned that building had code violations coming out of their asses and vacation houses in the Caymans. You know how much a new face costs? So yeah. Teddy earns his keep."

Michael gestured his apology. The last thing he wanted was to argue with this woman.

"So," she said, "tell me how you found me. I can't figure that out. It's been a long time since Trace and me have been associated."

He took the photo from his bag and handed it to her.

"Jesus. This clusterfuck. Look at me. The artist. Learn to smile, bitch. You dig this up at Klimov's gallery?"

"He's got Trace's archives there."

She looked at the photo.

"And there she is, lurking in the background."

"Do you know when it was taken?"

"Late 2005?" she said distantly. "Sometime around then."

Wessels stared at Justine's image for a while before putting the photo on the table. It was impossible to read the emotions on her face, though there was something there, something powerful. Michael decided to keep the nude under wraps.

"Tell me about you and the late great Desmond Tracey," she said.

Michael described the argument, his intervention, the white Mercedes speeding away. The late night text. The article in the *Call*.

"And you didn't hear anything from her after that text."

He shook his head. Coffee arrived. She took a sip and winced.

"The thing about ethnic coffee is—it sucks."

"Do you know where I can find her? Her work or an address? I'm having no luck with her phone."

"I haven't seen that sly bitch in over a year. I couldn't even say that she still lives in the city, much less where."

"Where did she live when she was here?"

She leveled a penetrating stare at Michael that actually made him squirm a little on the hard wood chair. She was barely over five feet, but played about a foot taller.

"Tell me about you and Justine first. I'm thinking, you come down to the city like this, cold-calling people, you must have been hooked up. Right?"

"For a while, yes."

"For a while is how it works with her. Come on. Spill. I need to figure out about you before I say anything."

"I met her up in Annville last January. She said she was an art dealer who was in town to show work to a client."

"Yeah, that sounds like something Justine would say."

"She wasn't an art dealer?"

"How long were you together?" Wessels asked, ignoring the question.

"Just a few days."

"That'll do it."

"And then she disappeared without a word. I thought I would never see her again. And then Saturday."

"And then Saturday."

She took a grudging sip, then gave the mug a surprised look, as if she'd forgotten she hated its contents.

"I'm not a stalker, Ms. Wessels. I really just want to see if she's all right. She asked for my help and I feel . . ."

"You feel . . ."

"I wish I hadn't let her go so easily. After the fight, I mean."

The tiny woman stared at him, her gaze pitiless as she decided. Finally, she shrugged and looked out the window. Having decided.

"Well, Trace would not have hurt her, if murder-suicide is your concern. Ever. In any way, shape, or form. Not his beloved Justine. And I *seriously* doubt she would off herself. That girl has a survival instinct the size of the Milky Way. But I must admit it's worrying that she would abandon him like that, even if he was dead. Those two were joined at the hip. There must have been a very good reason."

"You said beloved—were they lovers?"

"Trace didn't have lovers," she said immediately, categorically.

"Klimov said the same thing."

"That's because it's true. The man just didn't have it in him. Emotionally, physically. He just could not cut it. More power to him, say I. One less hard dick fucking up the program."

"So what was it between them?"

"Their relationship was, um, unique."

"I'm sorry, I'm not understanding this."

She took another wincing sip of her coffee.

"You really want to hear all this? Because you seem like a decent guy. A bit stressed, a bit lost, but that's cool. My advice is not to beat yourself up over letting Justine slip away. Because you're in pretty good company."

Michael stared at her. She saw something in his expression that made her smile. It was clearly an unfamiliar configuration for her face. He could see why she did not do it more often. Sinews and lines and small adipose deposits appeared. It aged her ten years.

"Yeah, okay. Gotcha. The Justine Story, in living 3-D technicolor. So. One day she just showed up . . . well, you saw the photo. You know, I'm thinking that may actually be the first time I ever saw her. Trace and I had been friends for like a decade at this point. I even lived in his palatial Chinatown apartment for a while before I got on my own two feet. The Zombie Birdhouse. We got to the city about the same time, me and the boy, trailing our sob stories behind us. This would have been early nineties. He got famous, I didn't, but he wasn't a dick about it. He hooked me up with Klimov. That show was Trace's idea. His money. It flopped, but, whatever. At least now when I lay dying I can say: I had a rotten show in a church basement in Queens where nothing sold."

She smiled again. Michael wished she would stop.

"Anyway, Justine started hanging around, this would have been about seven, eight years back. At first, I didn't think anything—there were always these fucked-up bitches on the scene. They loved Trace. That lost puppy thing beneath the Nick Cave exterior. Until they realized that his pain wasn't the cuddly motherable kind."

The waitress arrived and asked if they wanted food. Wessels ordered a pastry, any kind they had. Michael was all right, he said.

"But she stuck. Trace liked her. I did too. Well, I just wanted to fuck her, which is a kind of liking, right? She was such a pretty baby. All eager and lost. Said she'd just dropped out of college."

"Did she say where?"

"Arden," she answered immediately. "Down in North Carolina? I think she studied drama there. But she was only there for a little while. Evidently there was some big scandal associated with her departure."

"Did she say what?"

"No. She just indicated that some serious bridges had been burned."

The pastry arrived, color-drained and viscid, like an embalmed organ.

"Anyway, she had no visible means of support when she arrived here. I let her stay with me for a while at my place out in Brooklyn. I tried to fuck her, but she wasn't into it. What can I tell you, the girl liked cock. I know this because . . ."

"Because?"

"Look, stop me any time, all right?"

"Because . . ."

"The guys. She just always seemed to be involved in a passionate love affair. They'd last a while and then . . . poof."

The guys, Michael thought.

"Most seemed to be older," she continued. "Wall Street players, big-shot professors, film industry types. Handsome, put together. Like you. There was this guy who did something for Disney. And this Italian guy who taught politics somewhere. NYU? Though I think he was only there as a visitor. Don't get me wrong. It wasn't like she was some kind of money-grubbing slut. These were really intense relationships, as far as I could tell, though I would only catch glimpses of the guys. I don't think she wanted them to see too much of Trace's world. But she definitely fell for them and they *definitely* fell for her. They'd last months, some of them. She'd disappear, you'd see her occasionally and she'd be on cloud nine. And then, poof, it would end. Back to Desmond. Some of those guys were pretty pissed. They came looking, but what they found was Trace. Game over. She was always able to get away clean. She had this thing with her last name—what did she tell you hers was?"

"She didn't."

"Well, don't feel bad, because if she had told you, it would have been fake."

"Do you know what it is?"

"She told me it was Jackson. But it's not like I ever saw a birth certificate. In fact, there was something about Trace making her a false I.D. He was always using them for his work. To be perfectly honest, I'm not even sure her name was even Justine. In fact, I'd bet good money it wasn't."

She cut and speared a piece of the pastry, stared at it unhappily for a moment, then put it back on the plate.

"I once asked her, what the hell? Are you in Mossad or something? She claimed that some evil shit had happened to her when she was younger and she didn't want the people responsible to find her."

"She told me that some older guy had hurt her."

"Yeah, me too."

"And you don't know what it was?"

"No clue. But I think it was real bad. As in someone dying. She was definitely still freaked out about it. She said the guy was very powerful and that he would harm her if she came back on his radar. I thought it was bullshit at first, but after a while I believed her. To be honest, I think that's one of the main reasons she was with Trace. So he could protect her from this person."

They sat in silence for a moment. Michael thought about what Klimov had said about Trace's conflicts with the men who did bad things to girls. What had he called them? Shadow men.

"So what do you think Trace was doing in Annville?" Michael asked.

She picked at her pastry and shrugged.

"Prolly found a good connection and was taking a little drug holiday. Trace got around."

"But she'd been up there nine months earlier."

"These aren't exactly grounded people, Michael."

"Is there anything else you can tell me about Justine? Her family, maybe?"

"She never really talked about that except to say she was from some dump in one of the flyovers. And she was never going back."

"And are you sure that you have no idea where she could be living now?"

"My guess? She's probably with a guy. Who loves her so and does not know what's about to hit him."

Michael understood that this was as much as he was going to get.

He said, "All right. Thanks for your time."

"No problem."

She shook her head slowly. For a moment, it appeared that she was fighting back tears.

"It's just such a shock, him dying. You could see it coming from a mile off, but now that it's here . . . I mean, the guy could drive you crazy, but he had something. That honesty. Guess it got to him in the end."

She flashed that unfortunate smile.

"Which makes it kind of ironic that the one actual human relationship he had was with a girl who could not even tell people her real name."

"Maybe he's the person she told."

"Maybe."

Michael took out one of his cards. He crossed out his office phone, so only his cell number remained.

"Well, thank you," he said as he handed it over. "If you hear anything else that might help me find her, could you let me know?"

"Sure."

Michael scooped up the bill and stood to leave.

"If you see her," S. Wessels said.

"What?"

"Let me know what happened up there. I'm kinda into wreckage, as you may have noticed."

SIX

THE TURBULENCE WAS THE WORST MICHAEL HAD EVER experienced. It started with a shuddering jolt midway through the ninety-minute flight. This was followed by an interval of calm, long enough to suggest that the initial disturbance had been nothing more than an isolated rip in the sky's smooth fabric. But then the seat belt sign came on and all hell broke loose. The plane pitched and shook. Urgent chimes sent the attendants scuttling back to their jump seats. The pilot's voice over the intercom was too garbled to understand.

It got worse. There was a drop and a brief undulation; there was clattering in the galley, a yelp from the back row. Michael's hands were soon cramping from gripping the armrests. Five hundred flights had taught him that turbulence did not down planes. But after another sleepless night, his rational mind was proving a weak defense against the panic.

And then it ended. One moment they were being slapped silly by malignant unseen forces, the next they were gliding through the stratosphere. Passengers maintained a skeptical silence until the captain spoke, his drawl as heartening as the sound of a filling bath. There would be smooth sailing to the airport.

They landed in Greensboro a few minutes early. Michael rented a car for the forty-mile drive to Arden College, located to the northwest of the city, near the Virginia border. His exhaustion intensified as he drove, enabling his sense of folly to make its presence fully felt. He thought about how crazy Kim and his son would judge him if they could see him now. It was an accusation he could not contradict, at least not with his rational mind. And yet, beneath that, in a place that now felt much more important than his rational mind, there was a certainty that was becoming undeniable with every step he took. The only thing that mattered was finding Justine. Whoever she might be.

It had been a long night. After his meeting with S. Wessels, he'd done a search for "Arden College Justine Jackson." There was nothing. He had no luck on the school's website, either. He called the registrar and asked if a student named Justine Jackson had been enrolled there between 2003 and 2005. They had no record of her attending their school, in those years or any others. Michael guessed this was not definitive. She could have restricted the release of her information. Or Justine Jackson could not be the name she had been using in college. He went back to the Arden site and looked at the buildings, the faces, the classes and activities. There would be yearbooks and student newspapers in the school's archives. A person left behind more than just a name.

He'd found a seat on a flight out of LaGuardia the following morning. It left absurdly early and was very expensive. Too restless to sleep, Michael wandered the city before taking a bus to the airport, where he sat in a stupor at the gate until called. Traveling like this was new to him, after all those years of car service pick-ups and business class pampering. It felt right. It felt like he was moving closer to the life she might now be living.

The state highway to Arden was freshly paved. Detonated mammals glistened in the bright autumn sun. Bordering the road was a series of billboards that featured an apple-cheeked little girl who wore a party dress and clutched a terrified-looking clown doll. "Aren't You Glad You Had Her?" the caption read, followed by a toll-free phone number for women facing unplanned pregnancies.

The campus was five miles off the highway. The road to it passed through stubbled fields whose crops had been recently harvested. Smoky bonfires burned the residue. And then, without any prelude, there was a prosperous main street lined with cafés and bookstores, an organic supermarket and a co-op bank. Beyond this, the campus. In the visitor's lot, there was a map drawn in a style that reminded Michael of a Tolkien frontispiece. His destination, the library, was on the far side of the campus.

The predominant architectural style at Arden was Brutalist. The classroom buildings were concrete slabs, the dorms looked like they housed guest workers and soccer hooligans. Centering the quad was a great rusted slab of metal sculpture that might have been the wreckage of a fallen satellite. Michael had read about Arden after booking his ticket. The school had been founded in 1962 by idealists who wanted to establish an oasis of progressive education and racial tolerance in Dixie. Although it had started out as a training academy for young liberal paladins preparing to storm the region's lunch counters and drinking fountains, it was now a repository for smart misfits with lopsided SATs, spiky GPAs, and glowing recommendations from their English teachers. The curriculum was rich in the liberal and performing arts, while also offering math-free physics. If kids didn't go here, they went to Bennington or Bard or Oberlin. The only sports were Ultimate Frisbee and Quidditch.

The students Michael passed were dressed in pajamas and skinny jeans, hoodies and cunning T-shirts. They were not enjoying the perfect fall weather as much as indulging it, like an expensive gift they had known they would be getting all along. Michael's bewilderment increased as he moved among them. How had Justine journeyed from her Midwestern hellhole to this enclave of privilege? Who pointed the way? Who picked up the tab? Even if she had received substantial financial aid, the residual costs alone would have been beyond the means of the family she had described. That, of course, was presuming she had gone here at all.

The archive's main room, home to the most basic documents, was subdivided by shelving and carrels. It was empty except for the bored female student at the front desk and a woman in a glass-walled office. The student handed him a clipboard and explained that all he had to do was sign his name and show a driver's license. For institutional affiliation, he put self. The reason for his visit was simply "research."

He began with the student directories. He had decided to operate under the assumption she had enrolled in the fall of 2004 and left in the spring of 2005, a few months before turning up at the S. Wessels opening. Come on, he thought. Make this easy. Give me a Justine Jackson, class of 2008. Home address, phone number, and a mother who is only too happy to provide contact details for her child.

His start was not promising. As he'd feared, there were no photographs in the printed directories. Those would be online, behind the firewall, if they existed at all. There was no Justine Jackson. In the class of '08 there were no Justines at all. He went back three years, then forward three, in the unlikely event Wessels had been wrong about the date of the exhibition. Year by year, page by page, looking first at the Jacksons, then skimming over the first names. By the end of his seventh directory he had accumulated eight Justines, none of them named Jackson or coming from Indiana. He copied their home addresses and phone numbers and checked them on one of the library's public computers. He found enough information about six of the Justines to discount them. The remaining two were from Montreal and San Clemente. Not promising. He'd call them only if he struck out in the remainder of today's search. As he returned to the archive, he considered asking the student at the reception desk to help him access student records online, where he could look at faces. But that was a desperate move, best saved for the moment he understood his current search to be a failure. He presumed the campus police were local boys who would not be sympathetic to a stranger wanting to look at pictures of coeds.

He moved on to the yearbook, *The Mix*. The name was appropriate—it was chaotic, apparently assembled at random. It chronicled astrology clubs, home-building missions in Central America, an annual bacchanal in which students showed up dressed in togas. He went through six years, page by page. Once again searching the faces of strangers. He kept slowing himself down, working methodically. Willing her presence.

She was not there. He was so tired now that he briefly contemplated checking into the nearby hotel he'd reserved and resuming his search tomorrow. But he did not want to lose momentum. He did not want to encourage that voice in his brain that was accusing him of folly. He moved on to the student paper, *The Paper*. It was collected in large leather binders that looked like medieval tomes. It only came out once a week, which made it easier for him to flip through the years. He paid particular attention to the theater reviews—Wessels had said that was what she studied. But he also paused over stories of trauma and crisis. A rape, several suicides, including a philosophy professor who had hung himself immediately after a lecture on Wittgenstein. There had been a shooting in 2003, a murder-suicide involving a sophomore girl and her jilted hometown boyfriend. Michael wondered if Justine had joined the candlelight vigil. If so, it would have been somewhere out of frame of the four photos that adorned the extensive coverage.

He went on, turning every page, pausing over the photograph of any girl who might be her. Nothing. He could not find the theater department records in the open stacks. He asked the student, who grudgingly looked up from her smart phone long enough to tell him he would need to deal with the archivist. She was an edgeless woman in a yellow cardigan who simply handed him a call slip. He wrote in a request for all theater department records from 2002 to 2006.

"I'll bring them to you," she said, pleased to have something to do.

She returned ten minutes later, wheeling a cart that carried four moisture-proof containers. Michael carefully removed the lid of the one marked 2004/2005. Inside, there were five overstuffed manila folders, each labeled with the name of a production. The first was for the fall show, *Noises Off.* There was a permission letter from Samuel French, audition sign-up forms, rehearsal schedules, minutes from production meetings. Photos and playbills. Once again, Michael forced himself to work slowly, to look carefully at the made-up faces, to read every word in the hope there would be a hint of her.

The next folder was for the winter production, *Six Characters in Search of an Author.* Michael vaguely recalled the play from college. An imaginary family desperate to have their tragic story told. He shuffled through the copious printed sheets until he got to the production photos. The first one Michael had already seen in the student newspaper. It depicted a student actor in a nearly translucent veil kneeling between two children, both of whom were too young to go to Arden. The next one showed the entire cast, standing in a tight, terrified cluster, lit by a single spotlight. Two men and a second woman joined the characters from the first picture. All of them were dressed in black. They stared the camera, hands outstretched, beseeching.

Justine was second from the left. Young, in costume, heavily made up, but unmistakably her. She was dressed in a tight knee-length black dress, black pumps, a string of pearls. Her expression was haughty, seductive. He turned the photo over. *Tech Rehearsal— February 19, 2005.* The names were listed left to right. Hers was Jane Thomassen.

Michael's exhaustion and distraction vanished as quickly as they had during the turbulence. There were several more photos of her from the tech rehearsal. Arguing, flirting, mocking. He stared at each of them for a long time. Although she was in character, he could plainly see the woman he had known. The ironic sparkle in her eye, the unapologetic sensuality. It was only fitting that there would be similarities between the girl on stage and the one in his bed. She had been in character with him as well, playing Justine instead of the Step-Daughter.

Jane Thomassen.

He searched the entire file. In the master copy of the script, the Step-Daughter was described as "dashing, almost impudent, beautiful." That's my girl, Michael thought. The play's director was Vincent Batchelder. His production notes comprised over a dozen separate entries written after meetings and rehearsals. Justine—Michael could not bring himself to call her Jane, and knew he never would—was initially cast as one of the troupe of actors who is incidental to the play's action. Then the student playing the Step-Daughter broke her leg. "Slipped on ice!" Batchelder wrote. "And I hate pratfalls!" Justine, the understudy for both female roles, got her chance. Early reports were promising. "Kid's blessed with talent," the director wrote. "Old beyond her years." By the third week of rehearsals, Batchelder could no longer contain himself. He wrote that "she absolutely *nailed* the seduction scene at dress shop." He noted that her rendition of *Tchou-Tchin-Tchou* "had the boys straining at their leashes!" Dress rehearsal was a minor miracle. "Wish I'd taped tonight," he wrote. "Janey T. gave one of the best student performances I've had the honor of directing in nearly thirty years of teaching. When she screamed 'The truth!' it brought on goose bumps."

The performance report was next. It was dated 2/25/05. All of the boxes and sections and check-lists—Tech, House, Continuity—were empty. The only entry was in the Comments section. And that was one simple word.

"Catastrophe."

There was a clipping of the review Michael had already scanned from *The Paper* at the bottom of the box. It hinted that the production had been marred by Tiffany L. Schecter's halting performance as the Step-Daughter. Michael looked back at the production notes. Up until opening night, Tiffany L. Schecter had been the understudy for both female leads. Sometime between that miraculous dress rehearsal and opening night, Justine had left the production.

Michael put the pages neatly back into the folder and returned it to the box. He walked over to the shelves and took out the student directory for the 2004/2005 academic year. She was right there, as she had been all along. Jane Ann Thomassen. Her address was 99 Davis Street in Annville. Another shock, this one so powerful it took him several seconds to understand what he had just read. His exhaustion must have kept him from seeing the town's name during his earlier skim. Her parents were Neal and Nancy. He knew the street. It was just off River, a few blocks from the train station. Not far from his own house.

He walked over to the glass office and leaned in the door.

"I've just left the boxes on the table," he said. "I hope that's all right."

"Sure. Find what you needed?"

"Getting there."

He looked up Batchelder on one of the library's public computers. He was still at the school, the department chair. His office was in the Fine Arts building. Before logging off, Michael did a quick search for news of Jane Ann Thomassen, but nothing appeared in the first wave of information. She was not wanted for murder, she had not been reported missing or found dead. He was tempted to go deeper, but it was approaching four o'clock, and he knew that he should try to track down Batchelder as soon as possible.

Fine Arts was just a short walk. As he left the library, the reality of what he'd discovered finally registered. She was from Annville. She had probably attended Annville High, where she would have sat in the same classrooms where his son now sat, listened to the same teachers. Penny Bowman, perhaps, Michael's recent lover. Had Justine been staying with her parents when he met her in January? When he saw her on Saturday? Was it that simple? Is that where she was now, holed up in her childhood bedroom, a mile away from his house?

Fine Arts was the largest building on campus. Girders, glass, and jagged shards of concrete were arranged into an erratic dome whose crevices were cluttered with longstanding debris. The whole structure looked to have been frozen in time a split second after exploding. Michael stepped into a vast lobby where students lounged on benches beneath long banners. He could hear hesitant piano scales, giggles, a power drill. He asked a sleepy-looking couple if they knew where Vincent Batchelder's office might be. The directions were elaborate, plunging Michael into another labyrinth of corridors and stairwells before he finally found the drama department on a terrace directly above the lobby. Vincent Batchelder's office was the last one. A poster from what appeared to be an all-female production of *King Lear* hung on a door that was cracked open a few inches. Michael paused to listen. He detected a rhythmic snore. He rapped gently. There was an apneaic gasp, followed by a thud.

"Come!"

The voice was massive and brittle and loud, like a dead oak splintering. Michael gently shouldered open the door. The office was spacious, book-crammed, its walls covered with posters and photographs. The sanctum of a campus fixture. The single large window provided a view of the flat, harvested countryside, the smoke of occasional bonfires streaking the emptiness. The man behind the desk looked to be pushing eighty, perhaps older; he was jug-eared and bald except for sparse parcels of depleted hair emerging from dry scalp. Twin bladders of wilted flesh swayed beneath his strong jaw as he pulled himself upright in his massive chair.

"Well, hey," he said.

His voice was pitched at a thundering, pet-scattering volume.

"I wonder if I could have a minute of your time?"

"Well, sure. I was just . . ."

The man's eyes slipped into momentary confusion, as if he hadn't the slightest idea what he had just been doing. But then he rallied and flapped a large, liver-spotted hand toward the chairs arranged in front of his vast desk.

"Michael Coolidge," Michael said as he extended a hand.

"Vince Batchelder." There was stubborn, vestigial strength to his grip, as if it would be the last thing to go. "How can I help you, Mike?"

He had decided on his story while walking through the building's labyrinth. He was now convinced of what he'd only sensed when he started on Monday—lies were going to be an essential tool in finding the truth about her.

"I'm visiting campus with my son and he's very interested in theater."

The old professor's gaze traveled to the door.

"Oh yeah? Now where's our little thespian at?"

"He's with some old high school friends. I thought he'd be here right now."

"Well, that's all right. What's his name?"

"Will."

"Good theatrical name. So he's caught the performing bug, has he?"

"He sure has," Michael said, though nothing could be farther from the truth.

"Well, we have a very strong theater program here. Very strong. You see some of our alum photos out there?"

"I did. In fact, a former neighbor of mine came here as a theater major. That's really how we know about the school."

"Oh yeah? And who might he be?"

"She. Jane Thomassen?"

Michael might have just as well told him that the cancer had metastasized from his pancreas to his liver.

"Oh. Yes. Janey." The voice was no longer booming; his eyes had begun to vacillate slightly behind those glasses. "And how did you say you knew her?"

"Her family lived next door to us. She used to babysit my sons. The Thomassens moved away around the time she came here so we lost track. But I always expected to see her on television or something."

"Yes, Janey was, well, she was very talented and certainly made quite an impression for the short time she was here."

"She didn't graduate?"

"No, she left us as a freshman."

"Really? That surprises me. She was so enthusiastic about coming here."

"Well, it surprised us as well. Her departure was rather abrupt."

The old professor looked as if he was going to say more, but then caught himself. Michael could see the story lurking just beneath his skin, waiting to burst through.

"Actually, I have a confession to make," Michael said. "I'm not really that surprised. Jane always was a bit of a . . . thoroughbred. We loved her to death, but she was just too unreliable to use as a sitter in the end."

Batchelder held his visitor's gaze for a moment, then shook his head slowly. A lonely, bored, memory-steeped old man, taking the bait.

"Thoroughbred. That's one way one of putting it."

Michael gave him a complicit smile, a significant nod.

"Let me tell you what the girl did. She walked off stage during a scene break in the opening night of our winter production."

"Really? Why?" Michael asked.

"I never had the chance to ask!"

"You mean, walked off stage and didn't come back?"

"She just vanished. Ruined what was looking to be one of the best shows we'd put on here in quite a while. Quite a while."

"Now I feel bad bringing it up."

"You know, I think about it from time to time without any prompting at all."

"Do you have any idea why she did it?"

"The pressure, I guess. I blame myself for casting a freshman in the role. But she was such a rare talent. She just blew everyone away from the minute she arrived."

The old man was remembering now. Michael was nodding like a television reporter at the scene of a catastrophe.

"Opening night, well, the first act was sensational, if I say so myself. But then the second act starts and—no Step-Daughter. I was up in the booth and by the time I got backstage, all heck had broke loose. Somebody told me they'd seen her walking through the lobby

THE REAL JUSTINE

and out the front door. Just like that! In full costume, makeup, the whole kit and kaboodle. I wanted to go after her but I had a catastrophe to attend to. And we had them, too. We *had them*."

"Where did she go?" he asked him.

"Took her roommate's car without permission and drove down to Greensboro. Caught a bus to New York, we were able to figure out. Luckily the car was recovered without damage. And that was that for Janey. Never heard word one from her again. I suppose there's a story there I'll never know."

"Any idea what prompted all of this?"

"Well, that's the strangest thing. She did say something just before she left. Several people heard her. She said *I feel like he's watching*."

"Who?"

"That, we never figured out."

Batchelder caught himself. He looked at Michael. Something shifting in his eyes.

"Unless of course you know something I don't. What with you having been her neighbor."

"No," Michael said. "This is all news to me."

"You sure about that?"

Batchelder continued to stare at him and suddenly there was something new in his eyes, a lucidity, a squint of revelation.

"So where *is* that boy of yours, Mike?"

"How about I go look for him?"

He stood.

"These kids," the old man said, sage and suspicious now. "Always vanishing on us."

Michael called the airline from the building's vast forecourt—there was no chance of getting out that night, unless he wanted to travel through Houston and arrive at noon the following day. Better to take his original flight, which left at eight in the morning. As he headed to his hotel, he tried to shape what he'd learned in the past two days into some kind of coherent narrative. Her short, brilliant college career had ended on that catastrophic opening night. She'd fled to

New York, where she'd become involved with Trace. She would leave him occasionally for other men, but always returned to the apartment he kept for her. When he had succumbed to drugs and she had no one to turn to, she had come home to Annville. This must have been what had happened in January. Her choice of the Moon Temple made sense now. She was a lot less likely to be seen by anyone she knew.

But what about the nine months since January? He could not bring himself to believe that she had been in Annville. She must have gone back to New York after she left Michael. Last Saturday suddenly made sense. She had once again returned home after the unraveling of whatever relationship she had dived into after Michael. Trace had come to try to get her back, to regain his role as her savior. That was the scene he had stumbled upon in the alley. But she had spurned him because of the drugs. *You're ruining everything.* Rejected, broke, and desperate, he had camped out in the cheapest hotel in the county. Where he had overdosed. She had not gone to the police because there was no reason. She was sitting in her childhood room right now, grief-stricken and lost. While Michael, the lovelorn fool, was a thousand miles away, looking at photos of her in costume and makeup.

And all of it was driven by this terrible thing that had happened to her when she was young, this thing that must have happened to her while she was living in Annville. Home, perhaps, to the man who had broken her, the man she could not escape. Whatever it was, it had haunted her in college and in the restless years that followed. *As in someone dying*, Wessels had said.

He began a detailed search for her the moment he was in his hotel room. The only thing he could find for Jane Ann Thomassen was a progression of entries in the *Call* listing her on the Honor Roll for Annville High School. These stopped after her junior year, suggesting she had either lost interest in her studies or moved to another school. But there was no mention of her anywhere else. If she had used social media, it was not under her own name. There were no photos. He tried various permutations. Justine Thomassen. Jane Jackson. Nothing.

He moved on to the parents. Neal Thomassen worked in real estate; Nancy raised funds for charity and wrote short book reviews for a reading group's blog. They had a son, Jeremy, who was now eleven. They had moved house since Justine had been at Arden and were now living in Annville Heights, an affluent subdivision outside of town. Michael knew the place. There was a golf course, a fence to keep bad things away. She was not from some hardscrabble backwater. Her father had not been a petty thief, but a solid citizen who owned a house that must be worth well into six figures. Her mother was sane enough to write coherently about Barbara Kingsolver.

There was a phone number. A landline. He was tempted to call right away. *Can I speak to Jane? Oh, I just wanted to ask about the dead junkie up at the Valencia . . .* He managed a smile at the thought. He would need to go in person. Barring delays or cancelations, he would be at Annville Heights by mid-afternoon, where there was every chance he would be able to look her in the eye and ask her what the hell was going on.

SEVEN

HE MADE IT THROUGH THE GATE WITHOUT DIFFICULTY. Although he'd prepared a story about being interested in joining the club—he'd even swung by his house to dress in his best approximation of a golf enthusiast—all he needed to do was show his driver's license. All was quiet inside. The houses of Annville Heights were new and big. The golf course meandered among them. The broad sidewalks were empty except for women pushing sleek strollers. Few cars were visible.

The Thomassens lived on 14 Mozart Lane, in the subdivision of Symphony Woods. Hayden merged onto Puccini; he passed Ravel and Copland. Mozart was a long cul-de-sac; 14 was at the end. A pickup truck was parked out front. There was a three-car garage and a two-story portico bolstered by Palladian columns. Dormers and a chimney erupted from the slated roof. Behind the house was the golf course, where a foursome of bandy-legged men stood on a radiant green. Their putters flashed, one of them held a flag. They looked like conquistadors in pastel leisurewear.

Michael lingered in his car after pulling up behind the truck. Two men knelt over a narrow ditch in a front yard that was seamed with a network of trenches and excavated dirt. He looked at the house's stone facade, skirted by a tight laager of shrubbery, and pictured her arriving here after fleeing him in January. Perhaps one of her parents had collected her from Locust. He imagined her here after Trace died, crying quietly among the stuffed animals and framed photos of her youth, cloistered in a community where the greatest menace seemed to be a badly sliced drive. Doubt flooded through him. He pictured himself standing at that sturdy suburban door, a slightly haggard stranger trying to explain himself to a dubious parent as Justine descended the stairs, her expression collapsing into unhappy surprise. The story he'd prepared would sound ridiculous. Men like him didn't just show up unannounced at the door. Not with good intentions, at least. He should leave. But if he left, then he would not know. And that was worse than any sort of awkwardness that awaited him at the front door of 14 Mozart.

The men on the lawn had noticed him. This was not the sort of neighborhood where people lingered in parked cars. He opened the door and followed a woodchipped path to the front porch. The workmen nodded indifferently as he passed. One was tall and white, all tattoos and severe angles; the other short and brown, with smooth limbs emerging from a hard, rounded torso. They were laying PVC pipes in the trench, installing a sprinkler system.

An autumnal decoration hung on the front door, a few cobs of Indian corn surrounded by leaves and thistle. The entire assemblage had been shellacked. The doorbell chimed with surprising volume. Several long seconds passed. Michael's breathing had grown shallow; his heart churned within his ribs. He imagined her standing in front of him, confused and unwelcoming. He imagined her smiling.

There was no reason to ring again. The bell had been so loud he had probably ruined someone's putt. He was just about to ask the landscapers if there was anyone home when he heard the tread of footsteps inside. The door opened with the rending sound of an insulated seal separating.

It was a boy. Long-limbed and skinny, the pale skin of his forehead and cheeks parchmented with faint acne. Jeremy. The brother. He wore a brown hoodie. He was a couple years younger than Will. There was a faint resemblance to Justine, though Michael doubted he would have picked him out as her brother in a crowd. His expression was the mix of apathy and defiance typical of his age.

"Is this the Thomassen residence?" Michael asked.

"Yeah," he said, his face crumpling a little, as if the question was even more stupid than anything he had anticipated.

"I'm trying to get in touch with your sister."

"My *sister*?"

The word was drenched in baffled scorn, as if Michael had just suggested the boy waltz with him. He needed to talk to someone who was not eleven.

"Are your parents here?"

The boy turned his head slightly, keeping an eye on the stranger.

"Mom!" he shouted, his voice piercing and shrill.

There was no response. He shouted again. Again, there was nothing.

"Hold up," Jeremy said.

He disappeared into the house, leaving the door open. Michael looked inside. Figurines filled a glass-front hutch immediately to the right of the door; there was a small table whose sole purpose was to support a jade-green vase that held a single silk flower. The kitchen was at the end of a long hallway. Black pans hung from a rack above a tiled island like jerked carcasses. Beyond that, on a big redwood porch, stood a black barbecue large enough to roast a small horse. Nothing suggested Justine might belong to this house. Michael checked to see what the workmen were making of this. Nothing, it seemed. Their attention was still on the ditch.

When he turned back to the door there was a woman staring at him. She had arrived in utter silence. She was unmistakably Justine's mother. The same underglow to her pale skin, the same gentle slope of her nose. Her eyes were an identical shape and size and color as her daughter's, but there was no cunning in them, no wanting. Just weariness, beneath a gloss of courteous manners. She was neatly dressed, luncheon-ready, but Michael had the feeling she had no plans to go anywhere.

"Yes?" Nancy Thomassen asked.

He told the story he had prepared. He was Jane's friend. Her name—her real name—sounded strange, almost nonsensical on his lips. He explained that he had lost track of her and was hoping to get back in touch. The woman listened. Her veil of politeness fluttered but did not part.

"Jane has not lived with us for a number years now," Nancy said when he finished. "I'm sorry."

"I figured that might be the case. I was hoping you could tell me how to get hold of her."

Her gaze traveled over his shoulder.

"How does one get hold of Jane?" she said, doling out her words slowly. "My best guess is that she is down in New York City. And please don't ask me to be more specific than that."

The last sentence was accompanied by a softly self-deprecating laugh, but there a message in it. The conversation was over. Michael would not be invited inside for coffee. The photo albums would not be broken out. He wondered if others like him had come to this door.

"That's strange. Because I saw her here last week."

The woman's eyes widened a few millimeters; her painted lips parted.

"What do you mean, here?" she asked.

"In Annville. Right in the middle of town."

"That's . . . are you sure it was her?"

"Yes."

"But what was she doing there?"

Violently arguing with a man who would be dead of a heroin overdose in a few hours. Michael did not say this, of course, and not just because of a reluctance to terrify a woman he did not know. It was the same impulse that had kept him from telling the police about the slap. For reasons he could not fully understand, he did not want to betray Justine's trust.

"We didn't really have time to speak."

"Who *are* you?"

"Michael Coolidge."

She continued to stare at him expectantly, as if he had not answered her question. He pulled his wallet from his jacket pocket and removed one of the Grammaticus cards. He held it between them but she did not take it. Her gaze was still locked on his face. As if the answer to her question could not possibly be contained on a card.

"I'm afraid you are mistaken," she said.

"I . . . about what?"

"I seriously doubt she was in town last week."

"Mrs. Thomassen, I assure you that I saw her."

"Look, Mr. . . ." She finally glanced at the card. "Coolidge. I don't know what your business is with my daughter and quite frankly I don't really want to know. She's an adult and she does not live here. We have had no contact in years. So please, I would appreciate it if you would just go."

He stood his ground, still holding up his card. A shadowy figure had appeared at the end of the front hall. The boy.

"I just asked you to leave my house!"

Her words were said loudly enough to be heard by the workers. Although Michael did not turn to check, he knew they had stopped laying pipe to look at the interloper, who, come to think of it, had spent a little too long at the front door.

"If you should hear from her, will you at least tell her I was here?"

He moved the card incrementally closer to her.

"Have her call the cell because I . . ."

She snatched it from him so violently that one of her long lacquered fingernails scraped the back of his forefinger.

"Will you go now?" she said, her voice still loud, though there was a desperate quality to it now.

"Mrs. Thomassen?"

Michael turned. The smaller worker was standing. The one with tattoos still knelt beside the shallow ditch, figuring out what would be required of him. Michael held up a placatory hand. He was going. Behind him, the door slammed hard. He turned in time to see a cob of Indian corn landing at his feet.

Back in his car, Michael briefly examined his finger. It was the same one he'd jammed punching Trace. The scratch was not bad, a pink seam. He started the engine and drove back up Mozart. He had truly believed he'd find Justine here, or at least find the way to her. But Nancy had been telling the truth when she said that her daughter had not been home in a long time. And Jeremy's surprise at the mention of a sister seemed genuine, as if he had not heard her spoken of in a very long time. Once again, Michael experienced the vertiginous, dispiriting sensation of certainty collapsing into rubble around him.

His phone rang just as he pulled through the security gate. An unfamiliar number.

"Mr. Coolidge?"

"Yes."

"This is Neal Thomassen. I understand you are trying to get in touch with my daughter?"

The voice was smooth, suburban, accustomed to radiating positive energy onto strangers.

"I am," Michael said.

"Hey, you got a minute to swing by the office?"

"Now?"

"If it's not too much of a problem."

It was not far. Just across 44 and into the rambling business park of converted warehouses and factories by the river. Michael knew this area well; it was just a short drive from Grammaticus. Neal

Thomassen's agency was called the Property Mill. Michael had seen signs around town. It was located on a tributary as swift and slender as the one behind the hotel where Desmond Tracey had died. The similarities ended there. There was nothing untamed about this part of the county. Money oozed from the majestic trees and old stone. The address Thomassen had given him turned out to be, naturally enough, a converted mill. Or so it seemed. On closer inspection, it was a new building designed to look old. The gray stone was weathered and vined, but the mortar was bright and unbroken, and the copper cladding had yet to take on a verdigris patina. The signature millstone placed by the big glass front door might have been choppered in.

The Property Mill's suite of offices took up the building's second floor. The receptionist had been prepped; she led him immediately down a long corridor whose walls were lined with relief maps and panoramic photos of the region. In one of the offices two men in shirtsleeves sat on either side of a desk. A Nerf football sailed between them just as Michael passed.

The receptionist rapped twice on a door at the end of the hallway before pushing it open. Michael entered a large office dominated by a picture window that overlooked the river. Thomassen was on his feet, making his way around a large desk. He was a tall, broad-shouldered man in an expensive suit. There was little of Justine in his looks. Nothing, in fact. He was not fat, but there was something soft about him. His dull brown hair was just beginning to gray, and there was the making of a second chin. He made a dismissive gesture to his receptionist with his right hand, which he then offered to Michael as he introduced himself.

"We'll sit here," he said, nodding to a conversation area.

Michael took the sofa backing a stone wall; Thomassen sat opposite him, in a stiff-looking leather chair. He folded one leg over the other, exposing an Argyll sock.

"So, Mr. Coolidge, forgive me, but I'm not entirely clear on who you are. My wife was pretty rattled when she phoned."

"I'm sorry about that. That wasn't my intention."

Thomassen waved off the apology.

"How do you know Jane?" he asked.

"We're friends."

"Friends."

Michael let the conversational space the other man had opened remain empty. His gaze traveled to the formation of framed photos perched on the table beside the small sofa. Only one featured Justine. Jane. She was with her parents. She looked to be about twelve. Brown hair, radiant skin. Clear, uncomplicated eyes. Just a pretty girl having a family photo taken. The same human being he had met in January and seen in the alley, and yet something much more profound than the mere passage of time separated her from the woman Michael loved.

"From the city?" Thomassen prompted.

"I live here, actually."

"What, in Annville?"

Michael nodded. Thomassen was unable to hide his unhappy surprise.

"I thought I knew just about everybody in this town," he said with a dry laugh.

"I'm something of a newcomer."

"And you said you saw my daughter recently?"

"On Saturday. On Water Lane."

Thomassen's astonishment was as powerful as his wife's, though he managed it better.

"You're sure it was her?" he asked.

"Positive."

"Well, that's something of a surprise, as I'm sure you gleaned from Nance. We've grown apart from Jane over the years. I hear from her from time to time, we'll have lunch in the city. But I'm afraid when it comes to visiting home . . ."

Her made a gesture that Michael presumed was intended to evoke the difficulties facing parents everywhere.

"I'm sorry."

"Well, you know, children. You do what you can but the best intentions . . ."

An uneasy silence passed.

"And how is it you say you know Jane again? I'm sorry to press, but this is all pretty strange."

Something about the man—his lightless smile, the slightly tinny register of his voice—told Michael that he was full of shit. He did not hear from her from time to time. They did not have lunch in the city. The news of his estranged child's return to the homestead was not welcome. In the least. Justine would not want this man to know the first thing about her.

"I met her through work."

"And where is it you work, Mike?"

"I was at Grammaticus at the time. There was a meeting in New York and your daughter was there. She was working at a gallery. We got to talking and it turned out she was from here. Anyway, we saw each other socially in the city after that but lost touch. And when I glimpsed her the other day, I thought I'd look her up. I had a name but no phone number. I don't suppose you have a number for her?"

"I'm not really supposed to give it out."

The lie was so plain on his face that Michael almost pitied the man. He had no number. His daughter was lost to him. Michael glanced again at the photo of the pretty girl and her proud parents. He wondered what catastrophe loomed that would break them so irrevocably apart. He looked back at Thomassen. The two men smiled amiably at one another. All very friendly. Almost as if they had just been telling each other the truth.

Somebody hurt me.

"Can I ask you something, Neal?"

"Sure."

"Why are you lying to me?"

Thomassen actually recoiled.

He said, "Excuse me?"

"You don't have her number. You don't see her in the city."

"What is this?"

"She told me what happened."

Michael was not sure where the words were coming from. Only that they felt inevitable. Thomassen stared at him for a long moment. Weighing his options.

"I think you should go," he said finally.

"She told me that someone hurt her when she was young. So badly that she dropped out of college and changed her name and disappeared to the city. And I can see that you know what it was."

"Shall I call someone? Is that what you want me to do?"

"Was it you?"

"Right."

Thomassen stood and walked to his desk. He picked up the phone and hit a button. Michael stood as well. The man held the receiver against his shoulder and waited.

"I'm going to find her," Michael said. "I'm going to get her to tell me the truth."

He started to walk to the door.

"Mr. Coolidge."

He turned. Thomassen still help the receiver against his shoulder. There was something new in his eye. Something angry and wise and wounded. The radioactive residue of hard-won knowledge.

"Maybe you will find her," he said. "But getting her to tell you the truth is going to be another matter."

It had been him. Neal was the one who had hurt her. It would explain why she had changed her name, why she had cut off her parents. And why she had acted so strangely in town, going to the Moon Temple instead of the Tavern, staying in his house the whole time they were together. What it did not explain was why she had come back to Annville in the first place. Or what Desmond Tracey had to do with any of this.

He needed to find someone else in town who had known her. A childhood friend, a neighbor, a teacher. Penny Bowman. Of course. There was a good chance that the woman who taught AP English would have had smart, creative Jane Ann Thomassen in class. Her number was still in his phone. Penny answered on the second ring.

"Well, hello, stranger," she said.

She had spoken without him needing to introduce himself. He had not been purged. That was a good sign. He told her he had been thinking about her, and if she wasn't busy he'd like to see her for a drink.

"You sound funny."

"How so?"

"Like you have ants in your pants."

He laughed softly. This was how Penny talked.

"Well, you're in luck," she continued. "My dance card happens to be open this weekend. But fair warning. I'm seeing someone."

"Me too."

"Well, aren't we the naughty ones."

They met at the Tavern at eight. Penny was just getting out of her Prius when he arrived. She looked good. She was not a small woman, but her curves were emphatic and properly placed, and her lovely smile could take on an alluringly lascivious cast. He felt a pulse of guilt for using her like this, but he had no choice. She gave him a searching look after they embraced, as if she sensed that all was not well with her former lover. Still, she led the way inside. The place was packed but they lucked into a booth. She drank white wine so he ordered a bottle.

"So how have you been?" she asked. "Because you look a bit, I don't know, weary."

"Just coming off a long week of traveling."

She accepted this without comment.

"And this person you're seeing? Where might she be?"

"New York," he said. "For the weekend."

Their eyes held; the negotiation had been concluded. The night awaited them, but nothing beyond. They quickly warmed to each other, finding the old rhythms, the old allure. Michael kept her glass topped up, he stroked her hand across the table. Feeling like a heel, but also knowing this might be his only way to Justine. She discussed her boyfriend, who flew a Gulfstream for a man who had made a fortune selling scented candles; she told a long, funny story about her ex-husband's brief marriage to a fitness instructor in Orlando that ended with him in a truss.

"Oh, I was meaning to ask," Michael said in the first lull. "I bumped into an Annville girl recently and I was wondering if you knew her. Jane Thomassen?"

Penny's face underwent a rapid transformation. Nowhere near as severe as Nancy's, but the surprise was there, nonetheless.

"Jane Thomassen? Wow. Now there's a blast from the past. Where did you meet her?"

"I was freelancing for an arts education organization down in the city. She worked there."

"Sure, I know Jane. And you're saying she's doing all right?"

His heart quickened; the alcohol seemed to have evaporated from his bloodstream.

"She's doing great. Quite an impressive young woman."

"I'm really glad to hear that."

"You sound surprised."

"Well, Jane Thomassen is the stuff of high school lore."

"How so?" Michael asked, putting every ounce of his energy into modulating his voice.

She looked into her half-empty glass. Uncertain if she should proceed.

"I don't know, Michael. I don't want to cause trouble."

"I promise that anything you say will be kept in strictest confidence," he said, giving his voice an ironic inflection, like it was no big deal.

"But if you're working with her . . ."

"Job's over."

Penny ran her finger around the rim of her glass; there was a faint chiming. Come on, Michael willed her. Spill.

"Well, it's not like she did anything *wrong*. At least not that anyone knows about."

She drained her glass and he immediately refilled. She was remembering now. Penny was an avid gossip and the prospect of telling this story was clearly overwhelming her.

"So. Jane Thomassen. I had her as a freshman and then in Honors English her junior year. What can I say? She was the best. Smart girl. Pretty as all get-out. Great actress. She was an amazing Emily in *Our Town* and then she nailed, I think it was Helena, in *Midsummer.* A little withdrawn, a little aloof, but who wouldn't be with those looks and smarts? Popular in a *noblesse oblige-y* sorta way. Scared the hell out of the boys. Just a winner all around. One of those kids who high school just ain't big enough for."

She took a long drink.

"Okay, so. Fast forward to April, junior year. Jane leaves school." She snapped her fingers. "Poof. Just like that. Completely and totally. And there's no explanation as to why. Needless to say, the rumor mill starts working overtime. Jane was in the hospital, in a coma. She'd run away. The only consistent thing we hear is that she had been spotted by not one, but two different parties wandering around in the middle of nowhere up on 44 the night before she left."

"Where on 44?" he asked, a little too urgently.

Luckily, she didn't notice.

"Oh, somewhere up north, almost to the town line."

"And no one ever saw her again?"

She shook her head.

"Didn't she mention any of this to you?" Penny asked.

"Not a word."

"Huh. Because I'd love to know the truth of it."

Michael said, "So you never heard what happened? People must have had theories."

"It was so weird. I mean, this is not a big town. Yeah, we have a Trader Joe's, but at the end of the day, it's still just Grover's Corner with an attitude. But as far as I know no one ever heard anything definitive."

"What about the parents?"

"They got guidance to arrange for her to finish her classes at home. Or wherever she was. I gave her an A, for what it's worth."

"And you don't know where she went after that?" he asked.

"The most credible thing I heard was that she went to a boarding school her senior year, though which one, I do not know."

"People must have been dying to know."

Penny said, "Of course they were. Some of her friends went by the house but were politely rebuffed. Teachers would see her parents around town and ask, but no soap."

"There must have been suspicions about what had freaked her out so badly, though. The father, for instance."

"Obviously folks wondered. I know there were inquiries but nothing came of it. At the end of the day, there's only so much you can do. People moved on."

"What do *you* think happened? Because I know there's no way you don't have a theory."

She watched the dart players as she pondered this.

"I think she cracked under the pressure."

"Pressure of what?" he asked her.

"Being Jane. Being perfect."

"You just spitballing or do you have some hard evidence?"

"Just a feeling I had. There was always something about her that was, I don't know, too good to be true."

"I'm not sure I understand."

"It was like she had this image of a perfect girl she had to live up to, or else all hell would break loose. After she vanished, I kept on thinking, you know, she was just a girl with long legs and almost-perfect balance who one day fell off the highwire."

He said, "Well, she seems fine now."

"I'm really glad to hear that. I'd hate to think that we lived in a world where a girl that special could just vanish."

We might yet, Michael thought.

"Anyway, if you see her again, tell her Mrs. Bowman said hello."

There was a commotion over by the dart board. Cheers, high fives, raised glasses. Someone had just scored a bull's eye, or a treble, or whatever else was required to win at a game whose rules Michael did not understand.

EIGHT

HE DID NOT REALIZE HOW MUCH HE'D HAD TO DRINK until he sat up. Michael closed his eyes to stop the cyclone that had descended on his room, but that only sent him spiraling through darkness. It was just after eight A.M. Penny had left in the middle of the night. Although the particulars of her departure were still foggy, he knew that it had not been a happy one. By the time they left the bar, the night had begun to splinter. There had been more wine in his living room; there had been kissing and clutching and disrobing. And then it was the bedroom, where sexual failure and frustrated silence confirmed his suspicion that being with anyone beside Justine had become an impossibility. The date ended with the angry rustle of Penny dressing in the dark, followed by the sound of her hybrid whirring primly away.

He struggled out of bed. After pissing and brushing and showering, and avoiding eye contact with the mendacious bastard filling his steamy mirror, he limped to the kitchen. His stomach sounded like the debris of a house that had just burned down. There were run-offs and gurgles and minor collapses. He felt bad about Penny. A year ago such a predatory stunt would have been out of the question. Not to mention the way he confronted Thomassen. Now, he appeared to have become the sort of man who did such things. A major apology to Penny would be required, though all he could think now was that he needed to find out what had happened ten years ago to transform Justine from a happy, well-liked high school junior into the sort of person people could only speculate about.

His confidence that Neal was her tormentor had faltered over-night. It simply did not feel right. He did not match the description of someone who could still terrify her; someone powerful enough to force her into hiding. And Penny had said the authorities did not suspect him of anything. No, it was not Neal. Although that look he had given Michael just before he left the office suggested Neal might know who it really had been.

The problem was that he had no idea where else to look. The police would not tell him anything about what had happened back then, nor would doctors or social workers. And there was nothing archived in the papers. The only plan he could come up with was to get his hands on a 2003 yearbook and start tracking down her class-mates. It was a depressing thought, cold-calling strangers, especially with a toxic hangover.

He decided to drive to the area where she'd been found. That might bring a little clarity, if not to Justine's history, then at least to his whiskey-logged brain. Traffic congested the road out of town. Saturday morning was the busiest time of the week for the affluent precinct that began where River Road turned into Route 44. It was the sort of place you could get a Currier and Ives print or organic corn from a roadside stand, but a frozen burrito was out of the ques-tion. The sort of place where drug stores were called pharmacies, and struck animals apparently limped into the woods to die discreetly, since there was seldom any roadkill in evidence. There were no gas stations, no billboards. Nobody was in a hurry. People antiqued, they browsed, they cut in front of you with waves that were more entitled than apologetic.

After a mile of quaintness, wilderness began, or at least Annville's version of it. The forest grew increasingly dense, acre upon acre of trees, spreading from the hills in the west down to the river. The town's main floodwall did not stretch this far, so people tended to build on high ground, at least the people with enough money. There were hidden driveways, bed and breakfasts, a farm for Arabian horses, historical markers, some sort of rehab institute called Riverside. And, somewhere amid it all, the place where they had found her on the night everything changed.

Side roads up here were mostly terminal. Michael randomly followed a few. On those heading up into the western hills, fresh pavement gave way to rutted dirt. Those running east, to the river, led to luxury homes and the scattering of big estates where he had always imagined Justine's reclusive collector to live. One of the roads ended at a scenic overlook. Michael parked and got out, still feeling shaky. Pleasure craft crisscrossed the river below. A scull, whose eight-woman crew may very well have included his ex-wife, labored upstream. A quarter-mile to the north of the overlook, the remaining columns of the old ruined Annville rail bridge rose at regular intervals from shore to shore, their stone glistening in the bright autumn sun. Enterprising vandals had scrawled graffiti on the supports, the usual mysterious hieroglyphics, legible only to the initiated.

The river was at its widest here, well over a hundred yards across. Although not quite the size of the Hudson or the Connecticut, it was still the area's defining geographical feature. Most of the year it was a placid and reassuring presence, a sort of gurgling parkland, beautiful enough in places to inspire its own small school of eighteenth-century landscape painters. On weekends and bright summer mornings it was dense with fishing boats; its shores were latticed with hiking trails.

When it froze over, the huts of ice fishers appeared in its coves and backwaters.

But it had also long been the source of sudden, severe floods. These mostly happened during the spring melts, but there had also been some in the early autumn, when the area's unique microclimate subjected it to large amounts of rain. Although there had been no significant events since Michael and Kim had moved to town, people talked about past floods with an awe that bordered on nostalgia. There had been one in 1964 that had taken lives and damaged a significant portion of the town. Upstream dams and an elaborate system of barrier walls had largely controlled the problem in recent years, but with the ongoing changes in the climate, all bets were currently off. In fact, there were now near-daily reports about the possibility of another big flood.

But Michael was not really worried about floods. He wanted to figure out what had happened to Justine. He tried to picture her on that night ten years ago, wandering alone up here. If she had been alone. It would not have been warm in early April. Depending on the moon, the darkness could have been absolute. Cell phone coverage was sporadic now; back then it would have been nonexistent. He wished Penny had provided him with more specific details. A landmark. The name of her rescuer. It did not have to be much. Just one hard, undeniable fact. Something to anchor his whirling mind.

He pressed on, heading north, eventually reaching the Valencia. It was closed down completely now. A chain barred the entrance to the graveled lot, forcing Michael to park on the highway. He passed the playground, the chainsaw sculptures. The cabin door was bolted, so he had to settle for looking through the small window. They had taken the mattress away. Michael wished he had pushed the manager harder for information; he wished he had spoken to the tall red-haired man with the expensive suit and the Escalade. He had seemed too consequential for this place. Michael walked around back and watched the tributary flow down to the river. It brought to mind the old paradox, how you could never step in the same river twice. It also made him want a drink.

On the way home, he passed the road to Annville Heights, and was briefly tempted to pay a surprise visit to the Thomassens. Ask them what their daughter had been doing that April night. But that would probably only result in a conversation with the local constabulary. Whatever had happened to her was part of an amputated past. They had left her behind, as absolutely as they had escaped their modest little neighborhood.

Michael started to think about their old house on Davis Street. Perhaps there would be something there that would help make sense of things, since it was where she had actually been living on the night in question. The houses on Davis were pleasant enough, single-story for the most part, their yards small and neat. The cars had substantial mileage but were well-maintained. Roots erupted sporadically through sidewalks. Laminated notices hung on some of the larger trees, urgently seeking the whereabouts of family pets. Number 99 was a simple, ranch-style house, surrounded by brittle shrubbery. It was a quarter the size of the Thomassens' current place. Its walls were painted a self-effacing olive green. The guttering was dented; there were dun-colored curtains. Michael sat in his car across the street, imagining her growing up here, pretty and smart and well-liked. The girl in the photo at the Property Mill. And then something happened on a dark spring night and she was gone and her parents were living on the twelfth fairway, her father working in a big office that looked out over the water, her mother doing charitable work. The downfall of a beloved child usually shredded a family. But here, it had the opposite effect. It was almost as if losing her had allowed the Thomassens to prosper.

He drove home and searched her parents' past. He started by typing "Neal Thomassen" into the search engine. It was slow, frustrating work, but the rough outlines of the man's life gradually emerged. Neal had been a marginal presence before 2004, a struggling real estate broker trying to peddle two-fams by the railroad tracks down in Cheapside. His office had been in a mini-mall south of town, amid dry cleaners and appliance repair shops. This was during the late 1990s, one of the biggest housing booms in the nation's history. The only photo from this time was a head shot in which he sported a haircut that would have been fashionable during the Carter administration and the makeshift smile of a man trying to talk his way out of a speeding ticket. There were no golf tournaments or fun runs, no appearances at photographable social functions. Nancy was just a name in the directories.

After 2004, things began to change. The year following their daughter's disappearance from Annville High School had been transformative for the Thomassens. The well-fed suburban burgher in the power office at the Property Mill started to emerge. His company's polished, robustly interactive website showed Neal to be presiding over a pack of ravenous-looking young brokers. Their listings were split between commercial real estate and high end residential properties. In the ensuing years, Neal served on planning committees, raised funds for a community college, adjudicated membership applications for his country club. He joined a men's group called the Annville Leadership Forum. He earned an eight handicap. He arrived.

Nancy started showing up as well. In addition to joining the library's book club, she was listed on the board of a Cheapside charitable organization named Women in Transition. In its group photo, she lingered on the fringes, her smile fixed, her eyes a little hunted. Young Jeremy also appeared—Little League, a class trip to Montreal—but nowhere outside of the most basic demographic listings did it say that the Thomassens had a daughter named Jane. For the last five years, since she had turned twenty-one, there had been no mention of her at all.

Michael could find no indication of what powered all this good fortune. Neal's name was not attached to any big settlement, there were no headline-making business deals. It could have been an inheritance or a scratch card, but Michael doubted it. His rise was too inexorable to indicate a sudden visitation of luck. There was a solidity to it; the man Michael had met yesterday did not look like he was jetting to the Bahamas or making it rain at the Cheetah Club. He was an insider, a respected member of the community.

Michael briefly contemplated examining real estate records, but who was he kidding? He wouldn't begin to know where to look. Or what he was looking for. If there was a secret history behind Neal Thomassen's emergence, he would never find it by staring at numbers on the computer. And there was nothing to suggest that Justine's disappearance and her father's good fortune were even related. Maybe the guy had simply started doing better. Maybe he'd stopped drinking, or found Jesus, or read the right self-help manual.

Before switching off, Michael looked one last time at the available photographs of Neal. Most of the images came from the website of the Annville Leadership Forum, which clearly played a big part in the life of Neal 2.0. The site was amateurish in design but dense with information. The organization's brief charter spoke about "reinforcing core values of family, faith, and community among men of good will." There were roughly a hundred members, though there was no definitive list that Michael could see. According to their calendar, the Forum met biweekly. It all seemed harmless enough. They spent a lot of time doing good and having a blast. They cleared debris from the banks of the river, they hunted in the Adirondacks. There were seminars about being better husbands and fathers, led by inspirational speakers sporting golf shirts and goatees. There was a formal ball for the wives.

Neal, looking very much the new boy, first surfaced in the 2004 group portrait. Michael recognized a few of the beaming faces surrounding him. There was the lawyer who had represented him during his divorce. There was the man from the RiverBank who had organized the mortgage on Locust Lane. And others, familiar and anonymous, spotted in restaurants, at school events. He wondered why Kim's new husband was not among them—this sort of thing was right up Douglas's alley—but then he remembered that this would have been the time his wife had been dying of cancer.

And then Michael saw him. Front and center, in a position of honor. The tall red-haired man who had been standing outside the dingy cabin where Desmond Tracey had died. The Escalade driver. The photo was almost a decade old but it was unmistakably him. Tall, powerful, with piercing eyes and an intimidating smile. His name was listed as M. Munro. He was the Forum's vice president.

Michael twinned his name with Annville in the search engine and, in a fraction of a second, learned that he was Marcus Munro, a former chief assistant district attorney for Annville County and currently a senior partner in the firm of McNeil Whitty Munro. Douglas's firm. The biggest firm in town, probably in the entire valley. On its site, Munro's specialties were listed as Criminal Defense and Private Client. His bio also said that he was married with four sons and a daughter. Michael returned to the Annville Leadership Forum website. Neal and Munro were pictured together on a page titled "Installation Night 2004." Sponsor and initiate. Both men looked stiff and uneasy, like fighters after a draw, or fathers at a shotgun wedding.

Michael's hangover and his exhaustion and his confusion were suddenly gone. He had found his one real thing, a connection between Jane and Justine. A link between the Thomassens' country club idyll and Desmond Tracey's world of darkness and pain. One of the most powerful men in the county, benefactor and business associate of Neal Thomassen, had been at the Valencia Motel the day after Trace had been found dead in one of its rooms. Intimidating the manager and looking furious that Michael had seen him there.

Someone very powerful, she had said. The most powerful man in town. Who had everyone fooled, including her family. It was him. Munro was the one who had hurt her when she was young, the one she could not quit. He was the man who had broken her; the reason she could not love. What had S. Wessels said—she liked older men. Men who were put together. Munro had been her lover, and something bad had happened between them in the middle of nowhere when she was sixteen. Justine had fled, first Annville and then Arden, landing in the city, where she had found her protector. She was broken but it was a good place for broken people, especially if you had a brilliant adoring genius who would always provide you with a safe harbor. But then Trace had gone bad and she had returned to the man she could not quit. Yes and no, she had said. He was her lover and he was not her lover. Trace had come to save her one last time last Saturday, but he was no longer capable of being anyone's savior, including his own. She'd gone back to Munro and Trace had died and Munro had gone to the Valencia to clean up whatever part of the mess might lead back to him and his beloved. She was with him now. Michael was certain of it.

He could not find his address. There was nothing in the white pages or in any of the other listings. He got out his credit card but even a thirty-dollar search yielded nothing. Michael hunted neighboring towns. Nothing. He looked through real estate records, he searched the *Call*'s database. Nothing. Every path he pursued took him back to the McNeil Whitty offices on Water Street. It hardly seemed possible that there would be no listing for a man of Munro's stature. He had clearly gone to great lengths to keep anyone from knowing where he lived.

Douglas would have it. Michael set out immediately. He was counting on Douglas and Kim being out—they were not the sort of couple to waste the recreational possibilities of a crisp autumn Saturday. If they were at home, he would have to wait until tomorrow morning, when they graced a pew at First Presbyterian. And, if Munro's address was not in Douglas's home office, Michael would confront him at McNeil Whitty on Monday. Although confronting him might not be the best idea. Better to follow him home, or wherever it was he was keeping her. Whatever happened, he was going to wind up where the man lived.

He could tell the moment he pulled into the driveway that the house was empty. He checked the garage just to be sure—Douglas's car was gone. Getting inside was not a problem. He'd seen Will retrieve the spare key from its hiding place beneath a garage rain spout numerous times. There was an alarm, but Douglas only set it when they left town. This was not exactly a high crime area.

The house was tomb quiet. Douglas's home office was adjacent to the kitchen. He had built it so he could be close to his dying wife. Unlike Michael's office back on Locust, it was used often, and productively. Douglas still worked here whenever possible, even though it meant he would probably never get his name on the firm's shingle. Life was short, he'd said, and every moment he spent away from those he loved was a moment wasted. Michael had listened in tightly smiling silence, battling the urge to break a Sam Adams bottle over the man's head.

He hit the switch by the door, filling the room with lawyerly light. It was wood-paneled, dense with books. Michael lowered himself into the contoured leather chair and pulled the tiny chain of the desk's lamp. It was a very neat desk, dominated by Lucite-encased photos of Douglas's two families arranged in an egalitarian formation. In one, a post-divorce Kim perched in the doorway of a plane, her newly toned torso framed by the straps of a parachute. She wore goggles and looked brave as she peered over her shoulder at the camera, thumb jutting upwards. Behind her, the wild blue yonder, into which she was ready to leap.

Michael spun the thickly populated Rolodex. At first, he could see no listing for Munro in the M section. But then, at its very end, he found what he was looking for.

MM
Mud Creek Road—all way to the end—big black fence

Michael shuffled the index to cover his tracks. When he looked up a shrouded, ghostly figure watched him from the office doorway. His son, sleepy and confused by his father's unarranged presence.

"Hey, buddy," Michael said. "I didn't know you were home."
"No, I was just . . ."
Will did not seem inclined to finish his sentence.
Michael asked, "Is your mother here?"
"They're hiking. Dad—what are you doing in Douglas's office?"
"I just needed some papers."
"'Cause he doesn't want people in here. Not even Mom."
"I was in a rush."
Will's expression sank even deeper into confusion.

"Well, I better make like a tree and split," Michael said, as casually as possible.

He headed for the door. But Will stood his ground, blocking the way. Michael stopped just before colliding with him. He met his son's eye. Will stared at him with a vacant expression Michael had never seen before.

"Is everything all right?" Michael asked. "Are you sick?"

The question appeared to cast his son deeper into confusion.

"No. Yeah. I was just . . . resting."

The recent suspicion surfaced. Kim had got him into some sort of counseling without discussing it with him. He was being medicated and advised by experts. Michael would have to talk to her about this.

"Look, I gotta run. But I'll see you soon, all right?"

He added, "Sure."

"And, hey, no reason to tell them I was here, okay?"

Will shrugged, a gesture which could either mean assent, or that he was planning to sing like a canary.

"You forgot your papers," he said after his father had passed.

Michael tapped his head

"Got it all in here."

Mud Creek ran down to the river off the northern stretch of 44. It was not a road that Michael had explored when he had been driving this morning. It was easy to miss. The narrow entrance was shrouded by trees; the letters and background of the ancient street sign had aged into a uniform algae-green. For the first half mile, the houses were small and a little shabby. They appeared to be inhabited by old people, or people who were simply waiting to get old. The real estate changed once the road bent north to run along the river. Security gates appeared; there were warning signs and dense stands of camouflaging trees. The road grew even more narrow, until it was little more than a one-lane track. If Michael met a car coming in the opposite direction, someone would have to give way.

But he met no one. He passed more trees, more gates. And then the road turned abruptly back toward the river. It ended at a black fence. The one mentioned on the Rolodex. It was formidable—eight feet tall, opaque, made of heavy iron. The gate was firmly shut. Michael parked on the shoulder and got out of his car. Birdcall and leaf-rustle only made the silence feel more profound. There was an intercom speaker on a free-standing pole beside the gate. He did not want to press the call button, though leaping the fence was the only other way inside. The thought of hoisting himself up and over brought an unwelcome return of the feeling he'd experienced on Mozart Lane, that profound sense of his own improbability. Only this time it was worse. The man who lived here was a former district attorney, not a skeptical parent. How could Michael possibly explain himself to him?

And then he heard a gunshot. Michael knew little about guns; he had never fired one in his life. But there was nothing else the air-piercing clap that rolled over the fence could be. The thought was almost impossible to process. A gunshot. At the place where Justine was staying. It had come from down by the river, no more than a hundred yards away. The sound echoed away behind him, toward 44 and the hills beyond. When it was finally gone he could hear that the birds had stopped chattering. Even the breeze seemed to pause.

He looked around. The fence ran for well over a hundred feet in either direction before being swallowed by foliage. It would continue down to the bluff above the river on either side—it was that kind of a fence. The shot had come from within, so it couldn't be passing hunters. Someone was shooting a gun at Marcus Munro's house and Justine was there. Call the police and wait for the cavalry. He looked at his phone. No bars. He could retreat to one of the neighboring houses, but there was no telling how long that would take. He stepped up to the gate and pushed the hard iron but it did not give, not even a fraction of an inch.

Press the button. Let them know you are here. He reached out, but before he made contact there was another gunshot. Michael pictured her cowering. He drew in a deep breath and took two steps forward and leapt.

It was not until his hands had gripped the top of the gate that he thought about barbed wire, shards of broken glass, high voltage. But there was only cold smooth metal. He pulled himself up, his scuffling feet providing him with just enough leverage. He threw an arm over the top, then a leg.

Balancing there, he found himself looking at the biggest log cabin he had even seen. There were four vehicles in the forecourt. Two BMWs, a Mustang, and the late-model Escalade he had seen at the Valencia. He dropped down onto gravel, pitching forward a few steps but staying on his feet. He let his momentum carry him all the way to the side of the house. Thinking about alarms, about dogs. About bullets. There was no reason to try the front door—the shots had come from down by the river.

He froze in confusion when he reached the back of the house. Directly in front of him was a lawn that ran a couple hundred feet to the bluff overlooking the river. Standing at its edge were three young men. Tall and well-built. One of them held a rifle. They had gathered around a metal contraption. The armed man raised his weapon to his shoulder and then something flew up from the machine, only to disintegrate as the gunshot's report reached Michael. Pieces of the shattered clay rained out of sight.

There was movement to Michael's left, a man rising from a table on a redwood deck. Munro. He had spotted Michael. There were two women with him at the meal-littered table. One was Munro's age, his wife; the other was younger, with wild red hair that tumbled over her shoulders. She wore pajamas and a robe. Something about her suggested chronic infirmity. Michael took a stride toward the deck, but Munro held out his hand in a gesture so severe that Michael could almost feel it against his chest.

And then the women saw Michael. Munro's wife looked worried but in control; it was the younger woman who panicked. She rose from her seat so quickly that she almost toppled over backward.

"Dad," she said in a cracked, breathless voice. "Who is that?"

Munro kept his eyes on Michael as he said something over his shoulder. His wife was standing now.

"Mary, go inside with your mother," he said, his voice both soft and commanding.

She did as she was told. The sliding glass door thudded behind the two women as Munro turned his attention back to the intruder. Before Michael could speak, Munro crabbed his forefinger and thumb into his mouth and whistled to the three men by the bluff, then beckoned with a great expansive gesture. Michael remained perfectly still, understanding now that he was in actual danger. The three men were running up the lawn from the pier. The one with the gun held it across his stomach. At the ready. The others kept their hands low, palms down. They were spaced evenly. They had fanned out.

"Stay exactly where you are," Munro said from up on the porch. "I really just want to talk."

The others arrived. Munro's sons. Late teens, early twenties. Two had their father's reddish hair, but it was the black-haired one, the one who carried the shotgun, who most closely resembled him. He had the same strong jaw, the same mercilessly resolute eyes. A Dartmouth Crew T-shirt stretched across the plated muscle of his chest. Like his brothers, he was keyed up. Awaiting instruction.

Munro finally descended. He seemed even more commanding than he had back at the motel. He wore khakis and a sweater whose heavy cable knitting looked capable of stopping a blast from the shotgun. He pointed at Michael when he reached the bottom step.

Munro said, "I know you. From the Valencia."

"I don't want to cause trouble."

Munro's expression said the obvious—trouble had already been caused.

"I just wanted to ask . . ."

Munro stopped him with another preemptory gesture. He turned to his sons.

"Wait up on the deck while I deal with this gentleman. And Con, see if your mother needs any help with your sister."

The boys did as they were told. As they passed, each of them leveled a homicidal glance at Michael. Once they were gone, Munro led him toward a small assembly of wood chairs around a fire pit, a good thirty yards away from the deck. Out of earshot of his sons, Michael thought. There were remnants of a recent fire. Tumuli of ash, sticks blistered with charred marshmallow. Munro stopped beside the first chair. There was no question of sitting. Two of his sons were watching from the deck, the dark-haired one holding the shotgun in the crook of his arm. Con had gone inside to help with Mary.

"Who are you?" he asked.

Michael did not answer. Speaking his name would be a kind of surrender.

"All right. Here's the situation. You are trespassing. You have intruded on my family and terrified my daughter. If I call the police, they will respond quickly and in force."

Michael surrendered.

"My name is Michael Coolidge."

"What do you want?"

"I want to know what were you doing at the Valencia."

"What business is that of yours?"

"How did you know Desmond Tracey?"

"Be careful, Mr. Coolidge. You keep peppering me with questions, I am going to have to bill you. And I'm not cheap."

Michael simply stared at the man.

"You know what I do for a living?" Munro asked, a little weary now.

Michael nodded.

"Then you'll know that I am not inclined to discuss my business with strangers. Especially ones who leap over my wall."

"You were looking for her."

"Who?"

"Jane Thomassen."

This brought nothing new to Munro's expression. No surprise, no fear.

"Don't tell me you don't know her," Michael said.

"In case you haven't noticed, I'm not telling you anything."

"But you know her father. You sponsored him at your club."

Munro tilted his head slightly, as if only marginally interested in the fact Michael knew this.

He said, "I'll tell you what. Why don't you just tell me what you think you know. And then we can send you on your way."

"I think you have been involved with Jane Thomassen since she was a girl. I think you've spent a lot of time and effort buying off her father. Or making sure her father never found out. You've kept seeing her over the years and she's with you now."

"With me? Where, *here*?"

Michael did not answer. His certainty that Justine was with this man slipping further away.

"You aren't trying to blackmail me, are you?" Munro asked.

"No."

"Because that would be a felony."

"Just tell me where she is."

"All right. I'll set your overheated mind to rest, Mr. Coolidge, and then you can go. Yes, I remember Jane. And, yes, I know her father. I don't know what your involvement with her is, or what she's told you, but I think you should be aware that she is a disturbed person. At least she was ten years ago. As for the Valencia, my presence there has a straightforward explanation which happens to be none of your business. Although it does interest me that you say Jane was involved with the drug addict who perished there. What was she to him?"

A thought occurred to Michael, the same one that had come when he'd called the police moments after seeing the newspaper article. He was making a mistake.

"All right," Munro said after several silent seconds passed. "Have it your way. I'm going to have my sons walk you to the gate and let you out so you don't break a leg on that fence. That's the last thing we want, you getting hurt."

"I'm not going to stop looking for her," Michael said.

"That's your prerogative. The only thing I ask it that you please do it somewhere else."

NINE

KIM ARRIVED JUST AFTER DARK. HER VISIT WAS NOT A surprise. She'd already called a half hour after he left Mud Creek Road. Munro must have looked him up and made the connection. Michael had been foolish to give his real name, but that shotgun had made it difficult to lie. He had not answered her call; he had not listened to her voice mail. She'd phoned a second time, she'd texted. He'd ignored these as well. He did not want to hear a voice of reason. He was moving beyond reason now, drawn by something he could not control. All he could think about was how badly he had blundered with Munro. He was lucky he hadn't been arrested. Or cut to ribbons. Although, now that he thought about it, why hadn't Munro sicced the authorities on him? He did not seem like a forgiving man. And yet he'd let Michael go with a warning.

Michael tried to ignore the doorbell as well. He was in his dark office, his sanctuary, on his second big whiskey. It rang again. Kim would not be ignored. And she had a key. She drew back in unhappy surprise when he opened the door. Douglas stood beside her. His posture suggested anger, an emotion Michael had not thought the man could generate.

"What the hell is going on?" Kim asked immediately. "I've been trying to call you for the last two hours."

"Kim . . ."

She gave her head a terse shake, as if the notion of him actually answering her question was ridiculous.

"Will says you were snooping around in Doug's study. And then Mark Munro calls saying you trespassed at his place."

Michael closed his eyes and rubbed his forehead.

"I wasn't trespassing. I just went to talk to him."

Douglas almost said something but Kim silenced him with a curt gesture. This was her show.

"You jumped over the fence, Michael."

He shrugged, a maneuver he immediately regretted.

"He said you were being aggressive and flinging paranoid accusations. Those were his exact words."

"He's an eloquent guy."

"Don't take that tone with me, Michael. You cannot possibly be surprised we are angry. Marcus is Doug's boss. He thought Doug had given out confidential information."

"Look, I had good reason to speak with him."

"What reason?" Douglas said, no longer able to restrain himself.

"Why didn't you just ask Doug if you wanted to get hold of him?" Kim asked, not yet ready to relinquish her leading role. "Or set up a meeting, like normal people."

"It was urgent."

Michael said, "So you broke into our house?"

"Come on, Kim. Broke in? Really?"

"You really scared Will," she continued.

"Yeah, well, I didn't mean to do that."

"Marcus values his privacy," Douglas said.

"And why is that?" Michael asked, glad to have someone else to argue with. "I mean, why all the secrecy?"

"Because he used to be a prosecutor. He put rapists and murderers behind bars. His personal details are protected by law, Michael. Divulging them is an actual *crime*. And why the heck am I standing here justifying my boss's unwillingness to have people leap over his fence and accost his family?"

"I think we are owed an explanation here," Kim added.

Michael experienced a brief vision of his ex-wife's reaction if he told her the whole story.

He said, "I really cannot talk about this with you guys. I'm sorry."

"Does this have something to do with that fight you were in the other day?"

"Look, I'm sorry I used the spare key and I'm sorry I went into Douglas's office and I'm sorry I violated Marcus Munro's privacy. It won't happen again."

"Damn right," Douglas muttered.

Michael had had enough. He gestured to the empty house behind him.

He said, "There's something I need to do, so . . ."

Kim stared at him in astonishment.

She said, "But we're not done here."

"I'm sorry, Kim, but we are."

He started to shut the door.

"I don't want you coming around the house anymore," she said quickly.

This stopped everyone for a moment. Even Douglas seemed to be taken aback.

"But I'm supposed to have Will next weekend," Michael said.

"Do you honestly think I'm going to put my son in your care with you behaving like this?"

"You can't really do that."

"Seriously? You want me to make this official?"

"Kim . . ."

"I mean, Christ, Michael. You get fired from your job for embezzling money . . ."

"That's not . . ."

". . . and get into fights in front of our son and jeopardize Douglas's career—I have no idea what sort of weird place you are living in right now. But you cannot take Will there with you. Not with all the progress he's been making."

Michael wanted to ask her what that meant, progress, but she was already heading back down the path. Douglas stood his ground. He held Michael's eye, his gaze transforming into something very severe, very un-Douglas. A message was being communicated. A threat, a warning. Michael's first thought was that it was just a territorial assertion of his rights to his new family. But by the time the other man broke away Michael understood that this was a message from Marcus Munro.

Things fell apart after that. Michael drank two more whiskeys, he thrashed through a short restless sleep, and then he was lucidly drunk at four A.M., tortured by thoughts of his wanton stupidity in going over that fence, his inability to make sense of an accumulating body of facts. He had been convinced she was on Mud Creek Road. He had practically felt her presence when he heard the gunshots. But she was not there. And his certainty that Munro was the man she had described was now shattered. It had been exactly one week since he'd seen her and he had no more idea where she was than when he'd first read her middle-of-the-night text.

He finally fell back asleep just before dawn and did not get out of bed until late morning. For the first time since reading about Trace's death, he did not know what he would do next. Driving back up 44 would be a waste of gas; working his way through the 2003 yearbook would be futile. Her classmates would know nothing. Her story was beyond gossip.

He looked again at Munro's history. It had been almost twenty years since the lawyer had left the DA's office. In private practice, he represented both violent and white collar criminals, as well as participating in numerous civil suits. His most notable recent case had been defending a man who was accused of killing his wife, then making it look like a home invasion. The defendant had been acquitted after the jury had deliberated only two hours. But if he wasn't Justine's lover, what was he to her? And what was Desmond Tracey to him?

His phone rang just before noon. It was a New York number, one he did not immediately recognize.

"So, did you find her?" Susan Wessels asked without introduction.

"Not yet."

"Now there's a surprise."

"So I take it you've heard nothing."

"No. But I did hear something about what Trace was doing up in your picturesque little town."

Michael was very much awake now.

"Really?" he said.

She said, "So I was at this thing Friday night and I ran into a sculptor who lives out near the Gowanus. It turns out Trace was crashing at his studio all summer. He was in a bad way and my friend was about to give him the boot when all of a sudden Trace announces he's heading up to your neck of the woods. He said that he was going to set someone free."

"Set someone free? What does that mean?"

"Unclear. He just kept on saying *I have to set her free*. Kind of freaked people out. His solitary death in a cheap hotel makes me feel like his plan was not a roaring success."

"And your friend didn't know who this woman was? Or where he was setting her free from?"

"Not a clue."

"But it had to be Justine."

She said, "That's what I'm thinking. But set her free from what? Jail? A bad relationship?"

He remembered what Munro had said. *I think you should be aware that she is a disturbed person.*

"I don't know," he said.

"You doing all right, Michael Coolidge? You sound beat."

"It's been a rough week."

"She has that effect."

"Thanks for calling, Susan. I appreciate it. Seriously."

He remembered too late that he was not supposed to use her first name. But she didn't seem to mind.

"It's Sunday and I'm sober. What the fuck else am I going to do?"

He typed "Annville County" and "mental health" into his search engine. There was the psychiatric ward at the hospital. There was Annville Mental Health Associates, the pleasant suite of offices where he'd broken his appointments with a psychologist. And then there was the Riverside Institute, up on Route 44. He clicked on the website and was confronted by a nearly blank page, its typeface elegant, its background a calming blue. "The latest in mental health and addiction treatment for teens and young adults. Offering both residential and outpatient services." There was a phone number, an address. And that was all. There were no photos, no catalog of programs offered, no staff directory or testimonials. Just an invitation to call for a confidential conversation.

Michael typed "Riverside" and "Marcus Munro." The first hit was from an article in the *Call* four years ago. A man who owned land adjacent Riverside had sued the institute, alleging that construction of a new wing had led to blockage and pollution of a stream that ran through his land. The jury had found in favor of Riverside.

"My clients bend over backwards to be good neighbors," their lawyer, Marcus Munro, was quoted as saying. "Nobody respects the region's precious ecologies, both physical and human, better than this institution."

Michael searched for everything he could find about the Riverside Institute. It was a state-of-the art mental health clinic for teenagers and young adults ranging from the ages of 16-30. Private, though one article lauded it for its outreach into disadvantaged communities through a "scholarship" program. Other articles credited staff and board members with co-authoring articles in serious publications. One name came up consistently. Dr. Daniel Winter, the institute's director. Photos showed a trim, handsome man with eyes that managed to be both piercing and kind. The most commonly reproduced image was his author photo—he had published five books.

Michael had never heard of the man, although he was not exactly conversant with this world. He had not read anything dealing with psychology written after *Civilization and its Discontents*. Winter appeared to be a big deal. He'd been on nationally broadcast talk shows and lectured widely; he'd served on commissions and task forces, he held a visitor's chair at Cornell. His specialty was cognitive behavioral therapy for the young. Michael checked the Amazon page for his most recent book, *Excitable Boys: Anger Management for Your Son*. It was ranked 781 overall, 22 for self-help. There were 218 reviews. All but a handful accorded it five stars. In several of them, desperate parents credited the book and its author with saving their families. One of them claimed that Winter "had an uncanny ability to open lines of communication with our son, who we truly thought was lost to us." Another referred to his "profound understanding of the darkest reaches of the adolescent mind."

Justine was at Riverside. Even though he'd been wrong about so much else, he knew that this was true. She'd had a breakdown when she was sixteen, just like Penny said. And they had put her there. When she recovered they had packed her off to Arden. She had not cut it. She had walked off the stage. It all made sense now. Her rootlessness, her erratic and incomplete history, her false names. Her lies. The lover she had spoken of was not a man, but this place to which she kept returning. This was what she could not quit.

And it explained her relationship with Desmond Tracey, the Rembrandt of the locked wards. She had gravitated to him and he had been able to keep her afloat, keep her out of the sort of place he hated. But then he went bad and there was nothing for her to do but return to

Riverside. *Things are just so wrong with me right now.* That was what was happening in January. Her night with Michael had been her last one on Earth. She had been inside ever since.

Trace, wracked by guilt, crazed by opiates, knowing that he had failed the one woman he had loved, had come up to set her free. Sly genius that he was, he had managed to get her out, but they had only made it as far as Water Street before she had understood how gone he was. She had made him take her back and he had retreated to his cheap hotel to do the only thing that could take the pain away. Her text to Michael had been her last gasp before going inside. He wondered if she even knew that Trace was dead. Munro's presence at the hotel made sense now. A patient had escaped, the man who had freed her had died. He was the lawyer of an institute that clearly did not like publicity. Of course he would be there.

Michael cursed his blindness. He did not see it because he did not want to believe it. He wanted to think what happened in January was real, when it was nothing more than the invention of a woman's fractured mind. She was not to be trusted. She was not of sound mind. Wessels had told him and her father had told him and Marcus Munro had told him. She'd told him herself, if he had only been listening. She was broken. But he would not entertain the one hypothesis that explained everything, even though it had been there all along, in her lies, in her flight, in the reactions of those closest to her.

He closed down his computer and put the photograph of Wessels' opening in a manila envelope. He might need it—there was no telling what she was calling herself now. Before leaving the house, he took a long shower and shaved, but even then he still looked as if he had aged seven years in the past seven days. There was nothing he could do about that. Unlike the woman he was going to see, the face in front of him was the only one he had.

There was nothing about the sign to suggest it involved mental health. *The Riverside Institute.* The entrance to the facility came at the end of a mile-long access road that was bordered by thick forest.

Suddenly, twin brick columns appeared, the one on the right bearing the discreet plaque. There was no security shed, no impassable fence. Nothing warning off trespassers or directing visitors to report to reception. Just a small, state-of-the-art camera atop the pillar on the left.

The approach road ran through landscaped grounds. There were paths and picnic areas and volleyball courts. He followed a sharp turn and the main building came into view. It looked like a resort hotel, a place for doctors or businessmen gathered for conferences. He parked in the small visitor's lot. There were a dozen other cars. It was Sunday, a day to see troubled loved ones. He made sure to bring the manila envelope with him.

The front entrance was locked. Tinting made it impossible to see inside. He pressed the button beside a small speaker. Cameras nested in the upper corners of the portico, like slumbering bats.

"Welcome to Riverside," an effervescent male voice intoned through the speaker. "What may we do for you today?"

"I'm visiting a patient."

There was a buzz, followed by a click. The lobby did nothing to allay Michael's sense that someone was about to drape him with a lei and inform him of his tee time. There were coffee tables, potted plants, soothing colors. An aquarium filled with glittering fish. Two young men staffed the reception desk, both wearing polo shirts the same soothing blue as the website's background. One stared at a computer, the other watched Michael approach with an affable expression. He was blond and young and looked like he might have recently competed on the pommel horse. His nametag identified him as Jenner.

"Your name, sir?"

"Michael Coolidge."

"Okay. And who are you visiting today?"

"Jane Thomassen."

"Okay. Do you have an appointment?"

"No. I really just wanted to see how she was doing."

The man at the computer glanced briefly at Michael and then at the manila envelope before returning to his screen. His nametag identified him as Richard.

"Okay, we actually have a pretty set procedure here," Jenner explained brightly. "You have to schedule."

"Could I schedule now?" Michael asked.

"Yeah, no, we don't really do it like that."

"What if it's an emergency?"

"Is it?"

"Well, I'm concerned about her."

"Okay. What is your relationship?"

"I'm a friend."

"Well, Mr. Coolidge, the way we like to do it is, you call and you press option three to leave a message."

"What if I just called the number now and pressed three? Would I be able to schedule for today?"

Jenner deferred to Richard, who looked up from the computer again, finally ready to speak.

He said, "A client's care team would have to review any request. So I suppose in theory you could leave a message from here, but there would be no immediate decision on it."

"How long would it take?"

"Forty-eight hours. What with it being a Sunday."

"Could you at least tell me how she's doing?"

The man who had just spoken turned his attention back to the computer, forcing Michael to whiplash the question to Jenner.

"We cannot discuss our clients with members of the public."

"Can you at least tell me if she is even here?"

Jenner's bright patience was beginning to fade.

"That's the main thing we cannot discuss."

Michael contemplated showing them the photo, but knew it would do no good. He looked at the door beyond the desk. There was a small portal that was impossible to see through from this angle. She was in there. A short walk away. Staring glassy-eyed at a television.

Or sitting on a veranda, blanketed and sedated, watching the infinite river rolling past.

"All right," Michael said. "Thanks for your help."

"Have a good one."

The door buzzed just as he reached it. He paused on the shaded portico. Although there was a chill in the air, the sun shone intensely, bringing the sort of atmospheric clarity that only happened this time of year. He walked slowly to his car. This felt like the end. Her care team would never set up a meeting. Munro would have already given them Michael's name.

A man's voice drifted around the side of the building just as he reached the Sonata. Michael walked across the small lot. He paused when he reached the building's edge, then leaned forward to look. An orderly smoked a cigarette outside a propped-open door. He faced the river, his back to Michael. Smoke shrouded his head. He held a cell phone to his ear.

"Well, he's paying for it," he said. "And a new paint job."

There was an indecipherable squawk; the man inclined his head slightly and fingered a walkie-talkie attached to his belt.

"Gotta go," he said.

He took one last drag of the cigarette before dropping it into a bucket. He disappeared inside, leaving the door open. Michael started walking. He had no plan, he was just in motion. She was inside and now he was going to be as well. He'd only taken a few steps when an arm emerged from the door, an afterthought, jolting it to release the propping mechanism. Michael stopped so abruptly that he skidded a few inches on the muddy grass, but the moment the man's arm was gone, he started moving again. Running now. He grabbed the door with two inches to spare.

After waiting a few seconds, Michael stepped into a tiled, fluorescent service hallway. It was empty. He proceeded along it for twenty feet, expecting an alarm, a challenge. He had no idea where he was going, if he would end up in a kitchen, or the reception area, or standing face to face with her.

He reached a door. Through its small window he could see another hallway, this one residential. There was carpet, track lighting, a series of doors decorated with colorful signs. He tried the handle—it opened easily. He started down the hall. The first half-dozen doors were shut. There were small whiteboards on each of them. Bethany. Erin. Liz. Around the names, cheery insignia, flowers and peace signs, cartoonish figures. Clipboards were slotted into plastic holders. There was a minty tang in the air. Music played quietly somewhere, a man's plaintive voice, fire-and-raining through cheap speakers.

He came to an open door. The room was small and pristine, decorated with modular furniture. A girl lay on the single bed. She wore pajamas. She was awake. Sort of. The window above her bed overlooked a courtyard filled with potted trees. Scattered figures lounged on furniture, languid and ghostly. None of them were Justine.

"Excuse me," Michael said.

She looked at him without interest.

"I'm looking for someone. Jane? Jane Thomassen?"

She stared at him for a moment, then turned away, sinking even more deeply back into herself. He'd only taken a few strides down the hall when another door opened. A willowy girl stepped out and flashed him the sweetest smile he had ever seen. Fifteen, he guessed. She, too, wore pajamas. She held a stuffed giraffe.

"Hi," she said, her voice shaky and feathery and apparently untroubled by the fact she had no idea who he was.

"I wonder if you could help me."

"I seriously doubt it," she said with a self-deprecating laugh.

"I'm looking for Jane."

"Um, who?"

"Jane Thomassen."

Her smile diminished slightly as she shook her head.

"She may be called Justine."

Nothing. He took the photo from its envelope.

"This is her."

"She's pretty."

"Do you know her?"

"No. Hey, it's James!"

She was pointing at Trace.

"You know him?"

"Everybody knows James. James is the best."

"He was a patient here?"

She shot him an incredulous smile.

"He was a janitor. Wait—*custodian*. Everybody loved him. How is he? I miss him."

"When did he leave?" he asked her.

"Couple weeks ago. They fired him."

"Do you know why?"

Her gaze traveled over his shoulder.

"Oops." She giggled.

Michael turned. Two men in blue shirts were walking swiftly toward him, lockstep, their approach muffled by the carpet. Jenner and the man who had been smoking. Both gripped walkie-talkies. Neither looked happy.

"You need to leave this facility," Jenner said, his tone very different than it had been at the front desk.

"Let me just talk to whoever is in charge."

"I am not going to ask you again. Please comply."

Jenner grabbed Michael's arm. He pulled free.

"I just want to know if she's here."

The smoker reached for him and Michael swatted his hand away. Hard. Jenner raised his walkie-talkie and held it in front of Michael's chest, like a reporter wielding a microphone. For the briefest moment, Michael thought that he was offering him a way to talk to the person in charge. His next thought was that this was not like any walkie-talkie he had ever seen. And then there were no thoughts, only pain, more pain than he had imagined possible. Every nerve in his body popped, shooting doses of acid into his flesh and bone. The world went sideways. The floor had become a wall and people were standing on that. The girl was hurrying away—she had the thinnest white ankles. And there was the photo, right in front of his face, Justine and Trace and S. Wessels and that idiot with the beard. There was no sound, or rather everything was coated in a deep muffling gelatinous layer of white noise. Michael willed himself to stand and instead started to drool on the carpet. More sideways people arrived. He regained control of his muscles, but he still could not move because strong hands now held him down. The acid was replaced by simple pain. And then he was being carried.

They deposited him in a room that could have been in any hospital. The bed had rails; medical equipment lined the walls; the drawers of the cabinets were labeled. He was placed in the bed. Jenner and the smoker loomed over him. They told him not to move and he nodded. He was complying.

Finally, another man entered. Daniel Winter. The man who saved families. The five-star man. In person, he looked a little older, a little more careworn. He was Michael's height, with a trimly muscular physique, a forgiving gaze, a chin frozen in a slight jut.

"How are you feeling, Mr. Coolidge?" he asked.

"This asshole actually tased me," Michael said, his words slurred, too loud.

"Would you like to be transported to the hospital?" Winter asked. "This is a fully accredited medical facility and I am a licensed physician, but of course if you request transportation to the hospital we will call an ambulance."

"I'll live."

"That's a no?"

"Yeah."

"Can I have your permission to take your pulse?"

"Knock yourself out."

The man placed two fingers on Michael's neck. His touch was gentle. What he felt seemed to satisfy him.

Michael said, "I'd really like to know what the hell just happened."

"What happened is you trespassed and then refused to leave when requested to do so," he said as he removed his fingers. "After your actions were deemed threatening to staff and clients, you were forcibly restrained using approved techniques."

"Threatening? Are you serious?"

Winter nodded gravely. He was.

"I know you are feeling angry and confused right now. Believe me, I am not happy this happened. But this is a secure campus, Mr. Coolidge. We take intrusions very seriously. We recently had a fairly alarming breach of security and I'm afraid that has everyone on edge."

Desmond Tracey, Michael thought.

"There are young people here with severe addictive disorders," Winter continued. "Some of our clients have been the victims of the most horrific abuse. We cannot have men wandering the halls unmonitored."

"You could have just asked me to leave."

"I did," Jenner said. "You refused."

"I just wanted to see if she was here."

"I think our privacy policies were explained when you arrived?" Winter asked.

"Where is she?" Michael asked. "What did you do to her?"

Winter's expression grew even more sympathetic.

"I don't know you, Michael, but I do know something about you and your situation. There's not a lot I'm allowed to say, but I'd really like to urge you to stop what you are doing. For your own good. For everyone's good. Please."

There was a knock on the door.

"They're here," a woman's voice announced.

"Tell them to come in."

Michael asked, "Who's here?"

"The police."

"You're having me arrested?"

"Once a taser had been deployed, well, if we don't involve the police, there might be liability issues." Winter shrugged, looking a little embarrassed. "Sign of the times."

And then they arrived, two of them, bulky with Kevlar, their belts laden with gear. They explained his rights, just like on television.

They placed actual, intractable handcuffs on him. Everybody was very gentle; there was even a wheelchair to propel him out to the cruiser. He did not protest. He was complying. At the cruiser, they made sure he did not bump his head. It was not until they loaded him into the caged back seat that he realized he was no longer in possession of his photograph.

He had never been inside the Annville police station. His sole contact with them had been those two phone calls five endless days ago. Luckily, there was no one he knew in the lobby. Once inside, he was processed. There were fingerprints and photographs and a surprisingly exhaustive biographical interview. Several times, he was asked if he wanted to phone his lawyer, but the only lawyers he knew in Annville were the guy he'd used for the divorce and Douglas. And Marcus Munro, of course.

He wound up sitting alone in a small room with a table and three plastic chairs. There were posters on the wall detailing what to do in the event of various emergencies. Cartoon men choked, suffered heart attacks, had seizures. A man entered. He identified himself as Detective Maas. He was young and balding, with a fresh, plump face that looked like it only needed to be shaved every other day. He brought to mind an ex-athlete, someone who had played a stalwart position—linebacker, catcher, hockey goalie. He gave Michael the same look his doctor did when he walked into the examination room during check-ups. Cordial scrutiny with weighty undertones.

"So," he said as he dropped a dull green folder on the table and scraped out a chair. "We meet at last."

Something occurred to Michael. It was Sunday afternoon. Why was a detective working on a Sunday afternoon?

Maas said, "You know about lawyers and stuff."

"Yes."

"And we're good?"

Michael nodded.

"Because at any time, just say the word, you can get somebody in here."

"Understood."

"So. I'm really just trying to get some sense of what's going on with you, Michael."

He replied, "It's just a misunderstanding."

"According to what I'm hearing, they explained the drill pretty good up there and yet you still decided to ingress. You must know that you cannot just amble into a secure mental health facility, especially one with young girls in there."

"I understand now."

"We've also heard about your visit to Marcus Munro. And to the Thomassens. What's going on, Mike? Why are you so eager to find Jane?"

"I'm just worried about her. Like I said."

"You sure that's all?"

"What else would there be?"

"That's sort of what I'm asking you."

Michael said, "I'm not . . . wait, are *you* looking for her?"

"Should we be?"

"Do you think she's done something wrong?"

"Do you?"

Michael was suddenly tempted to tell him everything. Munro's visit to the motel. Penny's account of Justine's breakdown. Neal's sudden good fortune after his daughter's disappearance, his lies about being in touch with her. But he'd said enough. He'd done enough.

"I've made a mistake."

Maas raised his eyebrows.

"I'd just like to apologize to everyone," Michael continued. "Obviously, if there's some sort of fine I'll . . ."

"Whoa, let's not get ahead of ourselves here. Fines are above my pay grade."

"I just want you to know I'm done."

"And you're sure there's nothing else you want to tell me about what happened up at the Valencia last weekend?"

Michael shook his head. Maas stared at him.

"No," Michael said.

"Let me have a word with the people up at Riverside. See where they stand. I can't promise anything but, you know. You did get lit up pretty good."

"I'd appreciate that."

"A word of advice. She does show up, give us a call, will you? I can see you have feelings for this girl, but I'm starting to think you might have dodged a bullet on this one."

"Okay."

"You need anything now? Soda? There are usually baked goods floating around out there."

"No. Thank you."

Maas tapped the table.

"Okay. Let me see what's what. Sit tight."

He was out of the room before Michael realized he'd meant that last comment as a joke.

They let him go an hour later. Maas handed him a summons to appear in six weeks to answer a misdemeanor charge of disturbing the peace. Douglas and Kim waited for him on the other side of the locked door. Michael wondered who had called them, but was too exhausted to ask.

"Could you take me to my car?" he asked. "It's up at Riverside."

"Give Doug the keys," Kim said in a tone that precluded dissent. "We can drop him off and he can take it back to our house. We'll meet him there. You and I need to talk."

Michael complied. For the second time that day, he found himself in the back seat of a car. He did not look at the Riverside building during the ten seconds they spent in the visitor's parking lot. He remained in the back as Kim drove to the Tastee Diner. She said nothing, not a word, until they were seated in a booth.

"I know I am no longer your wife but I think I am due an explanation," she said.

He told her. Everything. There was no reason to keep it from her. It was over. Justine was in Riverside, or somewhere else beyond his reach. Kim listened without comment as he told her about the affair, Water Lane, Trace's death, his journeys to Manhattan and Arden. His confrontations with Nancy and Neal and Munro. The jolt that had taken him down.

"It's over, Kim," he said when he'd finished. "I lost it for a few days. I let my imagination run wild. But I'm done."

She replied, "I look forward to seeing that's true. You can start Tuesday afternoon."

He almost asked what was happening then, but luckily he remembered Will's race before he spoke. They drove back to her house in silence. The Sonata was there, as promised. Douglas met them at the door. After giving Kim a quick glance, he turned over Michael's keys. If Will was at home, he would not be greeting his father. Back on Locust, in the kitchen, Michael could see the accumulated debris of his spell of madness. Dirty dishes and glasses surrounded the sink, attended by an advance party of frantic ants. There was a slightly rank smell, old coffee and irradiated food. The microwave door was off the latch. He left it all for tomorrow. For now, it was all he could do to climb into the bed he had neglected for the last ten days and drop into an oblivion that lasted for sixteen hours.

His body still ached from yesterday's electrical disturbances as he made coffee and read the *Call*. His arrest was recorded in the police log. It gave his age and his address. Just another bad actor. Although he still felt a toxic exhaustion, he worked in his office for a while, updating his resume and sending out a few letters. When he was done he went out for a long, aimless walk. The sky was clouding over. Evidently some serious rain was on the way.

He passed the next twenty-four hours either asleep or sleepwalking. Just after noon on Tuesday, there was a heavy shower, as forecast, though the rain had paused by the time he made it to the high school. The ground was soft and muddy. Kim was among the small crowd of parents gathered at the starting line. She gave Michael a once-over and seemed at least provisionally satisfied with what she saw. Will was warming up with his teammates. His recent enthusiasm for cross country still baffled Michael. It seemed part of a larger agenda. He was no athlete. His stride was the lock-kneed shuffle of someone racing to the bathroom after eating tainted shellfish. He invariably finished out of touch with the leaders, gasping and raspberry-faced.

The runners were called to the line. Skinny and underdressed, they looked like prisoners awaiting the machine gun's rattle. Will's first step was backward—he slipped in the mud and went down on his right hand. He slipped again while trying to stand up, landing on his left hand this time. It looked like he was doing the soft shoe. By the time he finally crossed the starting line he was ten yards behind the others. He flailed through a storm of mud and turf but made up no ground by the time he vanished into the woods.

A pack of coaches and parents set off to watch along the course, but Michael did not have the energy to follow. Instead, he excused himself, saying he needed the bathroom. Once inside the school building, the enormity of it all struck him. She had been here. School plays and honor rolls, adoring boys and jealous girls, all of it. Before she'd fallen apart. Before she became the broken woman he loved.

He thought about the photo in Neal Thomassen's office. Her eyes on the vanishing point. Her future. He steadied himself with a hand against a cool concrete wall outside the bathroom as the tears came. He could not remember the last time he'd cried but here it was, sobs shuddering through his chest and throat. For God's sake, he thought. But he could not stop. It went on and on, for what felt like an eternity. Luckily, no one saw him. Classes were over and the race was happening outside.

He hurried back across the muddy field. Kim gave him a look but there was a shout before she could comment. The lead runner had emerged from the woods. Others followed. Small dramas played out. A minute passed, and then another. Slower runners appeared, some moving in liquid agony, others simply loafing it. And still, no Will.

"Do you think he stopped?" Kim said.

As if in answer, their son appeared, neck-and-neck with a tall runner whose legs were undergoing a laborious articulation, as if he were deploying a robotic limb. Both runners strained mightily. The battle was on. For last. Spectators noticed; the special cheer reserved for the inept went up. Michael, suddenly caught up in the race, ignored the ironic undercurrent. Kim was also getting excited. Will edged ahead, the tall boy caught up; the tall boy surged and Will reeled him in. Come on, Michael thought. Win this, at least. The runners were moving stride for stride. Twenty yards to go, ten, five. And then, Will managed a few organized strides just as the other boy's mechanical motion collapsed into chaos. His son had done it. He had not come in last.

Michael turned to Kim. Their bodies inclined briefly toward one another, moving on muscle memory, propelled by the good years. But then the bad ones intervened and they limited themselves to a shared smile. Michael led the way to Will, who was bent forward, hands on knees. He rose just as Michael reached him. His eyes met his father's. Michael smiled and hugged his son's hot, mud-flecked body. His embrace communicating the debatable message that any victory was victory enough.

They went out for pizza afterwards. Michael took the opportunity to apologize to his son. He had not been himself of late. He said he would be grateful if Will would be patient with him while he got his act together. His son looked embarrassed by the apology, but also genuinely touched.

The house was dark when he got back; he had not left the usual lights on. But the clouds temporarily cleared and there was enough of the moon to allow him to slot his key into the back door's lock. He twisted the knob but nothing happened. He'd just locked the door. He must have left it unlocked.

He stepped into the kitchen and hit the lights. Ants covered a plate he'd left by the sink. He went over and washed them away, then poured himself a glass of water—his whiskey days were over. For a while, at least. He headed to his office to see if his emails had received any response. A pale wedge of light shone beneath the door. He could not remember leaving it on. He really did need to get a grip.

He pushed open the door and there she was on his sofa. Her legs were folded beneath her, just as they had been the first morning. She looked up at him with a tired smile, and he knew in an instant that everything he had decided about her was wrong.

"You should find a better place to hide your key, Michael. There are some real fucking creeps in this town."

PART TWO

PART TWO

TEN

HE DID NOT TRY TO TOUCH HER. DESPITE THAT BRITTLE welcoming smile, there was a serpentine wariness to her that told him to keep his distance. Things still needed to be decided between them. She looked exhausted. The self-assurance and energy he remembered from January had vanished. Her skin was just as pale as it had always been, although there was something profoundly different about it now, as if it had been deprived of necessary blood.

"What were you doing at Riverside?" she asked. "Why did they arrest you?"

There was no hostility in her voice. Just a curiosity so deep it was almost like wonder.

"I . . . wait, how did you know about that?"

"It was in the papers, Michael."

She watched him. Awaiting her answer.

"I was looking for you," he said.

"Why?"

"I was worried. After I got your text and Trace turned up dead . . ."

There was no reason to complete the sentence; he let his silence catalog the grim possibilities.

"What do you know about me?" she asked, her tone soft but relentless. "What have you found out?"

He described his journey. Klimov to Wessels to Arden. Nancy to Neal; Penny Bowman to Munro.

"But how did you wind up at Riverside?" she asked. "It's really important that I know exactly what you were doing there."

"Susan Wessels said Trace had been telling people he was heading upstate to set someone free. Those were his exact words. *Set someone free.* Given his history, I figured he meant from an institution. Then I saw that Munro was Riverside's house lawyer. And that he was some sort of benefactor to your father. It all seemed to come together up there."

"And that's it? You don't know anything else about me and that place?"

"Only that Trace worked there. Until he got fired."

"How did you find that out?"

Michael said, "I guess I sort of broke in."

"I still can't figure out how you got by the palace guards."

"There was an unlocked door. But I didn't make it very far. I got tased before I could ask what he was really doing there."

"They actually *tased* you?"

"It hurts as much as advertised."

"Did you meet Daniel Winter when you were there? The guy who runs the place?"

"He dropped by to make sure I wasn't dying of a heart attack. He was the one who had me arrested."

"Did you talk to him about me at all?" Justine asked.

"It wasn't that sort of a conversation."

"So that's all you know about me and Riverside."

"Yes."

"I thought maybe you had . . ."

"What?"

"Look, I shouldn't have come. It's not fair to you. I'll go. Just . . . you're going to need to forget about me."

It seemed as if she truly was about to leave.

"Justine, wait—what's going on?"

She looked at first like she was not going to answer, but when she met his gaze, she saw something that caused her to relent.

"When I read you'd been busted at Riverside, I thought maybe you'd discovered something that could help me. But clearly you didn't. So we should just leave it at that."

"Justine . . ."

"I'm sorry, Michael. I know this seems weird and unfair and bat-shit crazy, but if you want to help, the best thing you can do is stop looking for me. I know you mean well, but you've already done more harm than good."

He asked her, "How have I done harm?"

"I was hoping Winter and Munro would not be able to connect me to Trace. But I take it you told them that I was with him?"

Michael nodded.

"But why shouldn't they know you were close to Trace? What was he doing at Riverside if you weren't in there?"

"Please, Michael. Don't make me tell you this."

"I can help."

"You can't. No one can."

"Try me."

Something briefly wavered in her expression.

"You don't want to get caught up in my shit. Believe me."

"I already am," he said with a grim laugh. "I mean, I did get electrocuted."

She did not share his smile.

"Once you know this, then you know."

"Tell me, Justine. Please."

She took a deep breath and looked up at the ceiling before speaking.

"Daniel Winter killed Trace on the night you saw me. He came to the cabin at the Valencia and found him semicomatose on that thermonuclear heroin Trace had been taking. Winter must have pumped him full of an overdose. Or maybe he just went old school and put a pillow over his face."

"Wait, you were there when this happened?"

"I was just outside. I did not want to be around Trace and his drugs so I went to cool off in this picnic area they have up there. I saw Danny come and I saw him leave and then I found Trace dead."

Danny, Michael thought.

"But why? Why would Winter do that?"

She finally looked back at Michael.

"Because he fucked me when I was fourteen years old. And he's done the same to others as well. Many, I think. Including one little girl who wound up dead in the river. And Trace was about to show the whole wide world what Winter was. That's why he was working at Riverside. And that's why I'm here right now. When I saw they'd arrested you, I thought you might have found out something about that. Which seems kind of crazy, I know, but I couldn't figure out what else you were doing up there."

"You were fourteen," Michael said from the doorway.

"And fifteen. It lasted six months. I was his patient. I'm pretty sure they all are, his girls."

"You were a patient at Riverside?"

"Outpatient. I wasn't *that* fucked up. My parents took me to him because I was having panic attacks. You ever have one of those?

"No. Not yet, anyway."

"I don't think you can understand how bad they are unless you suffer one. It's like the worst thunderstorm you can imagine breaking right inside of you. You're totally convinced you are dying. You cannot breathe, your heart races two hundred beats a minute. It got to the point where I couldn't shut doors in rooms I was in, I couldn't be in cars with the windows rolled up. Forget about getting on a plane. So my folks sent me to Riverside. At first I was in group. Afternoons, Saturday mornings. It was sort of lame. We talked, we role-played, we journaled. And then Danny invited me for private sessions."

She shook her head in dismal wonder.

"He made me better. That's what's so messed up about all of this. He knew exactly what I was feeling and exactly what to do about it. The guy is a wizard. He'd lock the two of us in a room and turn out the light and we would just . . . talk. Or he'd have me lie on his sofa and pile cushions on me. Confronting my worst fears, all that. It sounds messed up but it really worked. The attacks stopped, my heart returned to its normal cadence. He saved my life, as far as I was concerned."

She was completely lost in the memory now.

"I fell in love with him pretty much straight away. I mean, I was the perfect age for it. Who else was I going to have a crush on? Justin or Troy from Biology lab? And my real father died of a heart attack when I was young, so there was that whole daddy thing at work, too. Danny was the beautiful man who chased the crazy away."

Thomassen was not her father. Another thing he had missed. Her eyes narrowed.

"He played me like a fucking Stradivarius. Darkened rooms, pillows. I mean, on the one hand, it was pretty obvious what was going on. But he was always the perfect gentleman. He didn't even touch me, not even a pat on the shoulder. Not until the day he took me to his house, this cold stone mansion up in the mountains. He didn't explain why we were going. He just loaded me in his Lexus and drove me there. I presumed it was part of my therapy. And then he sat me on a big leather sofa and he undressed me and that was that. I was a virgin so it hurt like crazy. Though there was pleasure wrapped in all that pain."

She laughed quietly.

"He let me call him Danny. Which no one does, ever. It's Doctor or Daniel for everybody else. He told me I was special. His one and only. The rules didn't apply to us. We were outlaws, old souls. That whole routine. Although I sure didn't think it was a routine at the time. I knew all about perverts, of course. My Uncle Richard, he of the lingering hug. This was nothing like that. He was rich and powerful and famous and he'd saved my life. I wanted to please him so badly, it was almost like a physical ache. It didn't occur to me for a nanosecond that we were doing anything wrong. And the sex was amazing. Are you all right hearing this?"

"No. But keep going."

"He'd pick me up in a parking lot off River, which I guess was probably risky, though it wasn't like we were being watched. My mother and Neal were nuts about the guy. He'd turned their night-mare child into a well-behaved little princess. And I was quite the little accomplice. Having this big secret became almost as addictive as the sex."

She gave a fatalistic shrug.

"And then he dumped me. He let me down easy. He told me he was worried about getting caught. People had been talking. Which was bullshit, by the way. Nobody knew anything."

"Then why?" Michael asked.

"I was getting old. Literally. I was becoming a woman and the guy is simply not into women. Not that I knew this at the time. I thought we were . . . unique."

"And you never thought about telling anyone? Not even after he dumped you?"

"I'd convinced myself that we'd get back together the moment I became legal. Such are the delusions of a girl in love. To be honest, I'd have carried the whole thing to my grave if it hadn't . . ."

She looked up at him.

"I take it you never came across the name Natalie Chenier when you were searching for me?"

"No."

"She was in my group at Riverside. A real wild child. Couple years younger than me. She lived down in Cheapside with her drunk mother and her younger brother, this wannabe headbanger named Kevin. Their house was a pit. Smelled like cigarettes and piss. Guys in wife-beaters lounging around. She was a tiny little thing, Natalie. Beautiful, in her way. Totally messed up. She'd scorch her arm hairs with a lighter. Usually fried on whatever illicit substance she could get her hands on. But sweet with it. She had a monster crush on me. We'd make each other mix tapes. Neutral Milk Hotel. The Shins. Typical messed-up girl stuff."

She was slipping deeper into the memory. There was something desolate in her voice.

"We stopped hanging out after Danny took me out of group for my private sessions. I'd see her around—Annville's a small town. We'd say hello but that was it. I mean, Jesus, she was still in middle school."

Michael felt something sharp move through him. Middle school.

"So. Danny dumps me and I start my junior year. Still living in hope. And then I saw them together. Neal was giving me a ride somewhere, and he had to swing by one of the dumps he rented down in Cheapside, and I was sitting in the car waiting for him and there she was, riding in the passenger seat of his Lexus. *My* seat. It was just for a second, but they were definitely together. She didn't see me. But he sure as shit did."

She shook her head bitterly.

"My world collapses. The love of my life had left me for a younger woman. Who was thirteen. At first, I imagined doing all sorts of evil shit to her. But then I started to think rationally. It's not her fault. She's just a kid. And I have to tell her about the freight train that's about to hit her. I go to her house, it's the usual nightmare scenario there. Her mother's drunk, her brother's got music blaring in his room. I tell her what I saw, what I know. She denies she's with him at first but I can see it written all over that sweet little face."

"Her family didn't know what was going on?"

"Her family didn't know that they were on planet Earth. I tell her that the man is evil, that everything he's been telling her is a lie. She laughs in my face. No longer even trying to deny it. It's different with her, she says. They're soul mates. Blah blah blah. Same shit I would have said if somebody had confronted me a year earlier. I see there's nothing I can do. So I leave. Sensing that this is not going to end well."

"And she's the girl you said drowned."

"It happened just a few weeks after I saw her with him. I never got the chance to talk to her again after seeing her in her room. They fished her out of the river south of town. It was ruled an accident. They said she fell from the floodwall, down where those ruined factories are. But I decide what really happened is that she jumped."

"Because of Winter."

"He must have dumped her after I spotted them, just like I predicted. But I guess she wasn't as tough as me. Or as deluded. I wanted to tell everyone what happened, but I didn't have the nerve. Though I know I have to do something. So I get the brilliant idea of going to his house. On my own. I'm going to tell him I know what he's done. Tell him he has to make it right."

She shook her head in incredulity, as if she could not believe the brazen stupidity of the girl she was describing

"It took hours to walk there. It's night when I arrive. He's alone, working on one of his books that everybody loves so much. If he's surprised to see me he keeps it very well hidden. I just flat-out tell him what I know. He denies everything. Yeah, he worked with her, but it was all aboveboard. She had a lot of problems. Her mom whaled on her, guys molested her. He feels terrible about what happened. But the idea that he was responsible is just crazy. This from a guy who'd been fucking me a year earlier."

Her breathing was coming a little faster now.

"He offers to take me home. All calm and considerate. Only, I suddenly have the strong suspicion that home is going to be a windowless room over at Riverside. Or worse. So I go tearing into the night. I hide in the woods. Somehow, I make it to 44, where this old couple picks me up. I'm crying, babbling incoherently. Somehow I give them my address and they take me home. I'm ready to spill, tell my folks everything. Go to the cops, whatever. But Danny's already there, sitting in the kitchen with them. Drinking *tea*. I try to explain what he's done, who he is, but it's too late. I can see I've been pre-empted. So I opt for Plan B. I lose my shit. I have the mother of all panic attacks."

She sat in silence for nearly a minute. Her eyes so far gone that he knew asking her questions would be a waste of time.

"I spend a few weeks in Riverside, where they dope the hell out of me. My big time out. People with advanced degrees do a pretty good job convincing me that I really am imagining it all. Somehow, I managed not to slip into the abyss. I learn to keep my mouth shut. I don't want to spend the rest of my life wearing fuzzy slippers and humming Joni Mitchell songs to myself in some locked-down behavior modification facility in Utah. I never even see Danny. Once they are convinced I am *compliant*, they pack me off to this sketchy boarding school in Vermont, where I am closely monitored by the powers-that-be. And then I'm off to Arden, where fucked-up kids with lurid histories are a dime a dozen. It's a stretch for Neal but evidently business picked up."

"Because of Munro."

"Because of Danny. I'll bet you Munro doesn't know shit about his client. Nobody does. That's his genius. Parents, colleagues, he fools them all. Anyway, at college, I couldn't stop thinking about Nat. I wind up doing a play about a girl who drowns in a fountain and, surprise surprise, I melt down again. I run to New York where I meet this guy who *gets it*. I tell him my tale of woe and he takes me under his wing and I reinvent myself into this fabulous girl whose feet never touch the ground. Who never thinks about Annville. Because she was never there, right? She grew up in Indiana."

She shook her head.

"Trace was always telling me that I was just buying time. That I would have to come back and tell everyone what Danny had done. What he was doing. For a long time I didn't want to hear it."

"So why did you change your mind?"

"Trace. He forced the issue. He fucking hated Winter. Even though he never met him, he had it in for the guy. Winter represented everything Trace despised. So he came up with a scheme. He'd get a job at Riverside and reveal Danny for what he was. These places always need someone who can clean toilets."

Michael said, "But didn't they do background checks on him? I mean, I've experienced security up there firsthand."

"Sure. But Trace was brilliant at creating fake identities. That was as much a part of his art as actually taking the photos. Putting himself in a position where he could see things nobody was supposed to see. He'd made it into places a lot tougher than Riverside. He was loving it, deep down. It'd be like the old days, in Romania and Guatemala. Getting back in the game motivated him. Maybe not as much as helping me, but it was there. Redemption for us both."

She gave her head a few melancholy shakes.

"I was highly dubious, to say the least. Trace was not in the best shape at this point. And I'd seen firsthand how powerful Danny is, how good he was at protecting himself. That's why I was here in January, when you first met me. I hadn't heard from Trace in a long time and then I got this weird voice mail where he mentioned Winter—I thought he'd come up here. So I came to the last place in the world I want to be to figure out what was happening."

"That's who you were trying to get in touch with when you were staying with me."

She nodded.

"Turns out he'd gone on an epic bender and never even left the city. After that I didn't hear from him for months. Until ten days ago, when he calls again from out of the blue to say he'd cleaned himself up and had been working in Riverside and he had Winter dead to rights. I rush up here. Thinking—it's happening. I'm nervous and scared but also really, I don't know, excited. Only, when he picks me up, he's totally strung out. They'd fired him and he must have fallen hard after that. He needed money to buy drugs before we could do anything. He had to *get right*. Which is why you saw me so mad at him."

She shook her head.

"I should have driven him back to the city then and there, but I'm still thinking that maybe we are actually going to nail Danny. And Trace was very convincing. He'd found a girl at Riverside. He had photos. So I empty my wallet and he calls this local dealer he'd met at Riverside. We head up to the Valencia, where he promises to show me photos he'd taken of her. He doesn't say what they show. Just that she is what we need."

She scoffed bitterly.

"But Trace's guy is waiting for us at the hotel and so I go out to enjoy the scenery because I cannot stand being around that shit. The dealer leaves and I decide to give it a few minutes, and when I'm just about to go back inside I see headlights and I hear a car door slam and there he is. Dr. Daniel Winter. Trace's fake I.D. wasn't as bulletproof as he thought. Or maybe he'd just shot his mouth off to his dealer. I knew I should go to the room, protect my friend, but I'd frozen. The old panic setting in. When I finally get up the nerve . . ."

Her voice caught.

"His face, that beautiful face. It's . . . frozen. Agonal gasp. That's what they call it."

She took a deep breath and shook her head and kept going.

"Danny had taken Trace's camera, his phone. The case with his photos, everything. I was just lucky I kept my bag with me. Old habit around dopers. I slink back to the city, terrified that they are going to come for me next. But days pass and I begin to think they never even figured out the connection between me and Trace."

"Until I blew it for you."

"Don't tear yourself up, Michael. You didn't know. He'd have probably figured it out, anyway. "

"It was a big risk, coming back. You could have just vanished."

"I'd allowed myself to get excited about the possibility of actually doing it. Avenging Trace as well as Natalie. I'd convinced myself you'd found something. But now I see there's nothing I can do. Danny's got it sewn up. Once again. If I go to the cops, he'll just play the crazy card on me."

"So you're just going to disappear."

She nodded.

"And Winter just keeps on going? Untouched? What about this other girl Trace was supposed to have found?"

"Look, I hate it, all right? But there's nothing else I can do."

They shared a gloomy silence. He thought about helping her vanish. Raiding his savings account and sending her on her way. It was probably the sensible thing to do. But he could not let that happen again. It was something he could not endure. And then there was the thought of Winter. Those cool fingers on his wrist, taking his pulse.

Middle school.

"Let me help you," said Michael.

"Help me what?"

"Finish this thing Trace started."

She smiled hopelessly.

"You going to break into Riverside again?"

"What if I find someone who will tell the story you just told me? Someone they can't silence. Someone people can't ignore."

Her eyes narrowed.

"Are you serious?"

"Absolutely."

She looked dubious.

"So they publish this story and then he denies it."

"But it's out there. Other girls will come forward. Witnesses. Somebody has to know what this man is doing. But right now they are all afraid to be the first."

She held his eye. Considering it.

"You got someone particular in mind?"

"Jenna Fogg."

"You know her?" she asked, impressed now.

"I worked with her at Grammaticus."

He could map the transformation taking place on her face. Despair giving way to the understanding that this might be possible.

"God, she'd be perfect. How well do you know her?"

"She'll definitely take my call and hear me out."

She was close, but not yet decided.

"You came here because you thought I could help you," he said. "Well, I can. Like this."

"But why would you do this? I mean, you must know it's going to be a shitstorm."

"When you left in January—I wasn't necessarily ready for it to be over."

Their eyes held.

"All right," she said. "Call your girl. But I have to tell you something. If we're going to do this, we're going to have to go all the way."

"I understand."

"I mean, we can't mess around. Because Danny won't."

Michael did not doubt it. Even if he'd hadn't been tased and nearly shot, he need only to look at the fate of the last man she was with to see that this was true.

ELEVEN

SHE WENT FOR A BATH. HE DID NOT FOLLOW HER. IT WAS clear that she wanted time alone to get her mind around what they had just decided. What he, in effect, had convinced her to do. He sat perfectly still at his desk after she left the office. The tub filled, as raucous as a waterfall, and then there were faint splashing sounds. He, too, needed time to grasp what he had just heard. Two people dead. A legacy of broken girls. He could not stop thinking about Neal's clumsy lies and Nancy's incipient hysteria; Munro's refusal to call the police and the storm of the electricity from the taser at Riverside. People feared what she was capable of doing. And now he knew why.

The more he thought about it, the more deeply he became convinced that Jenna Fogg would be the perfect person to help them. She had credibility, she had an audience. And she liked Michael. He struggled to compose his email to her, knowing that everything he did now might become part of a closely scrutinized public record. He wound up sending just a few lines, telling her that he had become aware of a conspiracy by some very powerful men to cover up the abuse of at least two girls, one of whom had almost certainly committed suicide. There was no reason to mention Trace. Not yet. It would be better not to overwhelm Jenna. He sent it to the old address he had from when they were both at Grammaticus, as well as copying it to the one listed on the MorningFogg website.

He searched for Natalie Chenier. There was a brief, archived article about her death in the *Call*. Dog walkers had found her body washed up a mile south of town. The police had not yet been willing to go on record about the cause of death, but the tenor of the article made it clear that they did not suspect foul play. There had been a follow-up piece a month later. The medical examiner had officially ruled her death accidental. It was believed she had fallen while walking along the floodwall beside Prospect Road, a trammeled dirt lane that ran between the river and some abandoned warehouses down in Cheapside. Traces of drugs had been found in her system. Cannabis and painkillers. It was a miserable stretch of wasteland; Natalie had been spotted down there on previous occasions. Michael also found a twelve-year-old tax listing that showed her as being resident with her mother and brother on Station Road down in Cheapside. And that was all. There was no obituary, no memorial page. No candlelight vigils or ribbons. Following her death, Natalie Chenier had simply vanished.

Michael entered her mother's name. Marie Chenier had died four years after her daughter. There was no actual obituary, just a death notice in the *Call*, as tersely factual as a want ad. The cause of death was pneumonia. She was thirty-nine. Her profession was listed as food server. Her sole surviving relative was her son, Kevin Pierre Chenier. Michael found an article dated just over three years ago. He had been convicted in a local court of possession with intent to sell. He'd been twenty when they sent him away. He had received twenty-six months, which meant that he would have been released over a year ago, provided he had served his entire sentence. The only other hit Michael could find for him was the news that he had taken part in an Easter concert given earlier in the year by students at Jericho Evangelical, a Christian college fifteen miles north of town. There was no address listed for him, former or current; no evidence of him on social media. Just that one desultory mention.

He keyed in Winter's name. The phone rang just as he started to play a video called "Treating Adolescent Anxiety." He muted the computer before answering.

"Michael, what the hell?" Jenna asked without introduction. "Is this for real?"

"Very real."

"Who are we talking about when we say powerful men?"

"This is all in strict confidence, right?"

"Of course," she said impatiently.

On the computer, Winter lectured an unseen audience from a large stage. A university, a hospital, a convention center. A big screen loomed behind him. He wore an expensive suit. He was mic'd.

"Dr. Daniel Winter. He's the director . . ."

"Come on, I know who Winter is. I've got one of his books lying around here somewhere. What do you mean, abuse?"

"The girl I'm talking about was his patient and he had a sexual relationship with her. Same with the other girl. The suicide."

"How old were they?"

"Fourteen and thirteen."

"What's your source for this?"

"The first girl. She's been silent for a decade but now she wants to come forward."

"How do you know her?"

The camera panned over Winter's audience. Adoring faces. Rapt and ready to receive comfort.

He said, "That's kind of complicated."

There was a beat.

"Where is she now?"

"She's here, in Annville. With me."

"Living with you?"

"She's staying with me."

Another pulse of silence.

"And you think she's reliable?"

Winter strode the stage, confident without seeming arrogant. His smile was warm, reassuring, genuinely kind. He had done this a thousand times. A PowerPoint presentation played on the screen behind him, operated by the clicker held in his loose fist.

"Yes," Michael said. "I do."

"So how do you want to work this? You want me to come up there?"

"It's probably better if we come down to you. This place is getting a little claustrophobic."

"Can you come tomorrow?"

"Really?"

"Yes, Michael. Really."

They agreed to meet at her Brooklyn office. After hanging up, Michael turned the computer's sound on low, so Justine would not hear it. Winter spoke with easy confidence about topics like desensitization and avoidance; he mapped out techniques for helping troubled children with their black nights and crippling terrors. Everything ran smoothly. The projected images were in sync with his message. His mild jokes were met by warm laughter. Michael studied his face and his voice and his gestures. He pictured the man's gently expressive hands on the girl he had seen in the photo in Neal Thomassen's office. It was not easy. On the surface, he was just a soft-spoken, intelligent, authoritative doctor addressing a crowd that hung on his every word. Displaying the same decency as when he had looked after Michael a few days ago. If it had not been for what Justine had just told him, Michael would have never suspected him of doing harm. Not in a million years.

And that only made him more monstrous.

Michael crossed the house. Justine had fallen asleep in his bed, wrapped in towels, a bare shoulder visible. The hot water had put some color back into her skin. He badly wanted to touch her. The desire that had been driving him for the past ten days was almost overwhelming. But he stopped himself. Touching her had been different in January, when everything that had happened between them was destined to disappear like breath on glass. Touching her now would mean something very different.

She sensed his presence and woke. She greeted him with a soft, sad smile.

Justine said, "I fell asleep."

"Yes."

She sat up, willing herself awake. She tightened the towel around herself.

"What's going on?"

"I've been in touch with Jenna."

"Do you think she's going to print my story?"

"I imagine she'll want to look into it, but yes. I do. Absolutely." He snorted softly. "I mean, Jesus, Justine. Of course she will."

She drew back a little.

"What do you mean, look into it? She's not going to try to confront Winter or anything like that?"

"I think that's how it works. I mean, eventually."

She looked down at the tousled sheets. Worried now.

"And I presume she'll try to find other girls," he continued.

"She isn't going to find other girls."

"What about Natalie's family? I found Kevin with a simple search. They could know something."

"Kevin won't know anything."

"How can you be sure?"

"Michael, listen to me. If we get someone like Jenna Fogg up here asking questions, then Danny will figure out what we're doing and he'll stop us. Like he did with Trace. Right now, he thinks I've left town with my tail between my legs. The only way this works is if we blindside him. So if you don't think Jenna Fogg will print this without wasting a lot of time interviewing people who either won't know shit or are lying through their teeth, then we should forget about it. I'll just leave."

Michael thought about the man he had just seen on stage. His confidence. His invincibility.

"Let's just talk to her and see what she says. She's a good journalist."

"But you just have to promise me you won't let anyone mess this up. This is your world, Michael. I'm just hanging on by a thread here."

"I promise," he said.

Her wariness and impatience faded after that, although there was still strangeness between them. They had yet to touch. He opened a bottle of wine and they drank it in the kitchen, seated across from each other at the island. He asked her what happened after Trace's death and she said she had panicked, convinced that Winter and Munro had people out looking for her; that Riverside orderlies or the Annville police were coming to toss her into a locked ward.

Justine said, "It was just like the good old days."

She had fled back to the city, where she had a sublet under the name she hoped they had not learned. She had spent little time in the apartment, fearing a knock on the door. An irrational fear, per-haps, but that didn't make it any less potent. Mostly, she had stayed with friends or simply walked the streets. Thinking about Trace. Betrayed and unclaimed and alone.

After her first glass of wine she told him she was famished—she hadn't eaten properly since it happened. They decided on take-away from the Moon Temple. For old time's sake, she said with a heart-breaking little smile. As they waited, he described his trip to New York; he showed her the photo that he had bought from Klimov, the sleeping nude. She stared at it for a long time.

"Was this the only one?"

"There was a series."

"I think I remember when he took this. I was going through a bad spell." She laughed quietly. "One of many."

She handed it back to him without further comment. Wine and proximity were causing the strangeness to fade between them. He made her smile when he told her that Susan Wessels was now working as a chronicler of actionable catastrophe and then described Batchelder's ongoing mystification at what had happened on the opening night of *Six Characters*. But the smile disappeared when he described his few minutes with Winter in the exam room.

"I wish I'd known about this when I was in there with him."

"Don't you go all macho on me, Michael. I had plenty of that with Trace."

"I don't think I can rival him in the macho department."

She gently shook her head.

"You know," she said, "the funny thing is, he wasn't really like the person you saw. Most of the time he was very gentle."

"I still can't figure out . . ."

"What?"

He hesitated.

"Michael, say what's on your mind. This isn't going to work unless we're straight with each other."

"Klimov and Susan Wessels both said that Trace was impotent."

"Okay . . ."

And so she told him about Trace. She'd met him a few months after splashing down in New York. She was eighteen. It had been a dizzying, dangerous time. She'd often felt on the verge of extinction. On the bus fleeing Arden, she'd decided to become someone new. The first order of business was a name. She was still in costume, she looked European, so she chose Justine. In the city, she found a room, landed an off-the-books job as a hostess at an art scene bistro in the East Village. She went to parties and crashed receptions and told glittering lies about herself. She met Andrej, a 53-year-old set designer who approached her with a leer so forthright he was irresistible. He announced that he wanted her in his bed and would not take no for an answer. Which was convenient, because she'd already decided on yes. He was Polish, with a sweep of gray hair and icy blue eyes.

"The j was silent," she said. "As was Andrej."

She moved into his immaculate Brooklyn Heights brownstone, filled with exquisite things she dared not touch. Although rarely kind, he was unfailingly generous. He got her temporary assistantships in the shadow economy where she'd existed ever since. He also showed her another gray area, the one between being in love and simply hooking up.

She found a copy of *Varsa* in his library. Those girls rose right up off the page and whispered to her in a strange and familiar language. When she came to Madalina she almost fell off the ottoman. She knew those broken gypsy eyes. She had seen them just a few years earlier, on a girl who had wound up in the river. She needed to meet the man who had taken these photographs. His brief author profile said he lived in New York. She finally tracked him down at the opening of Susan's one-and-only show. He was amazing. Lean and tall and handsome and aloof.

"He was just beginning his decline. When that can be so beautiful."

At first, he kept her at arm's length. Nutty chicks were constantly circling him. Susan was much more welcoming, for reasons that soon became clear. Gradually, Trace warmed to her, even as her initial attempts at sleeping with him were rejected. Although he was obsessed by women, he rarely fucked them, and when he tried, it was the kiss of death for the relationship. No one ever said the word impotent, at least around him, but it was the subtext every time Trace's sexuality was discussed.

And so they became friends. Chaste and inseparable. She told him about herself. Not the elaborate construct she was still manufacturing, but the hidden girl, the one who had almost evaporated back in Annville. She finally revealed what had happened with Winter and Natalie. It just poured out one night. He listened in silence and then he told her he understood. His rage rippling through his body like a seizure. He was the only person she ever told. Until Michael.

She broke up with Andrej—one morning she found herself lying next to a grumpy old man with a silly accent and wires of gray hair sticking from his chest, like some busted robot. She lived first with Susan. She'd never slept with a woman and after a night with S. Wessels she understood why. She moved to Trace's place on Mott, perched at the top of five infinite flights of stairs. He let her have her own tiny room. There was no question of her paying rent.

"He was looking after me now."

They were together, off and on, for the next six years. He helped her become Justine. His journeys into prisons and mental wards and countries with corrupt regimes had made him a master imposter. There was a Bosnian photorealist who forged I.D.s for him, a computer guy who could keystroke you a whole new past. He conjured her an Indiana driver's license, in keeping with her story. Her real name never appeared in any record. The only jobs she worked were temporary, cash only. Setting up shows, personally assisting rich self-important women, whiling away the hours at gallery desks.

She did not date in the first months after moving to Mott, though she hungered for sex. Trace let her know that it was all right if she saw other men. He was never jealous, he never challenged her. He only had one rule. He did not want any of them around. He did not want to shake their hands. She could talk about them if she wanted, but she had to keep them away from him.

The men were different now that she was with Trace. Cruel daddies were no longer welcome. They were older, but not *that* much older. Sleek bond traders whose bodies were still buzzing from the floor, austere dotcom pioneers who knew their wines, tenured radicals who would take her to sit in the shadows so she could watch them be brilliant on WBAI before taking her to the apartment of a friend who was on sabbatical in Prague. She did not waste her time on art scene operators, Brooklyn boys with their Jonathan Franzen glasses, dive bar rebels.

"Nobody got mothered," she said. "Nobody got daughtered. Nobody got believed in. And nobody, *nobody* got loved. Danny's legacy, I guess."

She hated one-night stands, but there were inevitable mistakes, a few desperate getaways back to Mott Street. Mostly, she followed the same pattern. Flirtation. Seduction. Settling into a pleasing rhythm of dinners and movies and weekends away. And then it was over. The moment things began to get serious, she bailed. Sometimes it was smooth, sometimes ugly. Always, there was Trace, the only man who had ever loved her without demanding anything in return. Michael asked if it ever occurred to her that all of this was taking its toll on him; that the drugs were his way of managing the pain of not being able to be the only one.

"I only figured that out after it was too late," she said.

She understood what was happening with her. She was not trying to fill the emptiness left by what Winter had done to her so much as she was learning to embrace it. Her affairs—more than fifteen but less than twenty, although doing an exact count would have been gross— were vast glittering artifices she built around the void. Sometimes, she would look at herself in the mirror and know that the game she was playing could not last forever. There was going to be a reckoning.

"I just never really believed it would be Trace who made it happen," she said. "Or suffered for it."

He became a fully fledged junkie two summers ago. She was living with a man who owned restaurants at the time. After their break-up, she returned to find that the apartment on Mott had suffered a comprehensive collapse. It had always been messy; now it was filthy. Grime covered surfaces. Stenches lingered. Nasty characters arrived at all hours.

"I had to get out. I mean, any apartment where you have to carry your purse with you to the bathroom is probably not the best place to call home."

She found a place to sublet and despaired over what to do about Trace. It was then that he started to talk about the plan to expose Winter. He told her she would never be happy, truly happy, until she dealt with him. Justine knew Trace also saw it as a way for him to return from the land of the dead. And then he'd called and told her it was happening. He'd enlisted his Bosnian counterfeiter and his computer guy to forge one last identity, to make one last stand.

He'd snuck into the lion's den. He'd found what they needed for their mutual salvation.

"The effort it must have taken him to clean up and land that job . . ." Her voice caught briefly. "Which is kind of why we owe it to him to see this through."

The food arrived; they ate in silence, passing the cartons back and forth. Michael opened a second bottle of wine, though after just a few sips it became clear that she could no longer keep her eyes open. They went to bed together, though only for the sleep both of them so badly needed. She wore a T-shirt she borrowed from him, he stripped down to his boxers. She put her head on his chest; he ran his hand through her hair. But that was their only contact. It was still too early for sex. There was still too much that was unknown, still too much to come.

"I like that you still call me Justine," she said just before she drifted off.

He watched her as she slept. Thinking, what else would I call you?

The next morning, as they drove to the city, he explained Jenna Fogg. She had joined Grammaticus from the *Boston Globe* to work in the foundation's Public Truths division, her mission to fund projects that provided alternatives to corporate media. A basketball star at Dartmouth, Jenna was just over six feet, with a gangly frame and a broad, flat face. She was smart and aggressive and ill-suited for foundation work. She'd eventually left to start her own website, which focused on bullying, sexual abuse, and the ever-evolving dynamics of the war between the sexes. It was a hit. The previous year, she'd broken a big story about a serially groping venture capitalist who tried to buy off his victims with stock tips. It had been picked up by the mainstream press, making her star shine bright in the crowded firmament of the blogosphere.

MorningFogg's offices were like dozens of others Michael had visited during his Grammaticus days. Aggressively casual. A photo of the *Hindenburg* aflame hung in reception. There were partitions instead of walls; the only plants were cacti. Action figures and toy vehicles populated metal shelves, while books and magazines were left stacked on the floor. There was a dozing Lab. People worked from sofas. They wore skintight jeans and unlaced Chuck Taylors and T-shirts advertising things that were popular three decades earlier.

Jenna looked good. Her face had narrowed, an effect heightened by her large spectacles. Her height no longer seemed a burden, but rather a projection of self-confidence. She greeted Michael warmly, though there was also calculation in her magnified eyes, an acknowledgement that important business was about to be transacted. She was more formal with Justine; concerned and solicitous, though there was a reportorial wariness there as well. She took them to a small conference room that was thick with the smell of microwaved popcorn.

"So how are things?" Jenna asked.

"Well, I left Grammaticus a couple years back."

"So I heard. That surprises me. I thought you were the heir apparent."

"I'm doing some writing."

"Well, good for you," she said, dispensing with the pleasantries, much to Michael's relief.

She turned to Justine.

"Do you mind if I record this?"

Justine shrugged. She sat perfectly still as the iPhone was positioned in front of her. She had not said a word since their arrival. She was clearly not yet comfortable with Jenna, who asked her to introduce herself, for the record.

"I'm Justine."

"Last name?"

"It's probably best if we leave it at that."

Jenna took this in stride.

"So what's going on, Justine?"

She told the whole story, speaking with few pauses and little inflection. Michael watched Jenna as Justine spoke, but her face remained unreadable. Although he'd only heard the entire story once, Justine's narrative seemed nearly as familiar to him as one of his own memories.

At times, it was as if she was reading from a prepared text. The only deviation came when she claimed she had run into Natalie a number of times in the days and weeks following the scene at her house, even though she'd told Michael she had not seen her at all. Perhaps because the rest of the story was so similar to its first telling, the contradiction proved so jarring to Michael that he almost interrupted her.

"First of all, I'm sorry about what happened to you," Jenna said after she finished. "It must have been awful, living through that."

"Thank you. But it wasn't awful, at least until the end. It was actually amazing while it was happening. I was in love with a handsome, powerful man who I believed loved me back. It's important that you understand that. I really don't want to focus on what happened to me. Natalie is the real victim."

Jenna tapped the table with a long, strong index finger before speaking.

"Obviously, your story is something I'm very interested in pursuing. I do have a few concerns right off the bat. First, I mean, are you alleging that Daniel Winter actually *killed* Desmond Tracey?"

"I didn't see it with my own eyes. But I'm certain that Winter found him on the nod and pumped him full of an overdose. Or suffocated him. Or both."

"But—murder?"

"It may not have been Danny's intention going in, but he's pretty good at thinking on his feet."

"So, yes."

"Yes. Absolutely. That is what I am alleging."

Jenna said, "But why?"

"Trace was going to expose him. He had a name. He had a photo. He had an audience, or at least he could get one pretty quick. And he had me."

"That would just be such a monumental accusation to make."

"I'd be the one making it. Finally."

"My point is that there are two distinct allegations here, both of which are supported only by your testimony at this point. What I'm thinking is that it might be a good idea to focus on you and Natalie for the time being."

"I know what happened to Trace."

"And that's something we could certainly re-visit. I mean, I presume there's not been a ruling of homicide. We would have heard something, right?"

"Yeah, well, things aren't always out in the open up in Annville."

Jenna looked at Michael.

"I haven't heard anything," he said.

"I'll make a call when we are done," Jenna said.

Justine sat up straight.

"But you can't alert them to the fact we are doing this."

Jenna managed a wan smile.

"Don't worry, Justine. I've done this before."

Justine gave a single, distracted nod. She *was* worried.

"For the time being, it's my judgment that focusing on what Winter did to you and Natalie Chenier is the most productive way forward." Jenna tapped the table again. "Basically, we need to find someone who can corroborate what you are saying. What about this girl Trace found?"

"That's simply not going to happen," Justine said. "I'm sorry, but that's just how it is. I guarantee it. Those girls are either too afraid or too crazy to say anything. Or they still love him. When I was with him, they could have tortured me and I wouldn't have said a word. And then when I finally did open my mouth, they turned me into the walking dead. It's taken me ten years to get the balls to do this. And that's only because of Trace, what they did to him."

"But he found someone."

"Because he put his ass on the line. And because he was genius. You're not going to Google your way to the heart of this story. You really aren't."

Jenna said, "I like to go a bit beyond Google, but point taken."

"Look, Ms. Fogg. You're obviously a pro. But I was a popular white girl from a good family at a nice high school and they buried me like one of those guys at Guantanamo. If I had kept trying to fight them I'd be shuffling around in slippers somewhere, getting real good at arts and crafts."

"Still. I have to look. It's what I do." She frowned. "So there's no one you can think of who might have witnessed what happened to the two of you? Friends? Fellow patients?"

"There was nobody," Justine said. "I was basically alone. My parents thought he was a god. And Natalie's family—forget about it. That's how he operated. You came to him broken and he patched you up and then you were the only person in the world. Nobody's tweeting about this. There aren't any videos to share."

"What about Natalie's brother?"

"He was just a kid. And he was stoned out of his mind half the time, anyway."

"Your parents?" Jenna persisted. "You sure they won't come around?"

Justine looked at the table, shaking her head in frustration, a bitter unbelieving smile now shaping her lips.

"Neal is a spineless idiot who would sell his grandmother's soul for a decent tee time. And my mother worshipped Winter. I was this crazy kid driving everybody nuts and he turned me into Miss Perfect. And then when I suddenly fall apart, he tells her I'm not to be trusted. You see how he works? That's his genius. He only chooses girls no one will believe if they somehow find the will to tell the truth. It's the ultimate plausible deniability."

"I'm still not entirely clear what are you suggesting, Justine. You want me to print what you told me without corroboration?"

She replied, "Yes."

"I simply cannot do that."

"Even if that's the only way it is going to work?"

Jenna watched her for a moment from behind those big glasses, her long index finger tapping the table.

"I know we have to be careful," she said. "I get it. Winter isn't some slob chatting up twelve-year-olds from his basement."

The finger stopped tapping. She had come to a decision.

"Let me make some inquiries. Don't worry—I'll be very discreet."

"How long until you decide?"

"Till the end of the week."

"And then you publish?"

"We'll have to see where we stand."

"What can we do?" Michael asked as the silence grew uncomfortable.

"See if you can think of another witness. Other than that, for now, you're going to have to let me do my thing."

Justine stood suddenly.

"I'll wait downstairs," she said. "Nice meeting you. Thanks for listening. I'm sorry if I'm making this difficult for you, but this man . . ."

She shook her head in frustration, then walked quickly from the room, leaving the door open behind her. Michael waited for Jenna to speak.

"I gotta tell you," she said finally. "She's very compelling, but part of me also wants to call bullshit. Her resistance to finding corroborating witnesses is a definite red flag. Yes, I can see why she doesn't want me door-stopping Winter. But there could also be another reason."

He said, "No way she's making this up. You heard her. It's too real. I've met her parents. I've met Munro. People are shitting bricks at the thought of her being back in town. I got tased for simply asking questions at Riverside."

"Seriously? You walked into reception and said her name and they deployed a taser?"

"I may have gone through a couple doors I wasn't supposed to. But they are definitely hiding something."

She watched him before speaking again, her eyes unreadable behind those big glasses.

"I'll grant you there's a lot in what she says that's persuasive. Winter sounds like a classic top-of-the-line predator. Textbook. The grooming, the way he works the parents. And you believing in her counts for a lot. But I'll really need more before I even think about publishing. You know that, right?"

Michael nodded unhappily.

"Well, you should probably tell her, because nobody worth a good goddamn is going to run with this unless they have multiple sources. I don't want to blow my own horn, but she's not going to do better than us. And others won't have my scruples. They'd be camped outside Winter's clinic shouting questions in a heartbeat. Once this thing goes viral it can whiplash back on you guys in a heartbeat."

"She's just anxious and scared. Trace's death really rattled her."

"Don't get me wrong. I'd *love* to run this story. Dr. Daniel Winter? If he's guilty . . . are you kidding me? But it sort of has to be true. I'm funny like that."

"I just don't know how long she's willing to wait."

"Well, assure her I'm on it. 24/7. I'm all about Justine."

You and me both, Michael thought.

She was waiting for him on the sidewalk.

"So?"

"You've just got to trust her to do her thing."

"Trust doesn't come so easy to me, you know?"

She saw something in his expression.

"What is it, Michael?"

"Back in there, you told Jenna that you saw Natalie several times around town after you figured out she was with Winter."

"Did I?" she said after a moment.

"You said you tried to talk to her but she ignored you."

"And?"

"You told me you never saw her again after that day in her room."

"What difference does it make?"

"None, really. I just want to be clear on what happened in case we get challenged."

"What happened is he fucked her and made her love him, and then he dumped her and she killed herself, and they said it was an accident, so nobody would ask why. Are we gonna sweat the details or are we going to do something about that?"

They swung by her sublet on the way back to Annville so she could pick up some fresh clothes. Michael was surprised to find that she had been living in a tiny studio apartment with an obstructed view of the Queensboro Bridge. He had expected a bohemian grotto, perhaps a glassy penthouse. Instead, there were carpets and bookshelves and lamps, a pristine galley kitchen, and refrigerator lightly populated with yogurts and vegetables, too old to eat but not old enough to stink. As she packed, she described the time since her January affair with Michael, quiet nights with boxed sets of *True Blood* and *The Wire*; dates with men who would never know the first thing about her. All in a vain attempt to negotiate a different kind of forgetting than the breathless plummet into the future she'd performed when Trace was strong. Michael told her that if she wanted to stay here while Jenna did her thing, he would gladly join her. Or he could serve as her point man back in town. She said no—she needed to be in Annville or she would lose her nerve. And there was not a whole lot of that to begin with.

She fell silent during the drive out of the city. She was not gloomy, exactly. Just distant. At one point she closed her eyes and he thought she had fallen asleep, but they were soon open again, focused on a vanishing point far beyond the end of the road.

"He sounds like such a monster," Michael said, once the silence became too oppressive.

She looked across at him, as if she did not understand his words.

"Winter."

"It's hard for me to see him like that," she said, her voice flat. "Even after everything."

"Really."

"I loved him, Michael. Completely. You can't erase that. I can't, at least. Some people you love, and then it's over, and it's like it never happened. Or maybe there are some fond memories. But not him. I was too young. It was too strong. He was my world. His voice, the stubble on his cheeks, his smell. Waiting for him to pick me up—it was a kind of delirium. Bliss might be a better word. It was the happiest time of my life."

Michael could feel the sting of her words. He knew there were any number of things he could say to this. Things that would be true; counterpoints that she could not deny. And yet he also knew that none of it would matter.

"He doted on me," she continued. "He was never in a bad mood. He was never insecure or needy. He fed me and bathed me and made me come. He fixed me when I thought I was ruined. The thing about Danny is that he's a genuinely kind and gentle person. Except for, you know."

She was smiling now; it was not as grim of a smile as he would have liked.

"The best thing was the night he came to see me in *A Midsummer Night's Dream*. I was Helena. When it was over, he congratulated me right in front of Neal and my mother. I was still in costume, a girl in love pretending to be a girl pretending to be a woman in love. You cannot imagine how electric it felt, to be standing there in the school lobby, sharing this secret with him. Later that night I snuck away from the cast party and he drove me to his place in the woods . . . how do you forget something like that? What teaches you to hate it?"

"You sound like you might be having second thoughts about what you're doing now."

She looked at him, something very cold in her eyes.

"No. He has to pay. He has to be destroyed. But that doesn't mean I have to lie to myself while we do it."

A few miles south of Annville, she lifted the console's arm rest and removed her seat belt so she could put her head on his lap. An alarm sounded, warning that someone was unprotected. He thought she was simply being affectionate until they passed the train station and he knew what was really happening. She was hiding. Two weeks ago, the thought of someone having to duck for cover in this placid, prosperous town would have struck him as absurd. Now, he found himself longing for tinted windows.

Her caution proved prophetic—Michael almost hit Kim's car as he pulled into the driveway. She had parked in her old spot, beneath the basketball hoop no one had used in a long time. He had not considered the possibility of his ex-wife showing up unannounced.

"Damn it," he muttered.

Justine sat up.

"Whose car is that?" she asked.

"It's all right," he said. "We'll go."

Before he could put the car in reverse, Kim appeared at the top of the stone steps leading to the back door. Her eyes locked immediately on Justine.

"Your wife, right?"

"Let me talk to her." He killed the engine and gave her the keys. "You should probably wait inside."

"Think I'll use the front door."

Kim waited until Justine was gone before descending to the driveway.

"What is it?" he asked before she could speak. "Why are you here?"

She recoiled at the force of his questions.

"You seemed so down at the race, I was worried about you here on your own. Silly me, I guess. "

"Kim . . ."

"I guess you found your mystery woman after all. I can see why you'd feel she was worth getting arrested over."

"Kim, listen to me. You can't tell anyone she's here."

"What the hell are you talking about?"

"There are people who don't want her in town."

"I cannot believe you are still going on about this. Can't you see this woman is pulling your chain? Marcus said she was disturbed."

"Wait, you've talked to Munro about her?"

"Of course I have! You break into both of our houses on the pretext of finding her, I mean, what do you expect we'd talk about? The weather?"

"What she's saying is true, Kim. Munro is protecting Winter."

"I would hope so. That's what good lawyers do when someone blackmails one of their clients."

"Blackmail? He told you that?"

"Yes, Michael. He said that she and her wretched boyfriend have been trying to blackmail Dr. Winter with some cooked-up story of sexual abuse."

"If they believe that, then why haven't they gone to the police?"

"I'm sure they have their reasons. Marcus isn't exactly an amateur at this sort of thing. Maybe they don't want all that publicity."

"Winter is some kind of fucking monster, Kim."

She smiled incredulously.

She said, "Well, if he is, then we have a problem, since he's been treating our son for the last twelve months."

It took Michael several long seconds to register what she had said.

"What are you talking about? Will is a patient at Riverside?"

"Outpatient. Yes."

"Why didn't you tell me this?"

"Why didn't . . . because you were so dead set against it that I didn't want you undermining him. And he didn't want you to know either, Michael. He's heard your opinions. He thinks you'd see him as some kind of loser."

"I would never . . ."

"And you know what? He's a hundred times better since he started there. Dr. Winter has done a remarkable job with him. And now he's finally coming around and you want to blow it up with this insanity. Well, that's not going to happen, Michael. I can't stop you from disappointing your son, but I am not going to let you damage the one man who's been able to help him. If you saw them together . . . so just tell your girlfriend to take her toxic lies back to New York and be a drama queen there. I'm sure she'll have a much better audience."

"Kim, you have to stop him going there."

She waved her hands between them, erasing the conversation.

"Look, I'll make this simple. I want her out. I still own half this house. I don't know what you intend to do with the mysterious Jane Thomassen, but you are not going to do it where my son sleeps."

"You need to trust me on this."

"You see, Michael, that's the thing. I don't have to trust you at all. That's why people get divorced. The faith is gone. You no longer have to give them the benefit of the doubt." She pointed at the house. "I want her out."

"I can't do that."

"Are you serious?"

He did not answer. His silence making it clear that he was.

"In that case, can you at least move your goddamned car?"

She did not speed off. That was not Kim's style. Children lived on the street. But there was nevertheless something emphatic in her departure that suggested Marcus Munro and his client would soon know that the woman they were calling poison was a resident on Locust Lane.

TWELVE

"SO I'M GUESSING SHE WON'T BE JOINING US FOR COCKTAILS," Justine said when he found her in the office.

"There's something you need to know. Her husband works for Munro."

She flashed a bitter, unsurprised smile.

"God, I hate this town." She looked back at him. "So what does that mean for us?"

"I'm pretty certain she's going to tell them that you're here."

"Anything else?" she asked with a grim laugh.

"Munro is claiming you and Trace were trying to blackmail Winter."

"I figured they'd come up with something like that."

"We can still go back to New York. Stay at your place until Jenna runs the article."

She was shaking her head before he had finished speaking.

"You know what? Fuck it. Now they're just pissing me off. I'm not going anywhere."

"Are you sure?"

"Are *you*? Because I don't think I can do this on my own, Michael."

"Yes. Of course I am."

"Then we're staying."

He had worried Kim's arrival would drive Justine even further into gloom; instead, understanding that people knew she was in Annville charged her with energy. He could almost track it as it moved through her body. She was buzzing with the prospect of an imminent reckoning. The sight was not entirely comforting. Just a few hours earlier, on the ride up from New York, she'd been so gloomy and distant that she had actually hidden from view. Now, she was like an athlete getting ready for a big game. He was beginning to second-guess pushing her to come forward so quickly. Maybe they were moving too fast. He tried to imagine what she would be like when the questions and attacks started. If she would be the unflappable woman who had told her story to Jenna. Or if she would come undone like she had on stage in North Carolina.

They stayed up late. She opened a bottle of wine, and then another. No one bothered them. She relaxed. She smiled. She held his eye. There were no calls; nobody pounded on the door. He allowed himself to hope that Kim had kept Justine's presence secret after all. After a while, he could almost imagine it was January again, when it had been just the two of them. After the first glass of wine, they kissed. After the third, they went to the bedroom. His desire was more powerful than it had ever been, even during their first days together, when there had been nothing but desire. And yet there was something new there as well, something holding him back. The image of Winter's hands on her.

She looked at him through the darkness.

"It's all right, Michael."

Still, he hesitated, so she took him by the shoulders and laid him flat on his back. She kneeled above him, running her hand over his ribs. She kissed his chest and his stomach and then took him in her mouth. He touched her hair, but she grabbed his wrist and pressed his arm on the mattress. After a while she raised back up and ran her fingertips along his cock. She lifted a leg over him and directed him inside her. Her body was thin and strong. Before long she was moving into him with a ferocity that made it seem as if she was losing control. And then her body clenched and she stopped breathing; her back bowed and her fingers dug into the flesh on his shoulders. He came moments later, his breath leaving his lungs like he'd been struck.

She collapsed onto his chest and entangled his legs with hers. They lay still for a long time before she spoke. The silence settling over them.

Justine said, "Everybody is going to say I'm lying."

"It won't work. Not with me."

She raised herself onto an elbow.

"You can't just be smart, Michael. Not with Winter. He'll have you doubting me if you try to outthink him. You're going to need to believe."

He told her he did believe. Lying with her, he was no longer thinking about Jenna's skepticism and Kim's warnings and that small variation in her story about Natalie. He'd found her. She was right here. Her skin, her voice, her past. The heat coming off her. These were the things that mattered.

It was not until the next morning that the doubting began.

He woke to a gentle tapping. It came in muted, persistent bursts, like a craftsman diligently creating something fragile. Justine continued to sleep beside him. She looked utterly at peace now, as if it was all over. The wicked had been punished, the terrible burden of the last decade lifted. There was another rap, apologetic but refusing to be denied. It was the front door. He checked his phone. 8:10. There were no messages, no news from Jenna. He dressed quickly and quietly. He wanted to deal with this on his own.

If it was Munro, he would simply refuse to open the door. If it was Douglas, he would tell him to go fuck himself, and then refuse to open the door. He stepped into the dining room to look through the window. Nancy Thomassen, frail and terrified, stood on the porch. She appeared to be alone. Michael checked up and down the street. There was only one car. The smile she managed when he opened the door was as pressured and ominous as a crack in an aquarium wall.

"I guess it's my turn to arrive unexpectedly at *your* door."

The words came in a breathless, rehearsed rush. Her Hermès scarf was tied so tightly that it might have been a bandage.

"What can I do for you?" he asked her.

"I'm looking for Jane. Is she here?"

Michael simply stared at her.

She said, "You're not saying. All right. Could I have a word with *you*, at least?"

He stepped onto the porch and pulled the door shut behind him. "How is she?"

"Why are you here, Mrs. Thomassen?"

A jogger scraped past on the street. They both waited for him to pass.

"Can I ask you something, Mr. Coolidge? How well do you know my daughter? I mean, *really* know her."

"I'm sorry, but I don't see the point in our having this conversation. Tell them if they want to speak with me they should do it themselves."

"Oh, don't worry if you can't answer. No one really knows her. Including me. Well, there's her doctor. He knows. But she won't accept his help, so I guess we're back down to nobody."

She sighed and patted her scarf. This was torture for her.

"She's not a well person, is what I'm trying to say. You must see it. When she was younger, thirteen and fourteen, she'd have these spells. She'd just start to tremble. Like an earthquake. Her heart would race, two hundred beats a minute. I think all that commotion eventually fractured something deep inside her. She lost the ability to understand what was real. It was like her father all over again."

"What do you mean, like her father?"

"She didn't tell you? No, she wouldn't, I suppose. She wouldn't want you to know what's in her blood. My first husband, Jane's father, killed himself when she was three. Hung himself by an electrical cord from a water pipe in the basement. He was brilliant and he could be kind when the mood struck him. But he was a sick, sick man who was very good at hiding his various illnesses. Pathological lying. Panic attacks. Rage. He was an engineer, but he lost his job when the madness started to spread. Leaving us with nothing."

"Justine said he died of a heart attack."

"Would you like to see the letter from the insurance company, denying our claim? I still have it."

Michael did not answer.

"When Jane started to have her spells, I thought, here we go again," Nancy continued. "Thank goodness for Dr. Winter. He had her up and running for a while, but Jane decided to turn her back on his care. Sometimes the madness just wins."

"That's not what's happening, Mrs. Thomassen."

She dismissed his words with a terse shake of her head.

"I guess what I'm saying is that whatever she's been telling you should be taken with a grain of salt. Or a mountain of it."

"All right. Thank you."

"Yes, you don't believe me. It's just that you seem like a decent man, and . . ."

The door opened behind him, startling them both. Justine was wrapped in the blanket from the bed. Her hair was a mess, her eyes puffy. Looking every bit the disturbed soul her mother had just described. But when she spoke her voice was lucid and calm.

"Hi, Mom."

"Sweetheart, I . . ."

"You might as well come on in."

Without waiting for a response, she turned and walked into the living room, the room she hated. Michael sat beside her on the sofa. Nancy took the chair opposite them. She kept her coat on. Her purse was on her lap, like a weight to keep her from floating away.

"Did they send you?" Justine asked. "Because it's pathetic if they did."

"Nobody sent me, Janey. I'm just worried about you."

"Could you not call me that?"

"But it's your name."

"If they didn't send you, then how did you know I was in town?"

"Marcus Munro and Dr. Winter came to the house late last night. Nobody thought to include me in the conference as per usual, but it's not a big house. So my presence here is not as sinister as you seem to think."

Justine looked at her mother with a wonderstruck expression.

She said to her, "Jesus, you still have no fucking clue."

"About what?

"The night they found me on 44."

"You had a breakdown. Dr. Winter said . . ."

"He fucked me, Mom."

Michael looked at her in alarm, but she no longer appeared to know he was present. Her entire focus was on her mother.

"Sweetheart, you're not going to start that again . . ."

"Winter seduced me. He took my cherry. He deflowered me. He brought me to his beautiful mansion in the woods and fucked me senseless. He made me love him and then he threw me aside for the next girl."

Nancy was shaking her head.

"No? You want the nitty-gritty? He used to make me strip and then crawl away from him across the wood floor on my hands and knees. He used to give me baths to wash . . ."

"All right," Michael said. "All right."

She was breathing heavily. Tears welled in her mother's eyes.

"You honestly think I wouldn't know if that was happening?"

Justine said to her, "I understand why you didn't. I really do. You had a baby on the way and a messed-up daughter and the big medicine man made me all better. It's just that my ass covered the deductible."

"Darling . . ."

"Seriously, Mom. It's okay. Winter fools everybody. It's what he does."

"And so now you're telling this story again. You and that horrible man who died at the Valencia. This is why they are so concerned."

"There was another girl. Natalie? Do you remember her? "

"That tiny thing with the black hair?"

"She was his as well."

Nancy's face screwed up in confusion. For the first time, her certainty wavered.

She said, "But didn't she . . ."

"She drowned. Accidentally, they said. Convenient, right?"

"Why didn't you say something about her at the time?"

"I wanted to. But I could see that he had won and I was afraid what he'd do to me. But it's true. That's why I went so crazy."

"But she was just a little girl."

"So was I, Mom. I just had longer legs and a bigger house. You really believe I'm making all this up? Think back. Really, really, think."

Her mother said, "But that girl had all sorts of problems, sweetheart. That's what I remember about her."

"Okay, so what about Munro and Neal?"

"What do you mean?"

"Do you really think that Marcus Munro would befriend a pipsqueak like your husband if there wasn't something else involved? Neal helping cover up the crimes of his biggest client, for example?"

"There's things you don't know. Neal and Marcus have a lot in common. Dr. Winter brought them together. Marc's daughter Mary had many of the same problems you did and Dr. Winter was a big help to her."

"I bet he was."

Nancy did not bother to respond to the insinuation. She turned to Michael, who was thinking about the terrified girl on Munro's deck.

"Why can't you help her?" Nancy asked. "Why are you just sitting there?"

"I am helping her."

His words defeated Nancy. She sighed and looked out the window behind them.

"All right," she said. "I'll go."

She swayed a little as she stood. She touched her scarf, as if to make sure it was still in place.

"Take care of yourself, Jane. You should try to . . ."

But she had lost hold of her thoughts. Michael followed her to the door, locking it when she was gone. Justine was still on the sofa, draped in her blanket, like a disaster survivor.

She said, heavily, "That did *not* feel as good as I thought it would."

Michael sat and gently pulled her head onto his chest.

"Thank you for backing me up," she said.

They held each other in silence for what felt like a long time.

"I saw her," Michael said.

"Who?"

"Munro's daughter. Mary. When I was at his place. She was . . . she did not seem like a well person."

"Danny probably fucked her, too."

"But there's no way he could have fooled someone like Munro."

She was silent for a while before responding.

"I can see why you'd say that. Because I don't think you can understand Danny's genius unless you are one of his victims. The way he can infiltrate a family. The way he finds each member's weakness. Parents love their child and he makes that child better. Can there be anything more powerful? A young girl thinks she is worthless and he turns her into the most desirable woman in the world. His patience is astonishing. He does not move until each victim is paralyzed with gratitude or love. So it doesn't matter how strong Munro is. Danny would just use that strength against him. Shaming him for failing a child, this man who does not accept failure. And then taking that shame away."

She pulled back to look at him.

"We gotta publish. If we're going to do this thing, we need to do it now. If they are on the warpath having midnight meetings . . ."

He called Jenna but was sent to voice mail. He checked his computer for messages. There was nothing. They spent the next few hours wandering the house, feeling trapped. Michael found himself peering every few minutes at the street outside, expecting another car, another knock on the door, this one less tentative. He once again suggested they go the city, but Justine did not want to go anywhere. Her mother's visit had clearly rattled her. She did not want to eat, she did not want to be touched. She started to drink in the mid-afternoon, vodka this time. He had a few sips but did not really join her. He needed to keep his wits about him. This was his doing, after all. He had started it. She went to the bedroom after the sun went down, the blanket still draped over her shoulders. He desperately wanted to join her but one of them needed to be awake.

Jenna called a half hour after that. When he saw the 917 area code he was absolutely certain that it was all going to be fine. She had found a witness. Kevin Chenier, another patient. The article would run. He could wake Justine and tell her that everything was about to change.

He knew that he was wrong the moment he heard her voice.

Jenna said, "So I just spent several instructive hours with Daniel Winter and his attorney."

"Wait, you called them? I thought . . ."

"They called *me*, Michael. It looks like someone on your end told them that you had contacted me. I didn't really want to meet but Winter's lawyer said some things on the phone that were sufficiently alarming."

"What things?"

"Where is she now? Is she sitting there?"

No, he thought. She knocked back half a bottle of vodka and is catatonic in my bed.

"Just tell me what's going on, Jenna."

"Winter's position is that Jane Thomassen is a deeply disturbed former patient who has had an unhealthy fixation on him ever since he treated her when she was a sophomore in high school."

"That's . . ."

"Please let me talk, Michael. He says that during the course of her treatment for panic disorder she developed such powerfully inappropriate feelings for him that he was forced to discontinue therapy. She kept after him. He said he does not like to use the term stalking with his patients because it is reductive and derogatory, but that's clearly what it was. When that did not work, she accused him of having similar relationships with other girls. Finally, she had some sort of epic breakdown after showing up unexpectedly at his house one night. Several sources corroborate that she was a troubled girl with a long history of erratic behavior and fabrications. I've just been on the phone with her stepfather and I also spoke to a psychologist named Shelly Zintel, who treated Jane after her breakdown. She was limited by confidentiality but the thrust of her remarks confirmed Winter's account."

"None of that . . ."

"Winter went off the record and gave me a clinical overview of your friend's condition. He even let me look over his notes. It's called confabulation, what she suffers from. Fuzzy-trace theory, to be specific."

"What about Natalie Chenier? How did he explain her?"

"Winter was less inclined to talk about her for reasons of confidentiality, though Marcus Munro had no such qualms. He said that the girl had quite a sad history. He was aware of her family from his district attorney days. Evidently she had been abused from an early age by at least one of her mother's lovers. His office had tried to bring charges but the mother would not cooperate. Winter thinks Jane must have heard about this in group and mixed it into her fantasy. There were drugs in her body when Natalie was found. The thinking was she simply got wasted and fell in the river."

"But if Justine is lying, why would she risk exposure?"

"Because she believes her fabrications are real. Munro thinks Desmond Tracey exploited her illness to involve her in a crude blackmail attempt that ended when he overdosed. Evidently his arrest record is a lot more extensive and less noble than his rep as an art scene bad boy suggests. And he appears to have perpetrated some pretty major fraud to get a job at Riverside."

"But he had photographs of some girl at Riverside who was involved with Winter."

"Have you seen these? What exactly do they depict?"

"Jenna, listen to me. This is just Winter coming back at us. I mean, you said it yourself. He isn't some amateur. You must have known he'd have answers."

"They're pretty good answers."

"You haven't seen what I've seen. You haven't been with her."

"No I haven't. And that might not be a bad thing."

"So it's he-said, she-said, and you are coming down with the he."

The ensuing silence felt very profound. He thought he had struck a nerve. Right up until he heard the tone of her voice.

"Michael—what can you tell me about your departure from Grammaticus?"

It was his turn to pause before answering.

"What does that have to do with anything?"

"Munro claims you were asked to leave for falsifying an expense report."

"That was nothing, Jenna. I was just helping out some clients."

"They fired you with cause over nothing? How much did you get when you sued them for that?"

He did not respond. There was no reason. Even if he could make Jenna understand, there was the whole rest of the world to consider.

She said, "You see how this looks, right? You are dismissed for unethical conduct by one of the nation's most respected foundations. And then you turn up making explosive allegations in support of a woman who has a long history of mental illness and fabrication. Who says her name is Justine when it's really something else. And you both are allied with a drug addict who gained access to Riverside through fraudulent means and has an arrest record as long as the *Iliad*."

"So, what are you saying, that I'm her partner in crime?"

"No, that's what *they* are saying. And I don't see a credible contradiction to that assertion. Certainly not one that would stand up to the sort of scrutiny this story would get."

"Do you really think I'd do that?"

"It's not my job to answer that question."

"You're being played, Jenna."

"Being played is exactly what I'm trying to avoid."

"So what, we're done?" he asked her.

"Yes. No—there's one more thing before you go. If I see this story appear elsewhere, I will feel compelled to go public with what I have learned. About the both of you. There are a lot of real victims of predation out there who don't need their cause to be damaged by some fabulist."

He did not leave his office after hanging up. The call had not awakened Justine and he wanted to keep it that way until he could grasp what he had just heard. Kim had spied on him, he thought as he typed *confabulation*. Of course she had. She had come to check on his well-being and seen signs that there was someone here with him. Two wine glasses, a woman's clothes in the bedroom. Michael's computer was not password-protected; Kim would have read his email to Jenna. She told Douglas, who told Munro. And then, just to make sure that the bomb ticking in her house was completely defused, she had told them what had happened at Grammaticus.

Michael read about fuzzy-trace theory and Korsakoff's syndrome. He read about the frontal lobe and neural pathways and how the brain could reconstitute memory to impose order on a fractured world. What had Nancy said? It was like an earthquake inside her. He read case histories of fabrications that were far more richly detailed than her account. For ten days, he had been peeling back the layers of deceit in which she had encrusted her life in the belief that he would locate the true woman. He thought he had found her in the story she had told him, but what if this was just another layer, another lie, and the actual truth lay even deeper, explicable only in the jargon of men like Winter? What if her doctor was the dragon she needed to slay, not because he had fucked her on a hardwood floor or destroyed Natalie Chenier, but because he had spurned her ten years ago? That was why she had chosen Trace. He was her true believer because she had constructed a good part of herself from the photographs he took. To him, Justine and Natalie were not troubled girls who had been treated by a good-willed psychiatrist. They were beautiful victims. They were Varsa. Weeds.

Winter's version was becoming increasingly difficult to deny. Natalie was a messed-up kid who slipped and fell; Winter had never come anywhere near the Valencia Motel. Desmond Tracey was a con man and a junkie who had put one poisoned drop too many into his corrupted veins; Munro was simply a tough lawyer serving the interests of a wronged client. And Justine? He'd wanted to believe that her wild moods were symptomatic of the pressure she was under, but now he feared they were signs of something deeper, something that was about to engulf them both.

Michael turned out the light on his desk and crossed the quiet house, trying to come up with one thing about her that could not be doubted. Something to answer the doctors and lawyers and journalists and parents. She was asleep. He undressed and climbed into bed and gently pressed himself against her. Her body was so warm it felt almost feverish. She writhed and murmured but did not wake. He placed his fingers on her bare shoulder.

This, he thought as he touched her. This is what you do not doubt.

They called a few hours later. It was just after two in the morning. The darkness felt absolute; rain struck the roof and the flagstones of the back patio. Michael snatched his buzzing cell phone from the bedside table and crept as quietly as possible from the room, answering only after he'd closed the office door.

"Marcus wants to meet with you," Douglas said. "See if we can sort this thing out before she does something irreversible."

"Now?"

"Everybody's up. It's time to meet."

"Where?"

"We're at the office. And they'd like it to be just you."

"I'm not leaving her alone."

"Come on, Mike. Seriously. What do you think is going to happen? This isn't *The Sopranos*."

He repeated, "I'm not leaving her alone."

"All right. Hold the line."

There was the drowning sound of male voices in urgent conversation.

"They're driving over."

"No, I don't want to wake her."

"For God's . . ."

More muted conversation.

"They'll park in front of the house. You can meet in their car."

"I don't think so, Douglas."

"I gotta tell you, Mike, they're coming one way or another. If you don't want them pounding on your door, then you should do this."

"I'll call the cops."

"The police aren't necessarily your best option at this point in time."

"What the hell is that supposed to mean?"

Douglas said nothing. Michael remembered what the detective had said to him after his arrest. *You might have dodged a bullet on this one.*

"All right. They can have ten minutes."

He went back into the bedroom and collected his clothes as quietly as possible. She had not moved; her breathing was slow and steady. He closed the bedroom door tightly and took up a position at the front window. Rain filtered through the pale sodium nimbus from the lamp across the street. It came so slowly, so gently, that it could have been snow.

Munro's Escalade arrived, silent and emanating a dark light, like a barge from the underworld. Beaded rain glistened on its windows and hood. Michael stepped onto the porch and bolted the door behind him. The back passenger door opened as he approached. He hesitated. The vehicle's interior was illuminated by the dome light. Munro was at the wheel; Winter was in the back, directly behind him. He wore tan trousers and a black pullover and a dark blue windbreaker. He looked like a vigorous, popular governor about to tour a disaster zone.

Michael slid into the back seat. He shut the door, casting them into darkness. Winter reached up to turn the dome light back on and then locked eyes with Michael. He looked calm; concerned, but not at all hostile or angry. Rain sheeted over the glass behind him.

He said, "I'm sorry to drag you out of your home on a night like this, but I think we should try to wrap this thing up."

"Are you planning to confess?"

Winter smiled patiently for a few seconds, his eyes now on the window behind Michael.

"This rain," he said. "I think we're getting close to the point of no return with floods."

Michael did not respond. Winter finally turned back to him.

"Jane is profoundly delusional, Mr. Coolidge," he said. "What you are doing right now is not helping her. In fact, you are doing her immeasurable harm."

"She's not lying."

"Not like a normal person lies, no. Which explains your confusion."

"I'm not confused. I know exactly what's happening."

"It's a kind of genius, what Jane has," Winter continued, following his own train of thought. "Confabulators need to be seductive. They need to be charismatic. They cannot afford to prevaricate or leave loose ends. There have been experiments. Healthy people are shown an event and asked to describe it multiple times over a period of days, weeks even. Their stories vary. Always. Sometime a little, sometimes a lot. They meander, resequence, leave things out. But with people such as Jane, their stories are as well-constructed as a Swiss watch. They scarcely deviate from telling to telling. Even over the years."

Michael thought about the two times he'd heard her story. How incredibly similar they had been. And yet there had been that one unmistakable difference.

"My point is that you shouldn't feel bad about being taken in by her," Winter continued. "Desmond Tracey certainly fell for her fantasies. Luckily, we were able to get to Ms. Fogg before this all went too far. She's sufficiently conversant with this world to know about confabulation."

Michael said, "So you think lying gives Justine pleasure?"

"I wouldn't call it pleasure, no. I think she is following a compulsion that she cannot control and is in danger of doing serious damage to herself and those around her. "

"So you've come in the middle of the night because you are concerned for her well-being."

"Is it so strange that I feel immense frustration that I couldn't help her when she was younger? Look, Mr. Coolidge, obviously I don't want my name sullied. But I can weather that. I deal with troubled people. False accusations come with the territory. What won't survive any sort of glaring exposure is her psyche. Can I ask you a question? Was approaching Jenna Fogg your idea?"

Michael did not answer.

"I thought so," Winter said. "That was a mistake. The last thing she needs right now is to have someone she trusts urging her to make this fable public. Once that happens, she's doomed. Her world will be destroyed and she will be ruined."

"Then why is she doing it?"

"It's an addiction, this kind of lying. Like Tracey's heroin. The fabulist needs to tell bigger and bigger lies. To a wider audience. When you gave her the chance to tell her story to hundreds of thousands, she could not resist."

"So what do you want from me, exactly?"

"Isn't that obvious? I'd like you to use whatever influence you have over her to get her to stop this crusade."

Michael said, "And what happens if I don't? There seems to be a threat implicit in your visitation."

Winter stared at him in frustration, then looked at the man in the front seat.

"If we cannot come to some sort of understanding tonight," Munro said, his deep, rasping voice very different from the doctor's, "then this becomes a police matter."

"Yeah? How does that work?" Michael asked him.

"There's more than enough evidence for the authorities to open an investigation as to whether the three of you have been involved in a criminal conspiracy to blackmail my client."

"Bullshit."

"Have you ever been subject to a grand jury investigation, Mr. Coolidge?"

Michael did not answer.

"It's very unpleasant. I imagine you could probably muddle through. But are you sure that Ms. Thomassen could endure it? The subpoenas and the interrogations?"

"Obviously we don't want it to come to that," Winter added quickly. "We'd much rather see her dealt with in a clinical setting."

"I'm perfectly aware that you don't want the police involved," Michael said to Winter. "She was there. Outside the cabin. She knows what you did to Trace."

Michael saw something on Winter's face. It lasted for a fraction of a second, and yet it was unmistakable. The slightest disturbance in that flawless surface. Shock, fear, an unexpected loss of control. But when he spoke, his voice was as calm as it had been all along.

"What I did to Trace?" he asked.

"She knows you killed him."

"She's claiming that?"

"He died of an overdose," Munro said.

"Are you sure?" Michael asked.

"So let me understand this correctly," Winter said. "Jane is saying that I was there when Tracey died? That I was in some way responsible for his death?"

"You pumped him full of heroin."

Winter stared at Michael, his mind working. And then he looked at Munro and raised his eyebrows.

"What?" the lawyer asked.

"No, I'm starting to fear—what are the police thinking?"

"They haven't made any sort of call yet. Test results are pending. The APD has limited resources. What is this, Daniel?"

Winter's expression had taken on the same dispassionate cast Michael had seen in the YouTube video.

He replied, "I'm just wondering why Jane would say that."

"Because it's true," Michael said.

"Yes, but true in what way?"

"You think she did it?" Munro asked.

"She certainly had reason to be enraged with him. Using drugs, getting fired. Given his condition, it would not have been difficult for her to . . ."

He did not finish the sentence. An image passed through Michael's mind. Her hand striking Trace's face in the alley. Her words. *You're ruining everything.*

"She'd never have hurt him," Michael said.

Winter smiled.

He said, "Because she loved him? You should come meet some of my patients."

"Fuck you."

"You really do believe her, don't you?"

"Yes. I do."

Winter nodded a few times.

"You are an interesting case, Michael. I mean, the reasons for Jane's attraction to Tracey are obvious. You, on the other hand, were a mystery to me, at least until I learned about your history of fraud."

"This is ridiculous," Michael said.

"The question is . . ."

Winter's eyes widened. He'd seen something back up at the house. Michael turned. Justine stood on the lawn, her figure obscured by the water streaming down the car window. Michael fumbled with the door handle a few times before he was able to launch himself from the car, so violently that he almost pitched face-first onto the wet grass. She was just a few feet away. She wore his T-shirt but nothing else. Her hair glistened with rain, her bare legs were so pale they were luminous. She was staring past him, her eyes electric. Michael looked—Winter was out of the car, standing in front of the door Michael had left open.

"Justine, go back inside," Michael said as he turned back to her.

"Why is he here?" she asked him.

"Come on," he said as he reached for her. "Let's go."

"What is he saying? What did he tell you?"

She tried to slip by Michael, but he was able to grab hold of her rainslick arm.

"What did you do to Trace?" Her voice was loud now. "What did you do to him?"

She struggled to get to him but Michael did not let her go. Munro was saying something from inside the car; Michael could hear it through the open passenger door. *Get in.* Winter ignored him. He stared calmly back at Justine.

"Get help, Jane," he said. "Please. Before it's too late."

Mrs. Donald's light came on across the street and Munro began to speak more urgently. After holding Justine's eye a moment longer, Winter slipped back inside the SUV. It was gone in an instant.

The rain was coming harder. His neighbor's figure had appeared in her front window.

"Justine, we have to go inside."

She shrugged free of his hands and walked toward the house. He followed. She turned abruptly on him once they were in the front hall.

"Why were you talking to them? What were they saying?"

And then, in an instant, the anguish was gone, replaced by a fierce hope.

"Did Jenna publish? Is that why they came?" she asked.

"I'm going to tell you what's going on, but first you have to promise me . . ."

"For fuck's sake, Michael. Just tell me!"

"Jenna's not going to run your story."

"What? Why not?"

"They convinced her not to publish."

"How did they do that? She's supposed to be this big-time journalist."

"They told her that Natalie was abused by her mother's boyfriends. And Winter claimed that everything you are saying about your past is part of an elaborate fantasy and Trace was trying to blackmail them with it."

"And she just folded?"

"Yes. She just folded."

"There's something more. I can see it in your face."

Michael had to tell her about Grammaticus. But he could not bring himself to say the words. It would be too much for her. And for him, as well.

"I think they might try to implicate you in what happened up at the Valencia."

Although he would have thought it impossible, she looked even more stricken as she stared down at the water that had run off her onto the floor.

"We should go to the city," he said. "We should get you out of here."

"And then what?"

"We can find someone else. We can . . ."

He did not finish the sentence. He had no idea what they could do now. She had fallen into an airtight silence. Her eyes were open, but she did not seem to be aware of the world around her. It was all he could do to get her to change into dry clothes and sit with him in his office. She did not respond to his reassurances that going to New York was just a strategic retreat. Eventually, she put her head on his lap, as she had in the car, when she was hiding. Her breathing slowed, the tension left her muscles. Perhaps she slept, he could not be sure. He certainly didn't—it felt as if he would never sleep again.

As he watched her, he was thinking about Justine alone with Trace in that tiny cabin. He did not want to think this, but he had no choice. She had come up from New York to find that he had ruined everything. And so the madness had taken over and she had done it. Winter had never come to the cabin. It had only ever been her.

No. He could not think this. He stroked her hair and tried to summon the faith he had conjured in bed the previous night. He had to try to find a way to hold onto that. There had to be something else, something more than the words people spoke.

It was not yet dawn when she sat up abruptly, as if she'd been awakened from a nightmare.

"Take me to the city," she said.

"Really?"

"You're right. We need to find another journalist, somebody they can't get to first. Other girls will come forward when we publish. Witnesses. It'll be too late for him to do anything."

"Are you sure?"

"Of course I'm sure." She was watching him closely now. "Please don't bail on me, Michael. Doing this was your idea."

"I know."

"We can't turn back now. Winter knows I'm a threat. He won't stop until he silences me. Tell me you understand that."

"I understand," he said, even though he knew he was about as far from understanding as he had been in a very long time.

THIRTEEN

THE RAIN WAS STILL FALLING HARD WHEN THEY LEFT THE house. Even on high, the wipers were useless. Michael felt equally powerless. A few hours ago, he'd been making good decisions, making the right moves. He'd been helping a woman he loved battle a big, bad world. At least that's what he'd been telling himself. Now, he was just a man driving into the dark, accompanied by a woman who was becoming a stranger to him. He still felt the sting of Winter's accusation. He was doing more harm than good. He was only feeding her delusions.

In the end, his doubts were irrelevant. He did not even get her past the edge of town. Although it was just past six in the morning, a line of stalled traffic blocked River. A truck decorated with the colossal face of a happy girl idled directly in front of them, leaking diesel fumes and obscuring the view. Red and blue light from an unseen source played over the surrounding buildings.

"What is this?" Justine asked, her voice suddenly charged with fear.

"Nothing. Some sort of detour."

She pointed at the lights.

"Are those cops?"

"I think so."

"They're for me, aren't they?"

"No . . ."

"Turn around, Michael. Now. Please."

Rain pounded on the roof. The side windows were syrupy with water. The truck loomed in front of him. He checked the rearview mirror. Two cars had pulled up close behind him. Beyond them, an emergency vehicle approached, heading the wrong way past stalled traffic. If he tried to make a three-point turn he would block it.

"We're sort of stuck here."

And then Justine's door was open and she was out of the car. He called for her but his voice was swallowed by the sound of the rain. She walked quickly into the narrow street that ran between the CVS and an office block. Michael opened his own door. He started to rise from the car and was almost struck by the approaching emergency vehicle, which turned out to be a police cruiser. The cop at the wheel hit the brakes and gestured angrily for Michael to return to the Sonata. The truck with the smiling girl had begun to roll a hundred feet ahead; the driver behind him hit his horn. Michael had no choice but to get back in his car and put it in gear.

It was a small flood. That was all. No one was checking I.D.s; no one was looking for Jane Thomassen. A ten-foot stretch of the road was submerged in water that had percolated up out of a blocked sewer. Michael was diverted onto a side street that took him in the opposite direction from where she had fled. He searched desperately for a way back, all the while thinking about her slipping through the quiet streets, the relentless rain falling on her bare head. So this is the panic, he thought.

He spent the better part of an hour searching for her. He checked the station first; a train had left between the time she slipped into the alley and when he finally got there. She had probably been on it, and yet he continued to look, driving through downtown streets that were clotted with diverted traffic. Twice he parked and went through alleys and side streets on foot, walking all the way down to Cheapside. Dawn arrived during his search. The rain stopped. The only clouds were stragglers, racing east. Flattened leaves braided the sewer grills; the air seemed to have been scrubbed clean.

He headed home, clinging to the scant hope she had returned. There were two cars parked in front of his house, a black sedan, featureless and official, and an Annville police cruiser with a large radio antenna bowed across its trunk, like a rod that had just hooked a live one. The detective, Maas, was walking away from his front door, followed closely by a uniformed officer. They stopped abruptly when they saw him.

"I was beginning to think you'd flown the coop," Maas said as they congregated in the driveway. "Jane Thomassen around?"

"She's gone."

"You sure about that?"

"I'm sure," Michael said, even though he was not sure at all.

"You know where she went?"

The breezy sense of camaraderie the detective had displayed after Michael's arrest was long gone.

"I don't. She left abruptly."

Maas stared at him unhappily as he decided what was going to happen next.

"So how about you come over to the office for a talk?"

Michael thought about his rights, all the television shows he'd seen, the movies.

"All right," he said.

He followed them across town. The station was much busier than it had been after his arrest at Riverside. Three state troopers dressed in rain gear were locked in urgent conversation in the middle of the lobby. By the bullpen, a half dozen Annville officers had gathered in front of a large map of the region that had been perforated by dozens of colored pins. There was an intensity to them that suggested men preparing for the worst.

"We're gonna get swamped," Maas said to no one in particular. "You heard it here first."

He led Michael to the same room as before. This time, there was a video camera on a tripod. Maas gestured for him to have a seat in the chair at the small table. A manila folder rested in front of the seat opposite Michael.

He told him, "I really don't know what I can . . ."

Maas held up a silencing finger.

"Just let me get this contraption going."

Once the camera was operating, the detective sat and opened the folder.

"So I got your details from a couple days ago. Anything changed?"

Only everything, Michael thought as he told him no.

"You might want to repeat them anyway for the all-seeing eye here."

Michael did as instructed. Name, age, address.

"Occupation?"

"I'm currently unemployed."

"Okay," Maas said. "So I'm hearing you found your girl."

"She found me."

"But you've been staying together in your house."

"Yes. Briefly."

"So I'd like to revisit the exact nature of your relationship with Jane Thomassen. I recall you weren't so eager to discuss it last time we talked."

"We're friends."

Maas leaned back in his chair and raised his eyebrows.

"Would you say you were involved romantically?"

"We were."

"So it's all over?"

"Yes," Michael said after a moment.

"How long had it been going on?"

"Since the beginning of the year. Although we were not in contact for much of that time."

"What, was it an online thing?" Maas asked him.

"No, we lost touch back in January and I had no contact with her until Saturday before last."

"So you had not seen or spoken to her for, what, nine months previous to last Saturday?"

"No."

"Well, when you were together, did you ever discuss any plans she had regarding Dr. Daniel Winter?"

Michael knew before the detective had even finished speaking that he was going to lie to him. Whatever was happening with her, wherever she was and whoever she was, he was not going to say anything else that might harm her.

"No. Not at all."

"How about Desmond Tracey? How would you characterize your relationship with him?"

"Nonexistent."

"So you didn't communicate with him."

"No."

"And there's nothing you can say about what his business might have been up here in Annville?"

Michael countered, "Didn't he work at Riverside?"

"Jane tell you this?"

"Maybe. I might have read it."

"Kind of weird, don't you think? This world-class artist scrubbing toilets?"

Michael shrugged.

"Did she tell you anything else about what Tracey was up to? Any sort of plans they might have had? Particularly referencing Dr. Winter?"

"No."

Maas stared at him. Letting Michael's answer hover between them before moving on.

"How would you characterize the nature of the altercation Jane had with Desmond Tracey on Water Lane last Saturday?"

"It was heated. I told you about that when I called in, right?"

"Was there physical contact?"

"No."

Maas watched him with a slight, expectant smile. Michael remembered his son's terrified gaze. Will had told his mother. Who did not exactly have Michael's back.

"I guess there was a scuffle. It all happened pretty quickly."

"Any punches thrown? Kicks or scratches? Stuff like that?"

"She might have slapped him. It was all sort of a blur."

"A blur. Okay. And when were you next in touch with Ms. Thomassen after that?"

"There was the text I told you about when I called, later that night."

Maas read.

"*I might be needing your help*. And after that? Nothing until, what—did you pick her up somewhere? She just show up at your house?"

"Yes, she just showed up. And no, there was nothing."

"When was that?" he asked Michael.

"Three days ago."

"What did she say when she arrived?"

"I don't recall her exact words."

"You didn't ask her where she had been? What happened to Desmond Tracey? Why she was back?"

"I can't really remember what we said."

But he did remember. Very clearly. She said she had seen his name in the paper. Which raised the question—why had she been checking the papers? Had she been looking for evidence that the police suspected her?

"And when did she leave? Last night, you said?"

"Early this morning."

"And during this three-day period, she says nothing about the death of Desmond Tracey."

Michael shook his head.

Maas said, "I gotta say, I'm finding this kind of hard to believe. You see her fighting with a guy, she calls you a few hours later asking for help. And then he turns up dead. You're concerned enough to call us. And yet you weren't curious about what happened?"

"I know what happened. He overdosed."

"Is that what she told you?"

"It was in the news."

"But at no point did *she* explain to you how Desmond Tracey came to be dead, correct?"

"It was obviously a painful topic for her."

"And she didn't say where she went after Tracey died? Why she was in such a rush to get away? Why she waited a week to get in touch with you?"

"I presumed she was upset."

Maas leaned back in his chair and folded his heavy arms across his thick chest.

"You're not a very curious guy, are you, Michael?"

"I just didn't feel the need to subject her to this kind of questioning."

"You think *this* is bad?"

"Can I go?"

"One more thing. Did she leave this morning because you had come to suspect she and Desmond Tracey might have been involved in criminal activity? Or that she might have had a role in his death?"

"I don't suspect anything of the sort."

"That's right. You're the guy with no sense of curiosity."

Michael repeated, "Can I go?"

"As long as you don't go far."

Maas led Michael back across the bullpen, where the officers were still at the map, moving pins. The detective entered a code to unlock the door, but only pushed it off the latch.

"Mr. Coolidge, you are now part of a very serious ongoing criminal investigation," he said. "You need to make yourself available for further questioning. If you retain counsel, have them contact me. And if you should hear from Ms. Thomassen, let us know immediately. If you don't, you will be charged with obstructing a police investigation."

He waited for Michael to nod his consent, then pushed the door open the rest of the way.

At home, Michael retreated to his darkened office. He needed to slow his mind. Everything was coming at him too fast. There were too many theories, too many contradictions. He needed one undeniable thing. One fact. Until he had that, he would continue to stumble blindly.

Natalie's brother. Kevin Chenier might have been sniffing glue or worshipping Satan, but if he could provide even the smallest, most tattered shred of evidence tying Winter to his sister—a glimpse of her getting into his car, an overheard phone call, a stoned late-night confession—it would give Michael enough certainty to press on. Provided he could figure out where Justine went.

Jericho Evangelical Institute was fifteen miles northwest of the Annville line. Michael had never been clear of the exact nature of the school. Its conservatively dressed students appeared occasionally at the Saturday morning Annville market, selling depleted vegetables and functional furniture. You never saw them at Trader Joe's or the Cineplex. The school might not be entirely off the grid, but it certainly dangled at the end of one of its more remote strands.

It was early afternoon when he set off. Although there was an almost punishing clarity to the sky now, the radio said more rain was expected. A major flood watch was now in effect for the northern parts of the county. As Michael drove he slipped into a fugue state. He had passed beyond exhaustion. The road started to pull the car forward, as if he was following one long, steady decline, instead of the region's usual shuffle of small hills. Jericho Evangelical's entrance was marked by a ranch-style gate that consisted of two vertical fence beams, with a third laid horizontally across their tops. Similar beams—they might have been old railroad ties—had been used to construct a crude Calvary on a nearby hill. Near that was parked a portable trailer sign.

The Flood is coming. Get right before the rain.

Beyond the gate, a long dirt road led to a collection of rickety buildings scattered throughout a shallow valley of farmed-out looking land. Most were unadorned trailers and corrugated structures of indeterminate use. Classrooms or dorms—they could have been either. There was a vast barn, though no sign of livestock.

As Michael traveled down the access road, he passed a group of students walking in loose formation. They appeared to have just been disgorged from a bus, although no bus was in evidence. The boys wore baggy white dress shirts and thin black ties and trousers that ended well up their ankles. The girls wore knee-length gray skirts and wool tights and white shirts buttoned to the collar. Both sexes appeared to have gone to the same barber, one who hated hair. Michael considered rolling down his window to ask if anybody knew Kevin Chenier, but something about their unwavering forward gazes and dismal half-smiles prevented him.

He parked in a small square of gravel and clay that he decided was the visitor's lot. A thin path connected it to the only likely candidate for an administrative building, a structure that looked like a scaled-down version of the Texas School Book Depository. The front door was locked. No lights burned inside. In fact, the entire community felt deserted: those trudging students had vanished as suddenly as guerillas about to launch an ambush. The only sound was a dejected, sourceless bray that might have been an ineptly played brass instrument.

And then two young men emerged from a trailer a hundred feet away. They moved in rapid lockstep, their eyes fixed on the ground, even though they must have seen Michael as he headed to intercept them.

"Excuse me," he said.

They stopped reluctantly. Only one of them looked up. His tight smile oozed distrust. The other man continued to stare at the dirt path.

"I'm looking for a student. Kevin Chenier?"

The first student gave his head a single, emphatic shake.

"You don't know where he is? Or does he not live here?"

He continued to smile at Michael.

"Do you even speak English?"

The student sighed, then shrugged off his backpack and let it fall at his feet. He removed a pad and pen, then wrote something in big block letters on the top page.

SILENCE SATURDAY.

"You aren't allowed to speak," Michael said after the man held it up.

He nodded, affirming the negative.

"I still need to see Kevin. It's a very important family matter."

The second man finally looked at Michael. He pointed toward a prefab building near the barn. You could have just done that to begin with, Michael thought as they passed fluidly on either side of him, like he was a boulder blocking their swift and silent stream.

The front door was propped open with a rubber wedge; the lobby was crammed with broken furniture and cardboard boxes. There did not seem to be anyone around. A sweet, slightly rotted odor filled the air. Mold, manure, food—it was impossible to pin it down. There were two hallways, one of them dark, the other radiating erratic fluorescent light. Michael took the latter, his nervous system issuing cautionary reminders of the electric shock he'd received the last time he'd gone uninvited down a strange corridor. He passed three empty classrooms, shabby but neat, smelling of ammonia, before he came upon one that was occupied. Ten young men sat at desks facing a smeared blackboard, all of them perfectly still, heads down, eyes on the books in front of them. There was no instructor in sight.

Michael stepped into the open doorway. Only one of the men looked up. Michael sensed instinctively that this was Kevin Chenier. His uniform was disheveled, as if he had been sleeping in it. Michael almost spoke as he approached, but caught himself. Instead, he gestured to the notebook and pen in front of the student, who nodded warily, his manner more in tune with the state's correctional facilities than the pastoral setting around them. It took Michael a moment to find a page not filled with cramped, child-like handwriting. The pen was a marker; its squeak was as loud as a skidding tire.

Are you Kevin Chenier?

Michael held up the notebook. The young man's nod contained more menace than affirmation.

We need to talk about your sister.

As Kevin read, something wavered in his hard expression, something it took him a moment to master. He took the pen from Michael. Its shriek was even louder when he wrote, and yet none of the other students looked up.

I have no sister.

But he did not hand the pen back. He stared at what he had written for almost a minute before crossing it out and writing again.

Theres a gulf station. Turn left and go a mile.

They made eye contact and Michael nodded. Kevin returned to his Bible and Michael could now see a tattoo beneath his loose collar, something black and crude. When he left the building he once again heard that plaintive sound. It was coming from the barn. It was not a brass instrument after all, but a cow. It was really kicking up a fuss. Someone, it seemed, had not got the memo about Silence Saturday.

The Gulf station was impossible to miss. It was the only place of commerce Michael had seen since he left the campus. He filled up and bought a soft drink in case anyone tried to move him along, but no one noticed the man in the Sonata. Time passed. People came and went. Michael slept, he took short walks, he considered going back to campus. It was almost six P.M. when Kevin finally showed up. One moment he was not there and then he was, tapping on the glass with long unchewed fingernails. He slid into the passenger seat, a little winded from the walk, smelling of sweet cheap cologne. Michael extended a hand. The other man ignored it.

"Can you talk?" Michael asked.

"Who are you?" Kevin asked, his voice phlegmy from disuse.

"My name is Michael Coolidge. I'm from Annville."

"What's this about my sister? She's been dead a decade."

"Do you remember a girl named Jane Thomassen?"

Kevin simply stared at Michael

"She was an outpatient at Riverside with Natalie."

Recognition spread across Kevin's face like an illicit toxin dumped on the side of a highway.

"Jane. Yeah, I remember her."

He said, "She thinks she might know why your sister died."

"My sister died because she fell in the river. She got wasted and lost her balance."

"We think she might have killed herself."

"In that case she's definitely in hell and there's no reason to even talk about her. Damned is damned. There's no going back."

"We think someone might have driven her to do it, Kevin. So maybe she's not quite so damned, after all."

"Oh yeah? Who?" Kevin asked him.

"What do you know about a man named Dr. Daniel Winter?"

"Nothing."

"He's the psychiatrist who treated Natalie at Riverside."

"That's all devilry."

"I think I agree with you. But did you know him? Dr. Winter? Danny?"

"I didn't know about any of that stuff. Why are you asking about him?"

"We believe Winter may have been responsible for Natalie's death."

"How?"

"We think—Jane thinks—he had inappropriate relations with her."

"Shit, lotta people had those with Nat. My mother's boyfriends, in particular. There was this one guy. Donald Trump."

Michael repeated, "Donald Trump."

"I called him that because of his hair. It's like, dude, just shave the whole deal. But whatever. I caught some wicked beatings trying to get up in between him and Nat."

"Well, we think her psychiatrist did something to her that caused her to kill herself."

"You keep on saying *did something*—do you mean rape?"

"Yes. I mean rape."

"Your friend Jane tell you that?" Kevin asked.

"Yes."

Kevin emitted a brief laugh, one that was utterly devoid of humor or joy.

"What?" Michael asked.

"I wouldn't put too much stock in this Jane of yours. She hated Natalie. She tortured her. I remember one day, she came to the house like a crazy woman. I had to pull her off Nat. She was like to kill her."

"Are you sure?"

"I seen people try to kill people. You seldom confuse it with something else."

"When was this?"

Kevin said, "A few weeks before Nat died."

"But why?"

Kevin shrugged.

"There was something messed up between the two of them I could never figure out. All I know is that Natalie was terrified of her. And my sister didn't scare easy. She used to hide from her, especially after that day at our house. I mean, why anybody would want to give Natalie grief, I do not know. She was just this . . ."

His voice faltered, though the prisoner in him quickly gained control.

"She was just this crazy kid who wouldn't hurt a fly. Which I guess is why everybody used her so bad. The world seems to have it in for some people. I'd see it when I was inside. They wouldn't last a week. Out here, it just takes longer. But it gets them in the end."

"And you don't know what this conflict between the two of them was about?"

"That's probably a question for your friend."

"Did you tell anyone about this? I mean, after her death?"

"Nobody asked."

"Are you sure about all of this, Kevin? Maybe . . ."

"I'm sure, Mr. Coolidge."

The two men sat through a silence that felt very heavy to Michael.

"I brought this picture of her," Kevin finally said. "I don't know why. I just did. I haven't thought about her much in a while and when you said her name . . ."

He seemed to lose his train of thought.

"Can I see it?" Michael asked.

"Yeah, why not."

He took it from his jacket pocket and handed it to Michael. It was a Polaroid. Yet another Polaroid, although no one would ever call this art. In it, a tiny, unsmiling girl in torn jeans and too-big black T-shirt stared up at the camera. Her eyes were ringed by lines of kohl; a dozen bracelets dangled from her bone-thin right wrist. Her expression was poised between wonder and fear. She sat on a collapsing sofa, her legs folded beneath her. Michael guessed her age to be about twelve.

"When was this taken?"

"Not long before she drowned."

"She was just a child."

"She always looked young for her age. "

Michael handed the photo back to Kevin. He had to swallow a few times before he spoke again.

"Is there anybody else I could speak with?" he asked. "A friend?"

"Natalie wasn't real big on friends."

"Are any of the men still around? Your mother's men?"

Kevin looked at him, his expression stony now.

He said, "Are you serious?"

Michael did not answer. The gates had come down. They were done.

"I gotta get back and self-report. Every word I say today is breaking the rules."

Michael offered, "Let me drive you."

"No, I should walk. Get my penance on."

"You sure?"

He shrugged.

"We don't get out much."

Michael extended a hand. This time, Kevin took it. His grip was soft and distracted. He was thinking about his sister now. Who would not hurt a fly. Who was born to be crushed. Who was found dead in the river and nobody asked why. Kevin got out of the car and closed the door gently and then he was gone. Michael sat perfectly still for a long time before starting his engine. Thinking only one thing.

She was like to kill her.

He bought a bottle of whiskey on the way back to Annville. The exhaustion saturating his muscles and bones was becoming chronic, beyond the remedy of sleep. At home, he stood for a long time in the shower and then propped himself up in bed, drinking the liquor fast, sucking the sleep from it. The rain returned just as he felt himself slipping off. It was as heavy as it had been since the storms had started. What had Maas said? Somebody was going to get swamped.

He woke in the late morning. It was still pouring. He felt sick from the booze and yet he badly wanted to drink again. Somehow, he managed to stop himself. Instead, he made coffee and went into his office, where he stared numbly at his computer screen. Flood control barriers were about to be breached. The watch was now a warning. Local emergencies were being declared in the northern part of town, but central Annville itself remained safe. For the time being. People were saying that the flood had the potential of being unprecedented.

He wondered if the police were looking for her in New York; if Trace's body was being examined for signs that someone had killed him when he was helpless. There was a distinct possibility they were going to arrest Michael again, or at least serve him with a subpoena, as Munro had threatened. He had no idea how long he could maintain his silence once the real pressure started, or how much damage he would accept to protect a woman who appeared to have vanished completely from his life. Yet again. If Kim appeared at his door right now to accuse him of folly, there was no defense that Michael could mount.

But he did not do the logical thing. He did not pick up the phone and call Maas and tell him what he knew. He'd come too far. Before he did anything else, he had to understand the truth about her. And himself. Why he was still going long after he knew that he should stop. Justine had said that she had been broken when the most profound love of her life had turned out to be a lie. He needed to understand if he was about to suffer a similar fate. He had to get right before the rain. Until that happened, nothing else would be possible.

Uncertain what to do next, he called up the reports of Natalie Chenier's death in the *Call*. He focused on the article that said the chief medical examiner had determined her death was an accident. They said she had been walking along the floodwall down in Cheapside, a place she had been seen in the past. Michael got his raincoat and his car keys and headed out. Cheapside was quiet, but then it was always quiet. The neighborhood was a ragged mix of thrift shops and check cashing places; tattoo parlors and multiple-family units whose front porches were cluttered with furniture and busted appliances. It would never gentrify. You could feel it in the air. They could ring the neighborhood with a seamless laager of Crate & Barrels and it would still be home to stoop-sitters and scowling young mothers with their sniveling unwanted children.

He drove to Station Road, where Natalie had lived. He had no idea which house had been hers; it did not matter. They all told the same story. Duplexes and shotgun shacks. Fenced yards filled with weeds and dogs that barked as if they were accustomed to being ignored. Nobody was in sight. It was raining too hard. Rivulets of garbage-strewn rainwater crisscrossed the pavement, following the cracks and imperfections.

It was not easy to find a way onto Prospect. The first two alleys were blocked. He had to drive all the way to the southern edge of town before he finally found one that allowed him access. The road was long and narrow, speckled with shattered glass, scarred by pot holes. To his left, there was a row of abandoned factories and ware-houses, their windows broken, their walls covered with dull graffiti; to his right, the floodwall, and then the swollen river. The top of the thick stone wall was level with the road; the wall itself was a good five feet thick. In the northern part of town, where the riverfront was crowded with boutiques and restaurants, the floodwall was a scenic walkway, protected by a sturdy, handsome guardrail that ensured no citizen would accidentally topple into the drink. Here, there was a listing ten-foot-high chainlink fence that Michael guessed had been erected in the past decade, perhaps in response to the drowned girl.

He parked and got out and stepped onto the top of the wall. It was slippery with rain—he grabbed onto the fence to brace himself. The river was as high as he'd ever seen it. Usually it was at least a ten-foot drop to its surface; now, it rose to within three feet of where he stood. By his wet shoe, a starving weed struggled through a crack between mortar and stone. He yanked it out and dropped it through the fence into the water. It only took a few seconds for the current to carry it out of sight.

His doorbell rang just after sunset. He had been lying on his office sofa, paralyzed by confusion. His heart was pounding by the time he reached the door. He did not bother to check who was there before opening it. There was no reason. Whatever they had for him, that would be his future.

It was Mrs. Donald. She wore a clear plastic slicker over a floral housecoat; a Red Sox cap was perched uneasily on her permed hair. Her swollen lower legs disappeared into large rubber boots. Her umbrella was vast, the sort caddies held above squinting professionals in golf tournaments.

"I hope I'm not bothering."

"Not at all. What can I do for you, Mrs. D?"

"Well, I'm worried that darn gardener left the bulkhead unlatched again. And you just know that it will flood. I'd go down there myself but . . ."

"Let me get my jacket."

She shot him sidelong glances as they crossed Locust. He remembered her porch light flaring during his encounter with Winter and Munro.

"I'm sorry about the racket the other night," he said.

"Yes, well, I was all set to call the police."

"I've had a family friend staying. She's been having trouble with the men in her life."

"Well, I hope they sort it out, because this is a quiet street."

The bulkhead was sealed tight, as he knew it would be. He accepted her thanks and returned home. It was time to drink. He'd thrown his keys on the kitchen counter and rattled some ice into a glass before he understood that someone was in the house. The realization came without shock or fear. Just a dull sense of inevitability. Kim, he thought. Or perhaps the police. But there had been no car outside. By the time he heard the footsteps approaching from his office he knew that it was Justine. Her hair and clothes were wet. There was something wild in her eyes. She held a large manila envelope in her hand.

"The door was open," she said. "I couldn't figure out where you were."

He shook his head. Not yet able to speak.

"We've got him, Michael," she continued breathlessly.

"What do you mean? Where did you go?"

"The city. When I saw those flashing lights I just had to bolt. I'm sorry, that was bad, I know that. I was so freaked out, I was convinced they were going to bust me. I just wanted to get my stuff from my apartment and disappear. But then I remembered you saying that Klimov had more photos Trace had taken of me and I wanted those to remember him and when I went to see Klimov he said the police had sent him some stuff they found with Trace. Including these."

She pulled a small stack of photos from the envelope.

"These are the ones he took at Riverside," she said. "This is her. This is the girl he found."

"I thought you said Winter took his stuff."

"He must have hidden them in the room."

She handed the photos to him, one at a time. They were not Polaroids, but conventional prints, each of them of a single subject. It was the girl who had spoken to him just before he was tased. The girl holding the stuffed giraffe. There were eight pictures in all. In each, she stared at the camera with the same dreamy smile Michael had seen when they met.

"And Klimov just gave you these?" he asked her.

"Well, I didn't necessarily ask. He seemed to have bigger problems."

"I don't understand. I thought these were supposed to prove something."

"They do."

"Justine, these don't prove anything."

"She's one of his girls! I can see it in her face. Michael—we have to talk to her."

He placed the photos on the counter between them. Justine was studying him now.

"What's wrong?" she asked. "Something's wrong, I can see it on your face. What's going on?"

"I talked to Kevin Chenier."

"Why would you do that?" she asked, her voice shrinking.

"He said you attacked Natalie on the day you brought her home from school."

"He just didn't know what he was seeing," she said quickly. "The kid was a world-class stoner. Jesus—this is why I didn't want people talking to him."

"He said it wasn't just that day. Natalie said you tormented her. She was terrified of you."

She was shaking her head. It was as if she was denying something bigger than the words he was saying.

"Is it true?"

"Don't ask me this, Michael. Please. Let's just go find this girl. Danny is fucking her. I'm sure of it."

"You want to go up to Riverside," he said, his voice flattened by incredulity.

"Yes!"

"It's flooding up there, Justine. It's Biblical. You probably wouldn't get within a mile of the place."

"I don't care."

"Is what Kevin said true? Did you torment Natalie Chenier?"

"Please. Just do this last thing with me. Just believe for a little bit longer. You'll see."

Michael said, "I can't. I'm sorry, but I can't."

She held his gaze, pleading with him, before finally breaking eye contact.

"Okay."

There was a silence that extended for so long that Michael began to think she would never say another word to him. But then she met his eye. Her expression had changed. It had become cold and distant. There was defiance in it.

"I killed her, Michael. That's what happened. Okay? I killed Natalie Chenier."

"Justine . . ."

"No. Just listen. You want to know the truth so bad, all right, I'm going to give it to you." She took in a deep breath. "So, yes, Kevin is right. That day in her room was not the last time I saw her. And yes, I did see them together, but Danny wasn't the one who saw me. Natalie was. I went to her house the next day. I flipped out. I lost it. I think I probably *would* have hurt her if Kevin hadn't come between us. After that, I did everything I could to stop her being with him. I threatened to tell her mother, the cops, people at her school. Nothing worked. Natalie was battle-tough from years of cruelty. And she was a girl in love."

She shook her head in wretched wonder.

"But I didn't give up. I couldn't. Without Danny I was nothing. So I went to her house. I was going to have it out with her, once and for all. She was leaving just as I turned the corner onto her street. She didn't see me, so I followed her as she walked down toward the river. She wound up on Prospect; she cut through a derelict warehouse to get there. And I knew. This was where she waited for him. It was just like with me, only a different place. Somewhere no one would ever see them. I walked right up to her. I just wanted him to see us together. I wanted him to choose me."

She stopped speaking for several seconds.

"She hesitated a second, but then his orders kicked in. I knew them well. Anybody sees you, abort mission. She started to head back to her house but I blocked the way. I was going to hold her there until he rolled up. She tried to get around me so I grabbed her hoodie and we did this little dance. When we stop we're on the floodwall and she's smiling. In triumph. And then she says, *You're pathetic.* I lose it. I try to slap her, but she ducks out of the way and then my face is stinging and I'm thinking that little bitch just hit me. So I shove her. She's so small and light. And suddenly she's not there."

"There was no fence."

"There was no anything. Just the river."

She closed her eyes.

"It takes me a few seconds to get up the nerve to look. She's holding onto this greasy piling. And she's looking up at me with those eyes of hers. I can see the terror. She's just this scared little girl. Who can't swim because who teaches someone like that to swim? I know I have to do something, but I can feel the panic coming on. It was spring; the water was up. Not as bad as now, but it was enough. There's no way I'm jumping in. There are these steps a ways down, I run to those, but the water's covered up the bottom of them. I'm nowhere close. Meanwhile, she's losing her grip. I run back up to where she is and look down and tell her I'm going to get someone, but I just stand there. We both know there's no use. Our eyes hold for a minute and something passes between us and then she's gone. The current just sort of spins her away downriver. She hits the deep fast water and goes under. And that's that. The end of Natalie."

"Where was Winter?" he asked her.

"All of a sudden I do not want him to see me there. I run into the warehouse and hide just as he shows up. His tires crackling on the road. He's only about fifty feet away from where I am. He sits impatiently in his car for a minute. You can see he's pissed. And then he takes off. He never had a clue I was there. Or her."

"Jesus."

"I go home and lock myself in my room and basically lose my shit. The panic . . . God, you have no idea. But then I start using the techniques he taught me. I breathe. I visualize. And what do you know—it works. Irony of ironies. I'm able to make it through the night and then the weekend. Nobody kicks in the door. The sky does not fall. My mother does not even ask me what's wrong. I've killed a girl and no one gives a shit. It's in the paper on Monday, sort of an afterthought."

"No one asked you about her?" Michael asked.

"Why would they?"

Which was just what Kevin had said.

"And that was it?"

"That was it. Except it wasn't. Because deep down, I am basically going insane. My thought processes skew toward the abnormal."

Her mouth formed a cruel smile.

"I'm thinking, now that she's gone, I can get back together with Danny. So I walk up there. I don't mention Natalie. But I guess my general demeanor causes him to presume I have taken leave of my senses. He says perhaps I should come with him over to Riverside so I can get looked after. I bolt, these nice people take me home, where he's already turned Nancy and Neal against me. I'm on the starlight express by morning. I spend the summer there. I never mention Natalie. Not that anybody asked. She truly was an invisible child."

"And you never told anyone about what you did to Natalie. Not even Trace."

"Never."

"And Winter never suspected."

"Why would he? He never knew I'd spotted them together. He never knew I was tormenting her. She must have kept quiet about that for fear he'd dump her."

She finally met his eye and she saw his doubt.

"You don't believe me."

"Justine . . ."

The last vestige of hope left her.

"Okay," she said. "Okay."

She nodded once, then collected the photos from the counter. She stacked them neatly before putting them in the envelope.

"Goodbye, Michael. Thank you for trying to help. Seriously. You've been better to me than I deserve."

She picked up his keys as she walked past him. It was an act so smooth, so natural, that he did not understand what was happening until she was out the back door. He followed immediately, but she must have broken into a run because she was already in the car by the time he made it to the side of the house. The car's motor revved as he reached the steps; she was moving by the time he was in the driveway. There was no way of stopping her. All he could do was stand in the rain until the Sonata reached the end of Locust and slipped into the night.

FOURTEEN

HE WOULD NEED TO BORROW MRS. DONALD'S BUICK. HE had no choice. It would be absurd to try to get a taxi to take him into what was almost certainly a major flood zone. When his old neighbor finally came to the door, she looked as if she had been sleeping deeply, even though he had left her less than a half hour earlier. She was baffled and hesitant when he explained that the Sonata was not working and he needed to pick up his son immediately. But she turned over the keys. It was an emergency, after all. As if to underscore this, a helicopter flew directly over them, interrupting their conversation as it raced to the north, its searchlight probing the earth. Once it had passed, Michael promised to drive carefully; he said he'd be back in a few minutes. Two more lies to add to the mix.

Evidence of flooding began before he left the center of town. Deep puddles speckled the streets. Southbound traffic increased steadily, many of the vehicles directing high beams straight into Michael's brain. Some of the cars were laden with household possessions. On 44, several roads down to the river were blocked by emergency vehicles or sawhorses swathed with reflective tape. People drove with their flashers on. A policeman directing traffic stopped Michael to warn him that he could not guarantee his safety if he kept going. Michael was able to get past with the same lie he'd deployed with his neighbor. His son needed him. The rain continued to come hard, but Mrs. Donald's car had recently been serviced—its fresh blades renewed the world with every stroke.

Although there was almost no other traffic heading north, Michael's hope of a quick trip to Riverside was thwarted when he fell in behind a slow-moving bus decorated with Chinese characters. He was desperate to pass, but every time he ventured out of his lane, there was another car coming toward him, flashing its high beams and refusing to yield. The rain was falling in great whipping sheets now, reducing visibility to less than a hundred feet. On the radio, they were saying that flooding had begun to affect low-lying areas. Mandatory evacuations had been ordered in several riverside communities. There was talk about calling in the National Guard.

The bus's turn signal came on as it neared the Riverside turn-off. Michael followed it off 44. They were evacuating the facility. He hoped the girl in the photo was long gone, that Justine's frenzied mission would come to nothing. Her actions were simple desperation and madness. He pictured the fear and confusion Natalie must have felt when confronted by the beautiful, charismatic girl she had once admired. At her home, in the streets, and then finally by the floodwall. Neither she nor Justine had ever been Winter's lover. It had all been a product of Justine's broken mind. The seduction, the secret meetings, the hardwood floor. Everything except that plummet from the floodwall.

He was finally able to pass the lumbering bus. Riverside came into view. The facility was awash with light. Vans and cars circled the building like a besieging army, their crossing headlights creating a patchy radiant matrix. Rain sparkled around the building. Staff in ponchos had gathered by the portico entrance. Some held flashlights beneath large umbrellas, creating luminous traveling cones of light.

Michael pulled off the drive beside the last copse of trees before the main building. He did not want to make his presence known, at least not yet. He killed his engine and searched the visitor's lot for signs of the Sonata. It was nowhere in sight. Nor was Justine. The Chinese bus shrieked to a stop in front of the portico and, almost immediately, staff began to herd patients toward it through the front door. Some wore backpacks, others pulled suitcases. Michael searched their faces for the girl in the photograph, but they were too distant, too shrouded by glare and rain for him to know for certain if any of them were her.

He got out of his car, trying to decide on his next move. The front entrance was not an option. There were people around who might recognize him, who might want to know his business. Instead, he headed toward the side of the building, toward the door he'd gone through on his first visit. Emergency spots lit the way. He walked with purpose, trying to look official. There was a pneumatic shriek behind him just as he reached the building, so loud that it caused him to flinch. For an instant, he feared that it had something to do with him; he'd set off an alarm. But it was just the bus, starting its journey to higher ground.

As he turned the corner of the building he could see down to the river. It was illuminated by emergency vehicles on the far shore. A helicopter hovered steadily over some sort of industrial facility there, its powerful beam playing over squat buildings and long, elbowed pipes. The fractured, jumpy quality of the light on the water's surface showed how fast its usually placid current was moving. It seemed like a completely different entity now, an obsidian highway of destruction. Michael wondered if the flood really would reach Riverside's main building. Unthinkable just a few days ago, it was certainly possible now. The lawn leading down to the bank was flat. If the water jumped whatever sort of barrier they had, there would be nothing stopping the foaming tsunami from surging down those pristine halls. Even if it was only ankle-deep, it would do great damage.

The side door was unlocked. The hallway was empty, though urgent voices echoed toward him from somewhere just out of sight. He jogged to the hall where he'd met the girl, picturing himself on a monitor, ghostly but recognizably foreign, a virus that needed to be attacked by antibodies armed with nonlethal weaponry. He reached the meshed window. The doors to the individual rooms were open. Light spilled from each of them. There was no sign of staff.

Another unlocked door. He moved as quietly as possible down the hall. In each of the rooms, girls sat on their beds, dressed in warm clothing, patient to the point of stupefaction. Duffel bags and small suitcases rested in front of them. A few looked up expectantly as Michael passed, awaiting instruction and rescue. Others were locked in their own thoughts. There was no atmosphere of panic. Just a group of girls waiting, without evident hope or fear, for the next thing to happen.

Her room was empty, although the light still burned. He knew that it was her room because there was a stuffed giraffe on the bed. She had left in a hurry.

"Are you looking for Emily?"

A girl had spoken from the room across the hall. She was on her feet, but did not seem eager to stray very far from her bed, as if she had been tethered to it. She was very tall and impossibly thin. She had wild black hair and wore a burgundy tracksuit that hung loosely from her fleshless body.

He replied, "If she's the girl who lives in this room, yes."

"Her sister took her."

"Her sister? Are you sure that's who it was?"

"Well, I assumed. She wasn't one of us. She was pretty bossy but she didn't work here."

"And you don't know where they went."

She shook her head.

"When was this?"

"Ten minutes ago?" she said.

"Okay. Thanks."

"Um, sir? Do you know when they're coming for the rest of us?"

"Soon."

"Because they're saying the flood is getting pretty bad."

"You'll be fine. I don't think they'd forget about you."

"Somebody said the busses were Chinese. Those blow up. Did you know that?"

"I'm sure these ones are safe."

She sighed theatrically.

"Taken to my doom on a Fung Wah Bus," she said as she floated weightlessly back down onto her bed. "Typical."

Michael retraced his steps. He was running now, not caring who spotted him, afraid that she had got past him. As he left the building he saw that the rain had stopped, suddenly and absolutely, as if someone had cinched a great hose. Water continued to cascade from the gutters. He ran back to the front corner of the building, desperate to go after her, but not having the first idea about where she might have gone.

A new bus arrived, sighing and shrieking to a stop in front of the portico. A vehicle followed closely behind it. Marcus Munro's Escalade. Michael shuffled back behind the building's edge as the black SUV pulled behind the bus. Munro looked around as he got out, anxious but not alarmed. He gave no sense that he had come to deal with a dangerous woman on the loose. He looked like the chief counsel for a large facility that was currently in the process of an orderly evacuation.

Another line of patients was led from the front entrance, attended closely by Riverside employees. Winter was among them. He was giving orders, but broke off when he saw his lawyer. The two men spoke beneath the dripping portico as they watched the patients file onto the bus. Winter gave no indication that he knew Justine had been in the building. She was not here; she had escaped into her madness and delusion, taking some poor innocent with her.

And then another vehicle appeared on the driveway, an electric cart with a lone driver. It tore out of the darkness as fast as its small motor would allow, rolling to a stop just a few feet from the portico. The driver was speaking to Winter before he had even finished rising from his seat. It was Jenner, the orderly who had tased Michael. He carried a flashlight the size of a femur. He used it to gesture toward the bungalows and the thick black woods behind them. Michael could track the tension moving through the psychiatrist's body as he listened. Munro looked alarmed now as well. After a brief discussion, he and Winter climbed into the cart and set off immediately back up the driveway. Jenner followed on foot.

Michael ran after them. All he could think was that he was doing the most consequential and dangerous act of his life, and it involved chasing a golf cart. At least it was not hard to keep up with it. Everything seemed to be moving in slow motion now. The vehicle's wheels sputtered and spun in the mud, allowing Jenner to pull in front and light the way with that powerful flashlight. Michael tracked them from a distance of twenty yards. They could have spotted him if they turned around. But no one was doing that.

Just before reaching the bungalows, the cart joined a narrow service road. After several hundred feet the road curved to the east, into the black woods, toward the river. Michael now understood what was happening. Fearing she would be stopped on the main access road, she had driven this way. Her panic leading her into the darkness. She had run into a dead end. Or something worse.

They kept going, the flashlight's beam playing over the dark trees. Michael's foot caught on erupted pavement; he stumbled and almost fell. A vehicle came into view, just where the road turned sharply to the north, following the river. It was not the Sonata, but a parked pickup truck. Its headlights shone through an interval of trees and out over the river. Immediately to the truck's right was an angry divot of mud, fresh and deep.

The cart stopped behind the pickup. Michael did as well, twenty yards back, not wanting to blunder upon them, at least not until he figured out what was happening. Munro and Winter got out and joined Jenner, who directed his flashlight's beam into the woods. In line, silhouetted, the three men looked like sentinels, protecting the land from something evil that was threatening to emerge from the river. Michael understood what was happening. She had been driving crazily; she'd missed a turn. If she'd slid into the water, she was gone forever.

He rushed forward, no longer caring if they knew he was here. The Sonata appeared, lit by Jenner's flashlight. It was not in the water, but had wound up in the woods, wedged against a tree at the top of the sloping, tree-studded riverbank. Steam leaked out from beneath the hood. A shadowy figure stood near the wreckage; not Justine, but a heavy man, dressed in reflective gear. The pickup's driver. When he saw the newcomers he directed his own flashlight's beam at two figures standing upstream from the wreckage, their backs to the river. Justine and the girl, Emily. Jenner put his beam on them as well. The illumination from the two flashlights was so fierce that it looked as if they were lit from within.

The three men from the cart advanced in loose formation; the pickup's driver moved as well. Michael followed, closing on the men by the time they had encircled the two. Winter held his hands out in front of him. He was speaking, though his words were subsumed by the fibrillating beat of the helicopter as it raced to the south, to another emergency. Justine responded by grabbing the thin arm of the girl next to her.

From where he now stood, Michael could see that the steep slope behind the two was almost completely covered by the risen river. Just a few backward steps and they would be in it. The water moved fast, hurling debris downstream and flaring against protruding tree trunks. Although the river made no discernible noise, there was a subaudible crush in the air, as if the surging water was swallowing sound. A rotted sulfuric stench rose from the ground. Something hellish and alive.

No one noticed Michael. They were too intent on the scene before them. Justine put on a defiant front, but Michael could see the panic percolating inside her. A thin line of blood ran from the scalp above her left eye, over her cheekbone and chin. Her gaze traveled from man to man, assessing the threat, calculating her next move. She continued to grip Emily, whose terrified eyes were fixed on Winter, pleading for release.

Justine was the first person Michael heard after the helicopter had finally passed.

"I'm taking her away from you," she said, her voice shallow and breathless, close to hysteria. "That's what I'm doing."

"Let's just get everyone back up to the building," Winter answered. "We need to get you looked at. You're injured."

She laughed bitterly, as if a private joke had just been shared.

"Jane, please," he continued. "It's unsafe down here."

"Yeah, well, it's not so safe up there, either."

"At least let her come with us," Munro said, pointing to Emily. "She hasn't done anything."

"I haven't either!"

Munro had no answer for this. Jenner muttered something to Winter, who responded with a terse shake of his head, a denial that contained the possibility of imminent action. And then there was a new sound. A siren. It came from the west, back on 44.

"You called the cops?" Justine said.

"No," Winter said.

"Liar."

"He's telling the truth," Munro said.

"Listen to you," Justine said. "The truth. This guy hasn't told you the truth in twenty years."

"We all know what you're going through," Munro said. "We just want to help."

"You really have no idea who he is, do you?" she asked, her voice incredulous and mocking.

"Jane. Please."

"He fucked your daughter, Mr. Munro. Right under your nose. And I bet she still loves him. Your precious Mary is probably sitting back at your house right now, waiting for him to spirit her away."

Her words drove the lawyer into silence. From where Michael was standing, it was impossible to tell if was simple shock at the onslaught, or something deeper.

She turned to Emily.

"You have to tell the cops what's going on when they get here. Otherwise he's going to make you disappear. Do you understand?"

The girl directed a panicked glance at Justine before looking back at Winter.

"She told me she was helping with the evacuation," she said, her voice very small.

"It's all right," Winter said. "You haven't done anything wrong."

"I don't know what she's talking about. I told her."

"Don't worry," Winter continued. "We know who she is. We know all about her."

His voice was smooth and clinical. Justine's grip on the girl's arm tightened; she shook it a few times.

"You have to tell them! If you don't, he's going to break you. And then you'll be broken forever."

Emily appeared to shrivel in her terror.

"The photographs are in the car," Justine continued, though it was now hard to know who she was speaking to. "They show . . . they prove . . ."

She fell silent. She had lost her train of thought. She touched her forehead with her free hand, then examined her blood-smeared fingertips. She closed her eyes and swayed slightly. Jenner started to move forward but Winter stopped him.

"Jane, please," he said. "Let me help you."

She opened her eyes and stared at the ground in front of her. Michael was shocked by the transformation that had taken place in those few short seconds. The strength and defiance were gone. She looked weak and confused and very young; almost as young as the girl next to her. It was as if every vestige of the woman he had known as Justine had just vanished.

"Let her go, Jane," Winter said. "Please."

The siren continued to wail.

"Are they going to arrest me?" Justine asked, her voice brittle.

"I told you—nobody's called the police. We're going to work through this ourselves. Like we always did."

She released the girl. Just like that. So casually that it seemed like an afterthought. Once free, Emily stepped beyond Justine's reach, then looked at Winter for further instructions. He ignored her, his gaze locked on Justine as he walked slowly up to her. A sudden amplification of light made Michael wonder if someone else had arrived. But it was just the sky. The clouds had cleared, exposing a blazing moon that shone down with a post-storm brilliance.

Michael started to move toward her as well, but the big man from the pickup noticed him and quickly cut him off. He did not touch Michael, but his demeanor suggested he would with the next step. Michael held his ground.

"How does your head feel?" Winter asked once he was standing in front of Justine, his voice gentle and solemn, without a trace of anger or triumph.

"It hurts."

"I'll take care of that."

Justine nodded. Michael watched in stunned fascination. He could not believe that this was the woman he had known. It was all gone. Emily watched them as well; she looked to be even more confused than Michael. She said something to Winter that Michael could not hear; he continued to ignore her. He had started to speak to Justine in a low and intimate voice. Finally, Emily reached out and put her hand on Winter's forearm. He pulled away without looking at her. He turned to Jenner.

"Take Emily back up to the main building in the pickup," he said.

"You want her to evacuate with you?"

"No, she can go with the others."

Emily's mouth fell open. Her eyes widened in shock. Jenner came forward to get her. She ignored him, forcing him to place a hand on her elbow. She shook it off.

"But I want to stay with you," she said to Winter, her voice ringing through the clearing.

Winter looked at Jenner and jerked his head impatiently toward the road. He wanted the girl gone. Now. This time, the orderly did not hesitate. He took her in hand. The driver lit the way; Jenner handed Winter his flashlight before following. Emily looked back over her shoulder at Winter and Justine.

"Danny," she said, her voice almost a shriek.

That single word stopped everything, and then everything changed. An absolute silence descended on the clearing.

My God, Michael thought.

"Jenner, will you please take her out of here," Winter finally said, his tone thin and strained. "*Now.*"

The orderly did as told, dragging Emily up to the road so quickly that the driver fell behind them. She said something else that Michael could not understand. He looked at Munro, who had not moved since Justine had spoken his daughter's name. The lawyer's usual rigid mask had vanished, replaced by a stunned understanding. He had seen it on Emily's face. He had heard it in her voice. The love. The truth. If Justine had registered what was happening, it did not matter. Her collapse appeared to be complete.

"Let's go," Winter said to her.

She nodded. Winter placed a hand near the small of her back, not touching her, but nevertheless exercising complete control. He started to lead her toward the road. He was only able to take two strides before Munro grabbed his arm and pulled it so the two men were face-to-face. The flashlight shone up between them. There was something new in Winter's eyes. The beginning of fear.

"You son of a bitch," Munro said.

"Marcus . . . let go of my arm."

Munro did not release him. Back on the road, the pickup's engine fired loudly, its tires skidded as they found traction. The siren could still be heard, but it now seemed to be heading away from Riverside. It was just the four of them.

Winter jerked his arm free. The violence of his movement caused him to stumble backwards, almost to the top of the river-bank. The flashlight fell to the ground, its beam whipping crazily through the clearing.

"My daughter," Munro said, his voice cracking with fury.

Winter looked like he was about to respond, but he stopped himself. A small, incredulous smile twisted his mouth. He glanced at Michael before his gaze settled back on Munro.

"It's not something you'd understand," he said.

And then he looked at Justine, who was watching him as well.

"You were all so happy," Winter said.

Michael could see it on her face. The terrible emptiness of her victory. The end of the beautiful woman she had created.

And then Munro was moving forward.

"Marcus, wait . . ."

It was a short punch that carried great force. Winter staggered back. His arms clawed at the air in front of him, as if he was reaching for something that had been there only a moment ago. And then he was in the river. He did not make a sound; there was no splash. He was just gone. No one moved for an instant, until Justine started walking toward the water. Michael reached her just before she got to its edge. He wrapped his arms around her and he could feel the force of the river. Its immensity. Its inevitability.

The flashlight's beam began to play over the surface—Munro had picked it up from where it had fallen. He found Winter. The current had hold of him. It was as if he was on some great conveyor belt. His arms moved uselessly around him. Munro tracked him as he was borne away by the unseen logic of the currents, the layers of force and pressure handing him over, one to the other, like something unwanted. Winter reached the middle of the river and then he was gone. It was impossible to tell if it was the darkness or the flood that finally took him out of sight.

Justine had gone slack in Michael's arms. He was no longer holding her back—he was holding her up. She said something he could not hear. Her voice was not even a whisper. He thought maybe she had asked him for help, though he could not be sure. Michael told her that it was all right. He was here. He was still with her. The first thing they needed to do was get her away from the edge of the water. The flood was too close. It could take them at any second. And so he gently moved her back toward the dubious safety of dry land.

THE END